Let Me Get My Underwear On First

Written By

C.J. Striker

TABLE OF CONTENTS

Legal Disclaimser

This book is a work of fiction. Any similarities to real people, places, businesses, or events are purely coincidental or the result of common industry patterns. The characters and events depicted have been fictionalized for dramatic and literary effect. The author has taken creative liberties to blend imagination with universal themes of struggle, identity, love, and redemption.

While elements of the story may draw from cultural or emotional truths observed in the nightlife and adult entertainment industries, this work is not intended as a factual account of any real individual, establishment, or location.

A Note on References

Along the way, I tip my hat to movies, songs, and cultural touchstones that shaped my life. Those lines and names belong to their creators—I'm just borrowing them in the spirit of storytelling and respect.

Triggering Content Advisory: This book contains explicit depictions of sex, drug use, violence, sexual abuse, and other potentially triggering material. Readers should approach these pages with awareness. If you are seeking something soft, polished, or sugar-coated---this isn't it. These pages are meant for mature audiences only. Reader discretion isn't just advised---it's expected.

Readers should approach this book as an artistic exploration of character, morality, and consequence---not a representation of historical truth. The author and publisher disclaim any liability for perceived similarities or interpretations.

It's taken billions of years to get to this book---I hope you enjoy the ride.

Dedicated to the memory of my Dad, Dr. C.J. Striker. Sr.--my hero, my foundation. You gave me the wings to chase every dream, and the strength to survive the crashes. I carry your love with me always. Wish you were here. Love you, Dad. Your son, C.J. Striker. Jr

Prologue

Flight of the Aviator

Rocketman
Performed by: **Sir Elton John**
Written By: **Bernie Taupin**

Like the song Rocket Man, I shot to the top in no time---literally. I was thousands of feet in the air, moving seven or eight times faster than I ever did on the ground. And from that kind of altitude, with that kind of perspective, I finally had the chance to raise a middle finger to everything that once held me down.

As for Elton John---thank you for scoring the soundtrack of my life. If I had to reshuffle my catalog, it'd be damn near impossible. His music didn't just play in the background---it carried me. A once-in-a-generation talent, timeless and untouchable.

I stepped onto the flightline with that worn-in swagger you earn from logging years in the sky---not cocky, just carved from experience. But today hit different. There she was---a single-pilot jet, sharp lines and snarling engines, just waiting for someone crazy enough to push her limits. Not a G-Wagon, sure, but this bird had teeth. She could rip open the sky if you knew how to ask nicely... or rough if needed. As I closed the distance, boots thudding on concrete, eyes locked on her frame, a memory sucker-punched me---my first flight. That raw, addictive rush when I first broke free of gravity's grip. I didn't fall for the machine. I fell for the madness. For flying.

But don't check out just yet---this isn't your typical "I've been flying since I was in diapers" cliché-laced story. This one's got grit. Blood. Smoke. Regret. And a little redemption.

I caught the flying bug back in the '80s, when aviator shades were cool and danger still had swagger. Took a cheap discovery flight on a whim--- and that was it. One bounce in that rickety tin can and I was done for. Hooked. No going back. When I finally slid into the left seat for my first real lesson, everything below shrank into irrelevance. The world got small, the sky cracked wide open, and something in me finally woke the hell up. Flying gave me what booze, women, and business never could---pure, unfiltered freedom. A hit of adrenaline. Control over chaos. Confidence carved from thin air. It's not for everyone, and that's exactly the point. Most folks are too scared, too broke, or too sensible to ever touch that throttle. Lucky me---I never cared much for sensible.

It was like learning to play a musical instrument---but one mistake could kill you. That's the kind of discipline flying demands. It doesn't care how cool you think you are. You respect it, or it buries you.

My first solo flight came seven and a half hours into flight school. My instructor---a savage either drunk on confidence or just sick of my face-- -booted me out of the nest at Galaxy Beach airport. As I pulled back on the yoke, alone for the first time, "Always" by Atlantic Starr played in my head like a slow dance with a memory I hadn't earned yet. To this day, that song messes me up in the best way.

From there, flying wasn't a phase. It was a full-blown addiction. My first aircraft was a Beechcraft V-tail Bonanza---a slick little bird with just enough punch to make you feel like a badass, and enough forgiveness to keep a rookie like me alive. It gave me freedom. I could take off for dinner 200 miles away, land, eat, and still be home in time to kiss the kids goodnight. That plane was my loophole---business expense, tax write-off, and alibi wrapped in wings.

I remember one flight like it was yesterday---my instructor thought it'd be funny to introduce me to "cow tipping" from the sky. The plan? Drop altitude, fly low over a field, and let the slipstream or noise topple a few cows. Juvenile? Hell yeah. Cruel? Probably. Effective? Not at all. Thankfully, no cows were harmed in the making of that stupidity, but I walked away with a lesson: just because you can do something doesn't mean you should. And not every idea from someone with more hours in the cockpit is a good one.

From then on, I stayed grounded in the ways that mattered---kept my ego in check, flew smart, respected the limits. I brought younger pilots under my wing, let them log hours, kept them sharp while keeping myself sharper. Some of those guys are flying for major airlines now. They still call me up once in a while to say thanks. That part feels good. Real good.

Over time, the toys got bigger. The speeds got faster. The stakes got higher. Nine planes later, I wasn't just a guy who flew---I was living the jet style life. Private terminals. Red carpet treatment. Chauffeurs waiting on the tarmac with my name on a sign. This wasn't just flying anymore. This was lifestyle porn. And yeah---outside of sex, nothing gave me a rush like pushing that throttle forward and leaving the world behind.

But let's fast-forward to the day I climbed into the cockpit of that Phenom.

I met my co-pilot (an aspiring jet pilot) at the nose. Solid guy. Sharp. We exchanged the usual checklist, jokes, and caffeine-driven banter.

"You ready to get high?" I grinned.

He smirked. "As long as you're ready to come down."

We ran through preflight like pros. Got clearance. Taxied to the runway. And then that moment hit---the engines roaring, the acceleration pressing you back into your seat, the wheels breaking free from the ground... it never gets old. Not once.

Ten minutes in, we were cruising. Peaceful. The kind of quiet you only find up there. No emails. No phone calls. Just the whisper of altitude and the endless horizon.

I glanced over at him. I had something to say---something heavy---but didn't know how to lead into it. Finally, I just said it.

"I'm glad you're here with me, man."

He turned and smiled. "Me too. I love flying with you."

Then everything changed.

On our route to the destination---gear handle down as required---came the smell. Sharp. Chemical. Wrong.

Then smoke.

It slithered into the cockpit like a threat with teeth. Thick. Aggressive. Hungry. We locked eyes---no panic, just that quiet, cold focus that only comes from miles in the sky and too many close calls. "This isn't a drill," I muttered, already reaching.

"Mask on, mic on mask, grab the QRH!" I barked.

He moved. Fast. Trained. I stayed glued to the panel, scanning, hunting for the source. But the smoke wasn't waiting---it got thicker, bolder, smearing the gauges and sucking the oxygen right out of the moment.

We were possibly on fire.

"Mayday, mayday!" he shouted into the radio.

In that moment---when the air turned toxic and the future narrowed to seconds---I saw my life flash like a reel of broken film: my kids. My women. My sins. My wins. The clubs. The cash. The chaos.

Would my legacy be lap dances and leased jets? Would my kids remember my love or my absence?

But in the middle of that spiral, a strange calm settled in. A single thought cut through the static.

I always say, "If I die tomorrow, at least I've lived life. What a fucking life it's been."

Chapter 1

The Bitter End

It's Closing Time
Performed by: **Semisonic**
Written by: **Dan Wilson**

Like the song *Closing Time,* when 2:00 AM hit, it was *"Get the fuck out"* to all the customers. No exceptions. We had to put a hard stop to whatever fantasy was still swirling in their heads. Abrupt? Yes. Callous? Maybe. Necessary? Absolutely.

And just like the club shutting down at 2:00, it was also closing time for my marriage to Bridget.

Hang on to That Cliff

"Your flight is on time, Mrs. Walker," the counter attendant chirps, the kind of bright that feels like a slap. Her voice bounces off terrazzo floors and the ribbed metal ceiling. The printer spits out a bag tag that smells faintly like hot plastic. Somewhere nearby, a toddler wails, and a PA crackles with a boarding call for Group 3. Jet fuel taints the air even this far from the gates if you breathe through your nose.

Bridget doesn't look at the attendant. She looks at me.

"Are you coming to security?" she asks, gripping the strap of her purse like it's a lifeline. Her voice has that off-kilter wobble—half braced, half hiding.

It should be a nothing moment. Hug, kiss, joke about TSA pawing through her lotion, "Call you when I land." Instead, something sour blooms in my throat and swells until it feels like I'm trying to swallow a grapefruit. The terminal is all glass and gloss and noise, and somehow I can hear my own heartbeat.

"Yeah," I say. "I'll walk you."

We move as a unit through the predictable choreography of departure. An old couple argues over a boarding pass. A guy in a hoodie elbows a carry-on into compliance. A woman sprays perfume at a kiosk and sets off an invisible allergic reaction in three rows. Bridget breezes past it all like she's learned to walk inside a different weather system.

California. "Work training." Three weeks. New job—new words— new distance. We have never been apart longer than one, maybe two nights. Ten years. Whole empires were built and burned inside those ten years. Whole storms survived shoulder to shoulder. And then the four words that detonated a load-bearing wall: I'm not in love.

Not a crack. A charge wired into the studs. You don't patch those. You stand there afterward with plaster dust in your eyelashes and decide whether to rebuild or bulldoze.

The security line is a procession of gray bins and gray faces and gray patience. Shoes off. Belts off. Dignity off. She puts her phone in a tray like it's a fragile animal she's loaning to the universe. I watch the way she sets it screen-down. I know that angle too well.

"Text me when you get to Dallas," I say. My voice is steady. I hate that it's steady. I want the anger to show. I want the grief to show. I want to shake her and say, You're lying about what this is.

"Sure." Her mouth shapes the word, but her eyes are on the metal detector arch, on the agents, on the next thing.

When it's our turn, we look at each other like people who forgot how to exit a scene. Our hugs used to be a ritual, a muscle memory—my hand on the back of her head, her laugh at my shoulder, the way she'd pull away and then come back for a second quick kiss like she just remembered something important. This hug is technical. A demonstration. She smells like citrus shampoo and hotel laundry. Her bones feel calibrated for someone else's arms. I mouth "I love you." She gives me the kind of wave you practice in a mirror. "I'll call from Dallas," she says, and disappears into the machine.

I stand there until the agent clears his throat in my direction. "Sir? You're not going through?" No. Not today. Not with her.

Outside, the parking garage is a concrete cathedral. I get to my car like a man fleeing a crime scene. The pack of cigarettes is where I hid it—glove box, under the manual I never read. The lighter flares and throws a momentary sun on my knuckles. First drag in years. It scratches the throat and blooms in the lungs and spreads a familiar shame. I roll the window down just enough to let the guilt creep out.

Maybe it's good, I tell myself. Maybe it's the clean break. But truth isn't clean. It leaves a residue. It leaves fingerprints.

Because the fall didn't start at the curb, it started months back, in quiet rooms where silence got heavy and phones got slippery.

The night I decided to stop pretending, the house was museum-quiet. The hum of the fridge. A tick in the wall that turned out to be nothing. I sat at the end of the kitchen table with the phone bill spread out like a map of someone else's war. Numbers everywhere. Patterns, if you know how to squint right.

She'd been stepping into the bathroom to answer calls. The shh motion with the hand, like I was a dog that barks when the doorbell rings. Messages wiped clean. A fresh history every morning. Every time I dialed, that cold beep like a hospital monitor told me she was already "on the other line."

I traced the repetitions with a finger. One number was the spine. I *67'd it. My voice felt like someone else's when I said hello to the void.

"You've reached the voicemail of Ira…"

The name stopped everything. A pause that was a lifetime and a second.

Ira: a face I knew more from the margins than the center. Polished, older, clever in the way of men who play with people like they play with numbers. I remembered the first time I clocked him years back—dim bar light, a watch face catching it like a lighthouse. He held a room with the casual entitlement of a man who's never lost the big hand. Married. Always married, as if a ring is a valuable prop. Women looked at him like a practical joke they might be willing to go along with. I promised myself once, silently, in a bathroom mirror, not in my house. Not again. Not this time.

Now the name was inside my kitchen at 2 a.m. The oven clock glowed 2:17. I let the voicemail play twice, listened to the cadence you only get when a person owns his name, and started pulling line items. Three months. 5000 texts. 120 hours on calls. Ninety photos. The numbers were tidy like an audit. There is a particular nausea you get when the worst thing you can imagine arrives dressed as data. The body understands before the intellect signs.

The worst part wasn't the volume. It was ditto. Same phrasing. Same intimate idioms repurposed. Sexts that used to belong to me forwarded like templates. As if I'd been a rough draft and he was the final export.

I waited for morning to bring some moral clarity. It brought a sky the color of an old bruise and the kind of practical light that shows you dust you never notice. Bridget padded into the kitchen in a T-shirt and socks and did that thing where she reached for coffee without looking at me.

"I talked to Ira last night," I said, and let the sentence hang.

Her eyes finally found mine. For a heartbeat, I watched the calculus— deny, deflect, admit, cry—scroll behind her pupils. She chose the cool middle lane.

"I didn't call him first," she said. "He reached out. About the Pop Warner thing. Donations."

"We're past the donation part," I said. I slid the bill across the table. Numbers underlined in pen. The tethered cord of proof.

She barely touched the paper. Didn't need to. Maybe she already knew the plot twist and had a replacement ending loaded on a teleprompter behind my head.

"Are we going to do this blame thing all morning?" she asked, voice flat.

"Not all morning," I said. "However long it takes."

That was the thing about us: the fights weren't always loud. Sometimes they were surgical, cool hands and gloves, and scalpel blades that cut clean. Other times, screaming matches that could be heard in home town in Europe.

The week she rolled up in the BMW without a conversation, the message wasn't coded. Titled in her name. Terms I didn't see. She parked it diagonally in the driveway under the assumption that angles win arguments.

"We needed a reliable car," she said, palming the key fob like a coin trick.

"We have five," I said.

"I needed a reliable car," she corrected, and the pronoun clicked like a new lock.

Meanwhile, my spreadsheets bled. The runways of cash we'd flown down for years were suddenly gravel and potholes. I'm good in a fight— too good—and when money tightens, I sprint toward the next hustle like the answer is always forward. But momentum is not a bandage. Success doesn't cancel a debt. It only makes the collectors knock louder.

Before the marriage started smoldering, my new business empire had done it first. 2008 taught men like me about gravity, taught us that markets don't care about our mythologies. I had just opened two glass-walled temples, new motorcycle franchises, to combustion and chrome. Polished floors, banners that smelled faintly like vinyl, and promise, a coffee station that made customers feel like we were all family headed to the same cookout.

That morning, the raid came dressed in khakis and clipboards. I heard the forklifts before I saw them—the unholy backup beep that feels like it announces the end of something. Three white box trucks idled out back. Two men I'd never met introduced themselves with unearned first-name familiarity. They carried papers with a degree of authority usually reserved for coroners.

"Floor plan's note is being called in," one said, voice as bored as a weather report. "We'll be taking possession."

"Possession of what?" I asked. It sounded brave and ridiculous in the same breath.

"Of all this inventory," he said, and gestured like a pageant host at a hundred strangers I'd hand-picked.

My service manager, a good man with grease tattooed into his knuckles, stood with his hands in his back pockets and watched time in tenure and his loyalty get driven into a truck he couldn't afford to rent for a weekend wedding. We didn't look at each other for a full minute because I didn't know how to be a boss and a priest at the same time.

"Kill the lights when they're done," I told him, as if any light that mattered was still electric.

In one day, a million dollars evaporated with the gentle hydraulics of a liftgate. I signed my name wherever they asked and felt the way a man feels signing a polite confession to a crime he's sure he committed but can't remember the motive for.

Ira fell into a different register of theater. His seventy-thousand-square-foot appliance warehouse was a monument to volume, to the American certainty that bigger is safer. When it went, it went like a building implosion—planned, precise, a cloud that took a second to arrive and then swallowed whole blocks. As much as I despised him, I recognized that specific look in his eye the next time we crossed paths from across a parking lot: the look of a man inventorying losses without a ledger.

I lost friends that year. Not to business, to gravity the second time around. You don't talk about it at barbecues. You run your fingers along the gaps and pretend the fence was always built with spaces.

I crawled back by inches. An international rental car franchise said yes, where others had said, "come back when the blood dries." Counters. Schedules. A fleet of practical cars with names that sounded like household cleaners. Three locations. I learned the math of daily rates and weekly upgrades and the art of apologizing when a Camry smells faintly like the last man's cologne. It wasn't glamorous. It was oxygen.

The single-engine plane arrived like a confession and a cure. Part therapy, part freedom, part invisible middle finger to a world that tried to keep my feet on the ground. Climb to three thousand feet and the city shrinks to an idea you can fix with two fingers on a yoke.

Bridget didn't rebuild. She took her pieces and sharpened them.

Two weeks before California, she went out with Shay—chaos in heels, catastrophe with lip gloss. Time stretched cartoon-long and then snapped back. No text. No check-in. The night had that hollow sound the house gets when it knows something before you do.

I tracked Bridget's phone to a foreclosed property, the kind of house that looks embarrassed to be standing. The yard was balding. The windows had that blank film, like the eyes of a fish that lived too long. The front door was a rumor; we went around back.

Inside smelled like damp carpet and stale weed and recent anger. The living room had empty feedback. The lights didn't work. I said her name once, and the sound of it made me feel like I'd knocked on a church door after hours.

The bedroom door was half open. There are moments you walk into that feel like somebody ripped a page out of a book you never agreed to read, jammed it in your hands, and forced your eyes across the ink. This was one of them.

Bridget on her knees with Shay. Not worship. Not curiosity. A devotion that was all appetite and no reverence. A scene stripped of tenderness, stripped of partnership. Just an act meant to detonate something in me without even knowing if I'd be there to see it.

I didn't clear my throat. I didn't slam the door. I didn't give them the satisfaction of performance. I stood in my own skin, a furnace and a freezer at once, heat climbing into my ears while my hands went cold as stone. I let the scene burn itself into me and left without punctuation. Because sometimes the point makes itself, and you have to decide whether you're going to be a footnote or the next damn chapter.

Back at the ranch—my house, for those who don't live in cowboy metaphors—the violence didn't stop just because I walked away. It followed. My Bentley, gleaming in the garage like a loaded gun I never fired, took the punishment meant for me.

That night, Bridget came home with chaos still dripping off her. She set her jaw, gripped the key fob like a blade, and carved her shapes into the paint. Long, arcing lines, as if she were writing in a language only we could read. A private alphabet of betrayal. Keys scream differently depending on the pressure—there's a pitch somewhere between an apology and a murder. Metaphorically, of course.

I stood at the window and watched her like a sculptor chiseling at marble, convinced that if she pressed hard enough, she could carve out a new life right there in the steel and enamel. She didn't cry. She didn't shake. She just cut.

We sat in the silence that follows a siren, both of us waiting for cavalry that had no interest in saving either side. When the deputy finally pulled up, lights spinning lazy across the driveway, he shrugged like the whole circus was boring him.

"It's her property too," he said, flat. "If she wants to destroy it, that's between you and her." Then his eyes hardened. "But if I have to come back tonight, one of you's going to jail."

The irony? This wasn't his first dance with Bridget. He'd already cuffed her once before. More on that later.

She left again—Shay on one side, Shay's boyfriend on the other, like a twisted escort service. What that night turned into, I don't know. But I can paint the picture. I could paint it in oil, in blood, in detail you don't want over breakfast.

By morning, the damage glared back at me. The scratches shone in daylight, cruel lines catching the sun the way dust shows up in corners you never vacuumed. It was ugly. It was real. It was a mess that no wax or polish could hide.

California arrived with a smile and a brochure. "It's training," she said, eyes on the middle distance. "There's a girl—Jennifer—she's twenty-five and hilarious. You'd like her." She said, "you'd like her," the way a person tosses a hand grenade they know is a dud.

The night before she flew, we ate takeout and pretended to be a couple in a play about a couple eating takeout. The script was familiar, the timing rehearsed.

"Want the last sushi roll?"

"No, you take it."

"No, you."

The lines were placeholders, worn smooth from overuse, spoken without conviction. The sushi sat there until it went limp and gray because the food wasn't the point. The ritual was. The ritual of pretending we still shared things, that there was still a table between us worth sitting at. For a moment, we let ourselves believe it—our shadows against the kitchen wall said marriage even as the air said funeral. All the while, I kept my eyes off the Bentley in the garage, its wounds waiting for daylight. That's compartmentalizing at its finest—acting out a scene while the crime scene bleeds in the next room.

Day two of her California trip, we had a preset time to Skype. I shaved like an idiot with hope in his throat. Changed shirts twice like a kid nervous about homecoming. It's humiliating to admit the optimism—that thing with teeth that creeps in even when the facts are notarized, sealed, and stacked against you. Still, I angled the lamp the way she liked it, softer on the left side of my face. I practiced a smile in the black mirror of the screen, one that said I'm still here without begging, please pick me.

When she answered, the hotel lamp threw a warm circle on beige wallpaper and corporate art. She looked good—so good it twisted me up, made me proud and sick in the same breath. We did the routine banter.

"How's the weather?"

"Fine."

"How's the bed?"

"Fine."

"How's the food?"

"Fine."

She laughed at one of my throwaway lines, a bad dad joke that didn't even deserve the air it took to deliver. The laugh wasn't real—it was too quick, too practiced, the kind you give a stranger who holds a door but doesn't deserve more than a nod.

Then she moved. Stepped into the bathroom. The shower curtain was pulled just enough to make it a theater, not privacy. Steam stitched the air, curling and rising like something summoned. For half a heartbeat, my chest unlatched and something bright and stupid—hope, memory, love, take your pick—fluttered wild inside me, searching for an opening.

About the time I let myself drift into the rhythm—banter, fake smiles, the illusion of connection—he walked into frame the way a man does when he's not intruding: casual, confident, unannounced. Young. Shirtless. At ease in a room that wasn't his, and sure as hell wasn't mine. He didn't flinch at the camera. Didn't even hesitate. He belonged. My mouth was already shaping her name when the screen snapped black.

The silence that followed was so loud it crushed everything else. The hum of my office disappeared, swallowed by the sound of my own pulse hammering in my ears. I stared at the dark glass, my reflection glaring back—stupid, overdressed, like a man who showed up for a party that had quietly moved across town without bothering to send directions.

The next morning, I got to work with the efficiency of someone who has packed in a storm before. Her life collapsed into boxes under my hands. I folded her clothes with a respect that pissed me off. I wrapped the glass paperweight she loved in layers of yesterday's news, like I was protecting it for a future where it could still be heavy without drawing blood. Designer boots lined up on the floor—symbols of vanity, status, and nights she never spent with me. I tied each pair together with a double knot, set them in a neat row in the trunk, an accidental art installation, a gallery exhibit staged for a jury only I would ever face.

I'd like to tell you that was the end of it, that I carried out my duty with grace. But goodwill has an expiration date, and mine didn't last through the drive.

On the tall bridge outside town, the wind came sharp, knife-edged, the kind of wind you taste in your teeth. The river below churned quick and dark. One by one, I gripped a knotted pair and swung it over the rail. The arc of leather and laces was clean, almost elegant. Then a splash—small, pitiful, insulting in its size compared to the cost of the betrayal. I let most of the pairs go that way, sacrifices to the current. My Bentley sat in the garage back home, scarred but smug, and I imagined it enjoying the show, as if the car itself needed justice after what she'd done to it.

The pièce de résistance, my opus if you want to call it that, came last. A Louis Vuitton boot, hollowed of pride and packed with fresh dog shit, sealed and primed like a time bomb under the driver's seat of her uncle's truck. A gift set to explode not with fire, but with smell—the kind of lingering, inescapable reminder you can't wash out. People call that petty. People who've never had to invent a whole new language to speak the part of grief that doesn't cry.

Boxes delivered, I rang his bell like a courier waiting for a signature. Her uncle appeared in the doorway, face already drawn with suspicion hardening into something older. Behind me, his vacant truck swallowed Bridget's valuables—or half her valuables, depending on how you do the math. We stood there in the doorway like two men trading casserole dishes after a church potluck. Civility rehearsed. Civility dying in the gaps.

He started to speak, some sentence I could already hear forming, some judgment he thought he had the right to deliver. I cut him short.

"Don't," I said. "It's not your fight."

He clamped his jaw, eyes narrowing as he watched me carry the last box to the truck. His silence was a ledger. He was tallying scores, I wasn't playing anymore.

We haven't shared a beer since. And every now and then, when I let my imagination off the leash, I picture him opening the truck door, sliding in, and catching it—the smell, the shoe, the lesson tucked neat under the seat. I picture his face in that moment. And I'll tell you right now: I wasn't sorry.

There's something about a nice Georgia Beach; after, the beach is cheaper than therapy if you don't count the cost of honesty. I sat on cold sand and smoked until the tip glowed like a warning light. The ocean gnawed the shore with small, decisive bites. I made the kind of vow you know you'll keep because it's written in the hurt, not in your head.

No more toxic. No more making myself thinner to get through someone else's doorway. No more selling pieces of me at a discount because the buyer looks good in the mirror. No more idols with human teeth. No more survival disguised as romance. No more standing still for knives.

I thought about Scarlett's Secrets—the club that built our life and fed something in her I couldn't name without being cruel. Selling it had been my confession that I wanted a different kind of man in the mirror. She didn't want a different man. She wanted the perks. The shape of her love demanded a certain balance sheet, and when the math changed, she changed the subject.

I thought about the dealership raid and the employee with grease for fingerprints and how I had to look him in the eye and admit our ship got holed below the waterline. I thought about men who died because the fall was too far and how we whisper their names like children afraid of waking a parent. I thought about the plane and the clean horizon and how forgiveness looks easier from three thousand feet because you can't see the faces.

The smoke reached the filter and tasted like the end of something.

It's time to rebuild on my terms. With a hammer, I can lift, and a blueprint I'm willing to live inside. If love wants to move in someday, it can fill out an application like everyone else.

The thought hadn't finished settling when the doorbell rang back at the house. Sharp. Two shorts and a long like a code. The hangover the next morning had steel-toed boots and aimed for my temples. I splashed water on my face and watched a man who looked like he'd survived and had the courtesy not to brag about it.

Another ring. Closer. Insistent.

I pulled a shirt on, discovered I'd missed a button, and didn't fix it. My mouth was dry in the bureaucratic way—the dryness you get before you sign something that changes the day.

Through the glass, a man stood big and deliberate, a silhouette cut out of the morning. The badge on his chest caught the light and threw it back in a bright rectangle that landed in my throat. Gun belt, snug. Clipboard tucked like a gospel.

All the possibilities queued at once: papers, warrants, orders, service, summons, a past debt dressed in a new uniform. The mind is fast when it wants to scare you.

"Oh, shit," I said, hand on the knob, and felt everything in me gather.

Because nothing good starts with a badge and a clipboard at your front door.

Chapter 2

A Sinna is Born

Take My Picture
Performed by: **Filter**
Written by: **Richard Patrick**

Like the song *Take My Picture*---whenever I was met with doubt or side-eyes during a season of growth, my response was simple: go ahead, snap the shot. Freeze this version of me. Because soon enough, I won't just be climbing---I'll be rising into something greater, something I was always meant to become.

Well, look who decided to show up. You could be scrolling social media, neck-deep in a Netflix binge, or pretending to work---but instead, you're here. With me. So, thanks for that. I guess this is where I'm supposed to roll out the welcome mat and give you the classic "origin story." Think of it like the opening credits to a movie where things go south fast, but you just can't look away.

I'll keep it real. No sugar-coating, no guru-level life advice. Just some hard-won lessons, a few laughs, and maybe a gut punch or two along the way. If that sounds like your kind of ride, buckle up. We've got a lot to cover.

Let's rewind. Back to the beginning---the origin story. My roots, the raw groundwork. I was born in June, late '60s, in Rhode Island. A Gemini, if you believe in that sort of cosmic resume. Life back then didn't hustle the way it does now. It ambled. No iPhones chirping, no laptops glowing in your face, no TikTok wormhole sucking away your soul by the second.

Saturday mornings? They weren't for doomscrolling. They were holy. Cartoons that hit like gospel, and cereal so loaded with sugar it could've doubled as drywall paste. Social media? That was called going outside. And texting? We passed notes---real ones---paper creased with precision and packed with secrets too heavy for airwaves. You learned people by looking them in the eye, not through filtered selfies and heart counts.

Let me drag you back to the early '70s---when life was raw, rough around the edges, and proudly analog. TV gave you three channels, and if you weren't parked in front of the set at the right time, too bad. No streaming, no second chances---just a blaring test pattern and white noise once the station signed off for the night. News came in measured doses, not this 24/7 fear machine we've got now. And yeah, crime existed, but folks still left their doors unlocked---until the dead of winter reminded you it wasn't just people you had to keep out, but the fridged cold itself. Life didn't come at you so fast. Fewer choices, fewer distractions, and maybe because of that, it felt more solid. More real. You could breathe without feeling like the world was breathing down your neck.

Normal didn't just leave us---it entered witness protection. Mom was raised by foster parents, bless their unsuspecting souls. They thought they were signing up to rescue a child. What they got was front-row seats to a generational dumpster fire with no exit plan. She didn't even learn who her real mother was until she was grown---and by then, the damage was so baked in it might as well have been genetic.

And her biological mom? Jesus. "Colorful" makes her sound like a fun aunt with a drinking problem. This woman was chaos in a cocktail dress---part soap opera villain, part cautionary tale. She could've made the devil blush and still get invited back for Christmas. The kind of woman who'd blow up her own life for sport, then light a cigarette off the wreckage. You don't bring her up at PTA meetings---you don't even whisper her name near sharp objects.

Now the foster parents---our "grandparents"---were pure, unlucky gold. Church-going, casserole-baking, utterly doomed. Saints, really, in that tragic way where kindness becomes a liability. How they ended up in our family tree is still unclear. Some sort of cosmic joke? Courtroom roulette? Divine punishment? They walked into the burning building and just stood there, smiling, offering cookies. Too kind to leave. Too shell-shocked to notice the flames.

My dad never met his father. Raised by a single mom with a past so tangled it'd take a corkboard, red string, and a conspiracy theorist to make sense of it. That side of the family tree? Less "tree," more "haunted carnival ride." Our lineage reads like a mix of mystery novel, reality TV, and we don't talk about that.

Still, my immediate family was surprisingly "normal"---if that word means anything. My dad managed a Cadillac dealership, which meant the driveway was always lined with shiny new demos. Probably why I've owned over 200 cars myself. Like father, like son. We had a nice house with a pool---unicorn-level rare in New England---and my younger siblings, twins, and I lived a solid middle-class life.

The neighborhood was the kind where everyone knew everyone. Sundays were sacred for family dinners. Windows stayed open. Screen doors slammed with life. We didn't worry about locks. We didn't need fences. The street was our safety net.

It was Rhode Island---a transplant town full of New Englanders and their quirks. People added r's where they didn't belong and butchered them where they did. That accent, now fading, was a badge of pride. But in today's world, they're scrubbing it out like it's something to be ashamed of. I hate that. It's not just sound---it's memory.

Our neighborhood was a melting pot of loyalty and loud dinner tables. Thirty families sharing more than just yards. We were in and out of each other's houses like siblings. Kids ran wild, parents looked out for everyone's children, and no one worried. We had each other's backs. Through birthdays, barbecues, breakups, and breakdowns. It was messy, loud, and full of heart. But even in a place like that, darkness found a way in.

There was a predator among us. A trusted friend. Someone who laughed with our parents, clinked beers at cookouts, played poker on Friday nights, stood beside us at weddings and funerals. He was always there---part of the scenery. One of us. All the while, he was hurting the neighborhood kids. Stealing trust. Stealing innocence. Hiding in plain sight. No one saw it. Because sometimes monsters don't come in the night. Sometimes they walk through the front door with a smile and stay for dinner.

We didn't have the words to describe what was happening to us. We didn't know how to report it. The communication tools of today---texting, social media, instant information---didn't exist. Conversations only happened in person, and shame was a silencer.

His name doesn't deserve mention, so I'll call him Chester. Chester the Molester. Even now, over fifty years later, saying his real name makes me sick. His influence on my life, and so many others, remained buried deep inside me, unseen and unspoken, until one day, it all came rushing out.

It happened in marriage counseling. My first marriage was failing, and in one of the sessions, the counselor asked a simple yet life-altering question: "Were you ever physically abused or sexually molested as a child?"

The words hit me like a freight train. I broke down, completely overwhelmed by emotions I didn't even realize I had been carrying for decades. That moment shattered the illusion I had built around myself--- that I had moved past what had happened. I hadn't. I had buried it, let it fester, and allowed it to shape my insecurities, my trust issues, my self-worth, and my relationships.

Chester was a retired Navy man, outwardly respectable, with a wife, and two sons younger than me. He had a nice home, a pension, and a job as a school principal for those we now call on the Spectrum. To the outside world, he was an upstanding man. But behind closed doors, he was a monster.

Stephen---not his real name---was two years younger than me. Our families were as close as could be. That connection made me feel safe when invited on a camping trip with Chester, some other neighborhood kids, and students from his school. My parents, trusting Chester as much as anyone in the neighborhood, gave their approval. For me, I had no clue about any of this. I also had no idea I was being, what we now call, groomed.

One boy on the trip, Tim---also not his real name---was a student at Chester's school, Looking back, it chills me to think how easily Chester positioned himself among the most vulnerable. Tim was clearly Chester's favorite; they were inseparable, always sharing a tent. I didn't think anything of it---until Chester pulled out nude pictures of Tim and, with a disturbing casualness, described the things he did to him. I felt sick. I still didn't fully understand what I was seeing, but something deep inside me knew it was wrong.

That night, Chester handed out cigarettes by the campfire. It was a test. A way to see who could be trusted to keep their mouths shut. I was eleven years old, and that night, I had my first cigarette---a habit that would follow me off and on into adulthood.

The rest of the trip is a blur. I remember waking up in Chester's red station wagon as he sped down the road, passing a car. In a panic, I grabbed the wheel, causing him to scream at me. But I have no memory of how I got there. I can only assume now that I had been drugged.

Over time, Chester's tactics escalated. He had bought a motorcycle, as had my father. What had started as an innocent bonding experience between my dad and me soon became something much darker. On one of the rides, I was on Chester's bike with the notion that I would learn how to drive a motorcycle at 11/12 years old. Cool right? Until he reached around and started touching me while I was trapped at the controls. I was helpless. My father was nowhere in sight. I knew what he was doing. I knew it was wrong. And I knew I had no way to stop it.

By then, Chester had complete access to me. He assaulted me in my sleep in my own home while my parents were hosting a neighborhood party just feet away. He was confident, bold---too bold. And that would be his mistake.

One day, he took me on another motorcycle ride, with my father's resounding permission, still clueless of this fuck head, leading us to a secluded wooded area. I knew what was coming. Fear gripped every part of me. He forced me down to the ground, my helmet still on, as he loomed over me.

But fate intervened. A group of children stumbled upon us. Their horrified screams sent Chester scrambling. They saved me that day, those children. I never got to thank them, but if any of them are reading this, know that you changed my life and saved me that day.

I was just a child when my innocence was torn from me---quietly, violently, without warning. One day, I was small and whole; the next, something sacred had cracked wide open inside me. The way I saw life shifted overnight. When the very people who brought me into this world---my parents---couldn't protect me, it rewired everything. Security. Trust. The idea that adults were safe.

I told myself it was no one's fault that no parent could see the invisible. That you'd have to think like a monster to ever suspect monstrous behavior. But knowing that didn't change the damage. Any sense of real safety vanished, replaced by a gnawing insecurity that never quite healed.

Sleep became the enemy. I'd lie awake in the dark, my heart pounding like footsteps fleeing from something unseen, dreading the moment my eyes would close. Because when they did, the nightmares came. Not the kind with shadows under the bed. Worse. The kind where I was still awake. Still trapped. Still voiceless. Those nights made me question if I ever truly woke up at all.

It changes you, that kind of wound. Not just in childhood, but forever. It creeps into everything---every friendship, every relationship, every attempt at love. I learned early how to keep walls high and answers short. I laughed when I didn't feel like it. I told people I was fine when I wasn't. Because admitting the truth meant handing someone a loaded weapon and trusting they wouldn't pull the trigger.

Trust became a currency I didn't hand out easily. And when I did, it was with conditions, escape routes built in. Even as a man, I'd catch myself scanning for exits in restaurants, clocking people's tones, memorizing tells. I wasn't just living---I was bracing.

Love, when it came, felt like a gamble I couldn't afford to lose. I held women close with one arm and kept the other ready to shove them away if they got too close to the cracks. I wanted intimacy but feared it like fire---drawn to the warmth, terrified of the burn. And when betrayal came, it wasn't just heartbreak. It was confirmation. Proof that the world was just as unsafe as I'd always feared.

In the back of my mind, that child still sat awake in the dark, waiting for the footsteps. Waiting for the next nightmare. And maybe that's why I chased chaos as hard as I did---strip clubs, fast money, fast women, anything to keep me moving. Because standing still meant remembering.

Trauma doesn't leave. It mutates. Some nights it whispered. Some nights it screamed. And even now, all these years later, I can still feel the echo of that first fracture.

Because when innocence is stolen, it doesn't just take your childhood. It takes the map you were supposed to follow through life. And you spend the rest of your days trying to redraw it in the dark.

I stopped trusting people. And if I'm honest, I stopped trusting myself, too. Not just because I was broken, but because deep down I believed I should've been stronger. Smarter. More cunning. I torture myself with it sometimes---the ways I might have fought back, the words I could've said, the moves I could've made.

Retrospect is a cruel game. Monday morning quarterbacking at its finest. But when I let myself go there, I wonder if fighting back could've changed things. Not just for me, but for others. Maybe my retaliation could've stopped the cycle. Maybe it could've saved other lives from this same kind of hell.

That guilt isn't a visitor---it's a tenant. It sets up camp in the corners of your mind and refuses to leave. And I can't shake the thought that my silence, my inaction, gave the monster room to breathe.

Who knows? Maybe that backdrop explains why, later in life, I charged into rooms with arrogance, acting like the wise-ass young adult who always had the answer. Maybe that's why I made reckless choices that cost me opportunities I'll never get back.

Trauma doesn't sit neatly in a box---it slithers. It grows legs. It moves. It destroys. Not in the casual, promise-breaking way people like to talk about, but in the soul-deep way that robs you of trust.

That kind of trust doesn't just break---it vanishes. It was like living behind glass. I could see people. Hear them laugh. Watch them reach for me. But I couldn't get out, and they couldn't get in.

So I mimicked friendship. I smiled on cue. Nodded when the jokes landed. Played along like I was present. But I wasn't there. Not really. I was locked somewhere else---inside a room no one could see.

And I was angry. Furious, especially at my parents. I needed them to see me---not the version they wanted, not the grades and the forced smiles, but the quiet, haunted boy flinching at creaks in the night, drowning under a weight no kid should carry.

They were there---doing dishes, folding laundry, asking how my day was---but they were miles away from my truth. And that distance? That broke me more than anything.

I was already drowning in trauma I couldn't name. It pressed on my chest like concrete. I didn't understand what had happened, but I knew

I'd never be the same. And I couldn't tell a soul. Not a teacher. Not a friend. Not even my own reflection.

I had already learned the lesson: silence was safer than trust, and numbness was easier than hope. So I carried it alone. Quietly. Invisibly. Wrapped in armor, no one could see. Waiting for a rescue that never came.

Chester eventually stopped coming after me, but he didn't stop. Others in the neighborhood finally confided in me. We all knew. We all suffered in silence, finally together.

It wasn't until years later, during a heated argument in front of my parents, nothing related to them, that I blurted out the words I had kept inside for so long: "Where were you when I was being molested by your pervert friend Chester?" My parents were stunned. They had no idea. The guilt consumed them, but I told them what I now know to be true---there was no way they could have known. Chester was too good at hiding in plain sight, and I was even better at keeping my secret.

The scars did shape me in some ways that I didn't fully understand until much later. My trust in people was shattered. My relationships suffered. My sense of self was distorted. I sought escape in alcohol as early as twelve years old. I numbed myself and detached from the world.

As time passed, I refused to let Chester continue to define me. For years, Eres Tú by Mocedades stirred something in me---something dark. I didn't know why. Hell, I didn't even understand the lyrics---they're in Spanish. But that melody? It dragged me back to some shadowed corner of my past. A place filled with fear, helplessness... things I couldn't name, let alone face.

It took years before I had the guts to really listen---to sit with the words, line by line, and trace the ache back to its source. That song had teeth. And it never let go. It's just a song. But music doesn't need permission. It bypasses logic, punches straight through the armor, and lands where it hurts---or heals. That's why each chapter starts with a song.

A trigger. A memory. A mood. Because every story needs a soundtrack.

Eres Tú? Yeah, it used to trigger something buried deep. Not because of the lyrics---I didn't even know what they meant back then---but because of the timing. It played during those years. The dark ones. When everything felt out of my control. But I'm not that scared kid anymore.

Now I hear the words---really hear them---and they're beautiful. Soulful. Nothing like the fear they used to echo. The pain was never in the song---it was in what surrounded it. Today, it's still on my playlist. This time, when I hit play, it's not with fear. It's with peace.

I've taken that pain, that trauma, and forged it into strength because my childhood was altered in ways I couldn't understand back then. And in that confusion, I wasn't the son my parents deserved---or the big brother I wanted to be. I wish I'd been more honest with my parents, more present, and a better role model to my siblings. That truth weighs on me. But the reality is, I was fighting a demon that had me outgunned. My energy, my focus, my very being was spent just trying to survive---searching for answers in the dark with no map, no light, and no language for the pain.

To my parents and siblings, I'm sorry I couldn't be better when it mattered most. I was lost. And I hope, somehow, you've found it in your hearts to forgive the boy who was just trying to make sense of a world that never made sense to him. But I survived. And survival---that's the foundation of healing. The good news?

Google says Chester's most likely dead. Good!

Hopefully that bad seed is exactly where he belongs---some scorched corner of hell, burning alongside the rest of the fuckheads.

Knock, knock.

"Who's there?"

That question's chased me longer than I care to admit. And truth be told, I've rarely liked the answer. Hopefully, it's still you---still here, eyes on the page, curiosity not completely crushed. If so, bless your twisted little heart. That last stretch? Yeah... heavy. Like dragging emotional cinder blocks through molasses. But we made it.

We crawled through the wreckage. Now it's time to breathe, maybe even laugh---because life isn't just scars and sucker punches. It's also bizarre detours, half-baked miracles, and screw-ups so spectacular they deserve their own spotlight.

And trust me---I've got a few of those locked and loaded. If this were a movie, we'd cue the comic relief. That well-timed breather after the storm. So, in that spirit---let me tell you about the first time I fell in love.

She was in her thirties, effortlessly gorgeous, with that face you don't forget and a chest that defied gravity and reason. The kind of woman who could make a young teenage boy forget his own name. And the best part? She was the only woman I could have been completely naked in my room without my parents batting an eye.

We spent endless nights together. No words. No awkward silences. Just me, lying on my bed, staring at her like she held the answers to everything I didn't yet understand. It was simple. It was pure. But to me, back then? It was a full-blown relationship---with a woman way out of my league, and somehow, still all mine. And yeah... that was the moment I knew. Her name was Nadine.

Nadine shared my room for years---until my grandmother moved in. You, know, the saint I spoke of early that was vacuum-sealed into this mess of ours. She found Nadine highly inappropriate and waged a full-on campaign to banish her from my room. To me, Nadine was harmless, beautiful, and mine. But my grandmother saw things differently. She became relentless, making it her mission to rid the house of Nadine.

I'd head off to school, come home, and boom---Nadine was gone. Again. Sometimes it took me days to track her down. Closet. Under the bed. Once, rolled up behind the dryer like some shameful secret.

It turned into a full-blown turf war---my teenage hormones and loyalty to my first love, versus my grandmother, a devout woman with a Bible in one hand and a no-nonsense glare in the other. A clash of titans. She saw sin; I saw art.

By now, you've probably figured it out---Nadine wasn't exactly flesh and blood. She was real... in the form of a 24x36-inch poster that came home courtesy of my dad after winning a Cadillac sales contest. And to a teenage boy in the throes of discovery, Nadine wasn't just a poster---she was gospel. My heterosexual north star. A work of art with a perfect face, perfect body, and zero judgment.

After weeks of back-and-forth, I finally wore my grandmother down. Maybe she realized this battle wasn't worth fighting. Maybe she just got tired of dragging Nadine out of hiding. Either way, she gave in---with a dramatic sigh and a muttered prayer---and Nadine was granted full-time wall residency.

She stayed there, my silent muse, until I left for the Navy. When I came back? Gone. Disappeared. Vanished in a move like she never existed. I still miss her. Not in a creepy way. Okay... maybe a little. I still remember her. And if I could see her just once more, I would.

Looking back, I believe Nadine may have been a premonition of sorts---an early glimpse into one of the most financially rewarding, controversial, and, dare I say, colorful careers I would later find myself in. But I digress...

During the Nadine years, she bore witness to plenty of mischief. My sister---just a year younger than me---had a bedroom right next to mine. We both hosted our fair share of sleepovers, hers with her friends, mine with mine. And let's just say, once the parents were fast asleep, the walls between our rooms might as well have disappeared.

It was a time of exploration, of youthful curiosity, and---at least in our minds---completely appropriate for our age. It was an education of sorts, one that paved the way for future indulgences. While many puppy loves came and went, my beautiful Nadine will always be the first. And she will always have a special place in my heart.

And then there were the surprises---things I never imagined possible at the time but still look back on fondly today. Like the night I somehow found myself in a circle of eleven beautiful Cheerleaders, with me the only guy making out with each one of them. Stud never entered my sphere of thought of myself. Timing and lucky as hell, was more like it. I was never the most popular guy in high school, nor did I consider myself particularly more than average looking. But that night, surrounded by those beautiful girls, I felt like Hugh Hefner---if only I had known who Hugh Hefner was back then.

Then came my first 4 wheeled mode of transportation---a custom Dodge van.

Yeah, a van. And I was weirdly proud of it. Felt like I'd finally crossed some line into adulthood, like I owned a piece of the world. I tricked it out with a wooden partition, covered the thing in thick, shaggy fabric like some busted-down limousine divider---all to block the view of what I hoped would go down in the back. Hell, I even tossed in a foam mattress. Yeah… I really went there. And what happened behind that partition? Let's just say, I might be a lot of things---but I still believe in keeping a few memories just for me.

Now, on to the less "benign" moments---like getting run over by a garbage truck when I was four. Slow speed, thank God, but still enough to drag me under and leave some permanent souvenirs. Or the time I tripped and fell into smoldering coals at a construction site---hello, third-degree burns on my arm and chest. Those early ER visits? They gifted me a lifelong fear of doctors and anesthesia. Thanks for the trauma, ether!

Still, what doesn't kill you makes for killer cocktail-party stories, right?

By fifteen, I was already hustling---zipping around on my motorcycle with a mobile window-washing gig. Then came my first "real" job: detailing Cadillacs at the dealership where my dad worked. Not long after, his old high school buddy from Georgia dangled a big opportunity---partner in a dealership, real money, new life.

So we packed up and headed to Galaxy Beach, Georgia. Dad thrived. Mom chased her dream of becoming an OBGYN. And me? I crash-landed into high school with all the grace of a lawn dart.

Ah, high school. I wasn't exactly valedictorian, but I made it out with a diploma and memories of friendships, first loves, and plenty of shenanigans. Social media has been a blessing, letting me reconnect with those people and see where life has taken them---both the good and the bad.

Shortly after Nadine, I fell in love with a real person---the girl who would later become my future wife and, eventually, my future ex-wife: Regina. She moved into the next community over---just a few blocks from us in Galaxy Beach---and from the moment we met, I knew she wasn't like the others. She was different. Fascinating. Dangerous, in that beautiful way.

Five foot eight, legs like they were drawn by a man with too much time and not enough shame, and a chest that could've put Nadine to shame---sorry, Nadine. Long, sun-bleached blonde hair that looked like it belonged in a shampoo commercial. She was natural. Effortless. The kind of beautiful that didn't need filters or filler. People used to say she was a dead ringer for Farrah Fawcett. And they weren't wrong.

Fun fact? Her mom once dated Lee Majors. Yeah---that kind of bloodline.

There was just one problem---her boyfriend.

So, we struck a compromise: best friends… with benefits. For years, we played this twisted game of emotional chicken, toeing the line between loyalty and lust. We called it harmless. We called it special. But let's be real---cheating is cheating, and even if it was a half-step, it still put a bullet in her relationship.

She was eighteen when it stopped being innocent. I'd climb through her bedroom window after curfew like some hormone-fueled Romeo, and you already know where that road ends. I'd love to say I was a gentleman about it, but I wasn't. I was a teenage boy with zero brakes and too much access. But hey---growth is real. Regret too. Needless to say, after her boyfriend discovered what she was doing, Regina became a punching bag for her boyfriend, then dumped her. Good thing she didn't stay.

Then it all went sideways. Regina got pregnant.

My family? They stepped up, offered to adopt the baby. They saw a path forward that didn't end in trauma. But her family? They couldn't stomach the idea of me being permanently tied to their daughter. Not then, not ever. They wanted the problem erased, not solved.

So the decision was made---without me. The pregnancy was terminated. It wasn't mine to make, but it was mine to live with. My family mourned. I still do. We had a way out that wouldn't have wrecked anyone's future. But our voices were drowned out by fear, by shame, by her family's iron grip on control.

Still, Regina and I stayed together. Months later, we got engaged. The plan? Get married after I finished Navy Boot Camp. But something happened when I hit the fleet: I woke the hell up. No parents, no rules, no expectations---just me, 18, unchained and wide-eyed.

And then it hit me like a freight train: I was a kid, barely shaving, already shackled to the idea of forever. Marriage stopped feeling romantic and started feeling like a prison sentence. That hesitation? It was real and a mistake.

Because what Regina and I had was real, too. That reckless, first-love kind of real. But love isn't enough when your life is duct-taped together. We were kids with paychecks from fast food joints and dreams of escaping our parents' couches. That's not romance. That's survival mode. And you don't build a marriage on survival---you build it on something solid. We didn't have solid. We had chaos. Then came the second bombshell: Regina was pregnant again.

Just like that, every exit vanished. I was boxed in. Her family already had me pegged as the villain---the dumbass who knocked up their daughter and tanked her future. They weren't offering support. They weren't even offering decency. Their contribution to our wedding was pocket change and a pile of attitude.

I knew that if I bailed now, I wouldn't just be leaving Regina---I'd be confirming every horrible thing they said about me. And for all our mess, she deserved better than that. So we got married. I'd love to tell you it felt right. That I found peace somewhere in that honeymoon haze. But I'd be lying. Even on the honeymoon, I knew I'd made the wrong call. Regina was beautiful. Kind. Loving. She deserved someone all-in. The problem wasn't her---it was me. I hadn't lived.

No college. No real dating. No freedom. Just diapers, debt, and the echo of the life I never gave myself a chance to explore. I told myself we were doing the right thing---for her, for us, for our son, Bailey, who came into the world not long after the vows.

I'd already tasted business back in New England---young, scrappy, reckless in all the ways you can afford to be when there's nothing to lose. But now? I had mouths to feed. Dreams had price tags. Risk wasn't sexy anymore---it was survival. I didn't need a wild idea. I needed a paycheck. Something steady. Something that didn't break.

Because my Navy role was part-time---active reserve---a full-time gig was inevitable. So when we moved in together, I took the logical step: back to my dad's dealership. Ground floor again. Regina worked there too, managing the admin side while I scrubbed bug guts off bumpers and vacuumed crushed Cheerios out of back seats. It wasn't glamorous, but it was stable. Familiar.

Then came the curveball.

Regina started spending more time with a younger guy from her department---too much time. I tried to play it cool, but gut instincts don't lie. And sure enough, one afternoon, I walked in on them---mid-liplock. Not a goodbye peck. Not a misunderstanding. Full-tilt, eyes-closed, make-out session.

Game on.

Still, those early ventures---and the lessons---lit the fuse for something better. They laid the groundwork for everything that came next. Those early days? They were just the warm-up. It's about to get more interesting.

Chapter 3

Scarlett's Secrets Recipe

Ordinary World
Performed by: **Duran Duran**
Written by *Simon Le Bon*

Like the song *Ordinary World*---which, ironically, is the complete opposite of Scarlett's Secrets---I had to find a new way to survive. I went from having nothing to… well, you'll find out soon enough.

My dad, now well settled in his position as principal at a multi-line General Motors dealership, it felt like we'd hit the damn jackpot. Shiny new cars lined up like soldiers---Buicks, Pontiacs, Cadillacs---all gleaming under showroom lights. Hell, there was even a Lamborghini Countach parked out front, thanks to his partner's midlife-crisis-sized wallet. I never got to drive it, but just being around it was electric. My dad had made it. Big leagues. I was the lucky bastard riding shotgun.

Then I went and fucked it all up.

With my last name on the building, I acted like I owned the place. Mouthy. Entitled. Untouchable. I strutted around like I was GM royalty, treating the staff like background extras in my coming-of-age drama. I wasn't earning a damn thing---I was coasting. Arrogance wrapped in youth, sealed with a smart-ass grin.

Didn't take long for my dad's business partner to catch wind. The guy wasn't just his partner---he was his old high school buddy, and he didn't like what he saw. One conversation, and that was it. The axe dropped. Hard. I was out. No speech. No warning. Just gone.

At the time, I was working in the detail bay, scrubbing floor mats and pretending it was the first step on my rise to dealership royalty. The real plan---at least the one that lived on paper---was for me to rotate through every department, learn the ropes, and then head off to General Motors Dealer School. That was the pipeline. That was the legacy. And I pissed it all away. With a big mouth and a chip on my shoulder.

Once the dust settled, it hit me like a crowbar to the chest---what I'd lost wasn't just a job. It was the future I didn't know I wanted until it slipped through my fingers. The business, the path, the nameplate---it all shattered. And as long as that partner was still sitting behind the desk, I knew I wasn't getting so much as a foot back through the door. So I did the only thing I could: I left. Bitter, broke, and bruised.

They say, "Once a car guy, always a car guy." And yeah, the sound of a revving engine still does something to me. But the last name stitched on my shirt made me radioactive. Nobody in the industry wanted me around. They saw Walker and figured I was a spy---sent in to poach secrets and funnel intel back to the dealership I'd already been booted from.

They were wrong. I admired my dad's skill. Hell, I still do. But that doesn't mean I didn't carry a grudge.

I carried it like a badge.

Still, somewhere deep down, I had a gut feeling: fate had unfinished business. I figured sooner or later, my dad's partner---the one who pushed me out---would find his own exit door. And maybe, just maybe, the door would crack open for me again.

In the meantime, I landed a job at a Toyota dealership just outside of Galaxy Beach, selling cars while still doing my time in the Navy Reserve. The reality of unreliable income hit like a slap from life itself. I watched the sales team---seasoned pros, most of them---trapped in jobs they hated. Day after day, they showed up with the same tired look in their eyes, all quietly wishing the mirror would show them someone else. They weren't chasing dreams---they were chasing rent.

At twenty-three, I was married, already had two kids, and Regina was pregnant with twins---our third and fourth. I was scraping by on thirty to forty grand a year. Even in the '80s, that kind of money barely kept the lights on, let alone fed a growing family. Regina stayed home with the kids, and I was the whole show---the only breadwinner, the entire financial engine coughing on fumes. Every month was a balancing act between bills and basic survival. Something had to give, and I could feel the pressure building like a boiler ready to blow.

Between waiting for customers---affectionately known as "victims"---and dodging dealership poker games designed to fund "beer-thirty," I had a lot of time to think. I watched the owners rake in profits while the rest of us fought over table scraps. The dealership's owner, this so-called "astute businessman," spent more time being carried out drunk than actually running the place. This couldn't be the endgame.

So, I started looking around. Asking myself: What business makes money no matter what? The answer came fast and clear---alcohol. The problem was, I didn't have the money to back an idea like that. So, I did the next best thing: I mapped out a bold little plan on paper and sent it off to the state of Georgia. No money, no connections---just a long shot. And to be honest, I never expected a response.

Then came the infamous Camry Wagon moment.

I'd pitched a couple on the car, but they were torn between ours and a Nissan across town. So, I took a page out of my own playbook---bold and borderline stupid. I drove the Camry Wagon straight to the Nissan lot and parked it nose-to-nose with theirs. The couple laughed. The Nissan salesman looked like he was about to have a stroke. Their manager came out, veins popping, and physically escorted me off the lot.

Back at the dealership, my manager was caught between pissed and impressed. "You've got guts, Walker," he said. And just like that, I was Employee of the Month.

Oh---and the couple? They bought the Camry, and from there, I was confident in my ability to carve my own pathway forward, that I won't let anything stand in the way to make my way.

A few months later, life threw me a hell of a curveball: my liquor license application was approved. Just like that, I had a shot to change my fate.

Enter the saloon---a grimy, 10,000 square feet of half-dead beer-and-wine joint that hadn't seen a mop, a fresh coat of paint, or a sober customer in god knows how long. It had all the charm of a crime scene with a liquor license. The kind of place where the air was thick with regret, spilled beer, and whatever else the barflies were marinating in that day. I had my hands full, but I was stubborn---determined to make something of this sorry excuse for a building.

I locked it down with sheer hustle, a $50,000 loan from my dad, and an old owner who'd finally agreed to finance the rest, though, let's be honest, he was more interested in getting out than handing me the keys. My old man, ever the cautious type, threw me a hell of a lot of side-eye. He wasn't thrilled about the whole thing. But like most dads, he was too proud to show it---outwardly, he grumbled and resisted every step of the way, but in the end, I knew he was all in. Behind that stubborn exterior, he had my back, even if he didn't exactly know what I was trying to do with a rundown dive in the middle of nowhere.

The place itself was a wreck. Dirt parking lot, peeling paint, the kind of building that seemed to sag under the weight of its own poor decisions. The regulars? Well, let's just say they treated deodorant and dental care like optional luxuries. It was the kind of crowd you wouldn't catch dead bringing your grandmother around. But I saw something in it---something most wouldn't. Potential, or maybe it was just desperation wrapped in neon lights. Either way, I had a vision.

Reality slapped me fast. The staff were loyal to the previous owner, and theft was the house specialty. Booze vanished by the case, the register looked like it hadn't seen a dollar in days, and even the cleaning crew joined the looting spree. I had no choice but to fire everyone and start from scratch.

For a while, it was just me---working 7 a.m. to 2 a.m., learning the business one broken bottle and bloodstain at a time. I dodged fights, cleaned bathrooms, kept the lights on, and tried not to drown in debt. Glamorous? Not even close.

Then came a turning point, courtesy of a part-time DJ I'd hired to liven up the dead-end weekends. He leaned over one night and said, "Why not hire topless dancers?"

At that point, I was broke, exhausted, and out of ideas. So we did our research---meaning we hit up every topless joint within driving distance. What we saw was undeniable: these places were packed. The energy was electric, the money was flowing, and the women running the show were professionals who knew how to keep a room alive.

That's when it hit me---this little dump of a bar could be reborn. Not as just another watering hole, but as a full-fledged gentlemen's club. The blueprint for success was right in front of me. And best of all---it wasn't illegal.

People called me crazy. Some still do. My wife, Regina, and my mother both threatened to disown me. The warnings came hard and heavy--- moral lectures, whispered gossip, veiled threats. But I ignored them all. Because deep down, I knew this could work. I had no safety net left. Only guts, blind ambition, and a credit card with just enough left to light the fuse.

So I took the plunge. Sold anything that wasn't nailed down. Cleared the legal hurdles. And then, Scarlett's Secrets was born---my shot at reinvention, wrapped in red lights and unapologetic hustle.

Enter stage left: makeshift construction. And when I say "makeshift," I mean a one-foot-high plywood stage slapped together with linoleum flooring, 2x4 railings, and the unmistakable aura of something built by a drunk uncle at a backyard barbecue.

Fun fact: it was built by a drunk guy---balding, toothless, and as questionable as his carpentry skills.

And the pole? There wasn't one. But no pole, no problem. We hired three dancers---none of them exactly pageant queens, but they could move, they showed up, and they knew how to work a room. Add a fully stocked bar and the right mix of desperation and curiosity, and suddenly, we had a formula that filled the place fast. It wasn't art---it was survival with a G-string. And it worked.

The clientele? Let's just say fresh clothes and functioning livers were still in short supply. But the cash? That started flowing like a busted fire hydrant in August.

Scarlett's Secrets didn't just become a gentlemen's club---it became a full-blown financial resurrection. Within 30 days, I was out of the red, shelves fully stocked, and twenty grand sitting fat in my checking account. For the first time in a long time, the light at the end of the tunnel wasn't a train barreling toward me---it was opportunity, flicking the high beams.

The dive bar was dead. In its place, a legit club was being born---new name, new layout, new rules. I'd gone from slinging used cars and babysitting a booze-soaked dump to running a top-tier gentlemen's club pulling in damn near seven figures. In the '80s. Ferdinand Porsche once said about his cars, "We are what nobody needs but everybody wants." The same goes for strip clubs. Nobody needs 'em. But damn if everybody doesn't want 'em.

My role quickly shifted into talent scout, quality control, and keeper of the velvet rope. Let's just say some auditions were… unforgettable---for all the wrong reasons. Without getting too graphic, I'll put it like this: not every asset belongs under a spotlight.

Mother Nature hadn't been generous to every woman who stepped on that stage. And to be blunt, not all dancers should've been fully nude---

even when the law said they could. I mean, come on---some things are better left to the imagination. Mystery can be sexy. A biology lesson at eye level? Not so much.

Back then, the "landscape" situation was like spinning a roulette wheel blindfolded. A clean trim was rare, and some of the ladies were rocking what I can only describe as rainforest chic. Full-grown brush---lush, untrimmed, prehistoric. I'm talking vines that looked like they hadn't seen daylight since the Reagan administration.

One girl had so much overgrowth, I swear if you leaned in close enough, you could hear birds nesting. Another had what I can only assume was a territorial squirrel. I'm not saying it was a fire hazard, but if someone lit a match too close, we'd need the sprinkler system and a priest.

And it wasn't just the foliage. There were nights I caught myself questioning my own manhood. A couple of the dancers looked like they were smuggling extra gear. Maybe that was jealousy. Maybe it was fear. All I know is, when a customer pays for a private dance, he shouldn't leave with self-esteem issues and a nervous tic.

But honestly, the real buzzkill wasn't the Amazonian growth---it was hygiene. Some of the girls just didn't take care of themselves. And guys, being guys, still wanted the full face-dive like it was all-you-can-eat shrimp night.

We had to draw a line. Because when you're running a club and a dancer walks by and you suddenly understand what the word "funk" really means… it's time to set boundaries. At some point, it stopped being sexy and started feeling like a public health crisis with stiletto heels.

So we made the call. For the safety of the customers---and for our own sanity---we started restricting and regulating some of the nudity in our club. It wasn't about being uptight. It was about survival.

Because nothing empties a VIP room faster than cheap perfume, stale smoke, and the sudden, horrifying realization that you're face-to-face with something that smells like it lost a custody battle with a sponge.

But this was business, and I had to sort through it all---Mother Nature's sense of humor included.

You know that saying, "Some things you can't unsee"? Yeah, I've got a whole playlist. God made some fine tools---and some that not even the loneliest soul with a pocket full of singles could pretend to love.

As the club grew, the old freeloaders started noticing the change. The mooches---the ones who used to drink cheap beer and hang out for free---realized their gravy train had derailed. I even teamed up with a rival bar owner to give them a new home. Poetic justice? You bet.

The remodel kicked into high gear, and the operation exploded. What started as duct tape and bar fights turned into a full-fledged machine---25 staff members, 75 entertainers, and real momentum.

But with growth came new problems. That's when George showed up. A seasoned vet in the business, he saw the blind spots I didn't. Thanks to his guidance, I dodged more bullets than I care to count---employees with hidden agendas, dancers with sharper instincts than Wall Street sharks, and customers who smelled opportunity like blood in the water.

Without George, I'd have been chewed up and spit out. But with him in my corner, I stayed in the game---and kept building something that was finally bigger than my past.

With a tidal wave of staff to manage, running the entire operation solo was a fantasy. I had no choice but to build a management team---people to oversee security, DJs, waitstaff, bartenders, and dancers. : The problem was, I'd never run a business this size before. No playbook. No blueprint. I was winging it---pure trial and error. Mostly error.

Luckily, George stepped in when he could and offered some much-needed guidance. To bring order to the chaos, I hired three managers--- one for days, one for nights, and a part-timer for weekends and fill-ins. My gut told me the only way to keep them honest was to pay them well.

Real well. These were the people handling thousands in cash every night.

So I sweetened the pot---fat salaries, bonus plans, health insurance, and for the cherry on top, I bought each one a brand-new Cadillac from my dad's dealership as a company vehicle to drive. The goal? Lock down their loyalty. Make them feel too valued to steal from me.

Wrong.

Despite everything, they skimmed. They all found their angles--- bartenders pocketing cash by skipping rings, doormen charging at the door but never counting the heads, DJs stealing VIP dance money and squeezing dancers for under-the-table gratuities. Everyone had a side hustle, and most everyone was in on it. And still, somehow, gross profits hit nearly 90% margins during my run. It was insane. They lined their pockets and laughed behind my back. It gutted me. Infuriated me.

But I wasn't one of them. I didn't hang after hours. I didn't party, didn't chase drugs, didn't screw around---yet. I was married. I played by the law. Theft just wasn't wired into me. So I couldn't fully grasp how easily they robbed me blind, like it was just part of the job description. My first attempt at trusting people to help run my business was a crash-and-burn lesson in betrayal. I had to fire two of the managers. But before I could lower the axe, one of them played a dirty little card.

Turns out, one of the cocktail waitresses had developed a thing for me. Nothing happened---never crossed the line---but there'd been just enough casual friendliness to be twisted into something it wasn't. And that's exactly what he reminded me of.

That manager, in a final act of retaliation, saw his moment. As a parting gift, he tried to blackmail me. Demanded the car I'd provided as his company ride---threatening to "blow the roof off" a scandal that didn't even exist.

I was blindsided. Naïve. Still learning how twisted the rules could get in the world I was now neck-deep in. I didn't cave completely, but I didn't walk away clean either. He didn't get the Cadillac---but he did drive off in a pretty decent consolation prize, now titled in his name. And trust me--- it only gets better from here.

Let's talk about one of humanity's oldest hustle models: good old-fashioned prostitution. Too risqué? Maybe. But if you're not here to rattle the cage a little, what the hell are we doing? Opinions on the subject are as varied as the ways to burn a soufflé, and if we gotta agree to disagree, well... welcome to adulthood.

Now picture this: A guy buys a lap dance. The dancer does her thing, grinds his dick until he gets a little too into it and---boom---wardrobe malfunction. Nip-slip, ass-out, the whole damn buffet. Technically, is that sex for money? Is it prostitution? That legal brainworm bounced around my skull more than once. But thank God it never crawled into a courtroom---at least not on my watch. And let's not pretend it was always the guys pushing the limits. Some of the girls got just as carried away. They'd get off on each other right there in the VIP room or at a table--- no shame, full display, and the crowd ate it up like it was dessert. And I'll be honest---once that energy gets rolling, it's hard to throw the brakes on without killing the whole vibe.

But here's the rub---no pun intended. If the line ever got crossed---if fantasy tipped into something real, even once---I wasn't just some bystander. I was the one with the target on my back. Not just the dancer. Me.

Enter the RICO Act. That's not just some obscure statute you hear tossed around in mob movies. RICO---short for the Racketeer Influenced and Corrupt Organizations Act---was passed in 1970 to bring down organized crime. Think mob families, drug cartels, criminal syndicates. But here's the kicker: it's been expanded and weaponized over the years to take down all kinds of businesses, including adult clubs, when certain illegal activities happen under their roof. How it works is chilling.

The law allows prosecutors to charge owners, operators, and even employees as part of a criminal enterprise if a pattern of illegal conduct happens repeatedly, over time. You don't need to be the one turning tricks or dealing drugs. You just need to be in charge while it's happening---and not stopping it. Suddenly, you're no longer just a business owner. You're the head of a criminal operation, whether you knew it or not.

Let's say one of my dancers crosses the line---offers a little "extra" for a client in the champagne room, behind closed doors. That's prostitution. Now let's say it happens again. And again. Add in a bartender dealing blow in the bathroom or a bouncer turning a blind eye to it because he's getting a cut. That's a pattern. That's enough to build a RICO case.

Under RICO, that one dancer's decision becomes everyone's problem---mine especially. Because they don't need to prove I told her to do it. All they need to show is that it happened under my roof, on my watch, and I should've known. That's the part that stings. "Should have known" is all it takes. The burden of ignorance doesn't protect you---it convicts you. It's not a stretch. It's already happened.

Take the case of Rick Rizzolo, the former owner of the Crazy Horse Too in Las Vegas. The club was a moneymaker, famous for its high rollers, celebrity clientele, and wild energy. But beneath the neon and champagne, there were persistent whispers—claims of illegal payoffs, violence, and ties to organized crime. Eventually, federal investigators brought a RICO case. Rizzolo pled guilty to tax evasion connected to that broader investigation and served prison time. The club? Shuttered. Millions gone.

Another example: Michael Galardi, the owner of several strip clubs in Las Vegas and San Diego. His venues became the center of a sweeping public-corruption scandal—cash payoffs, influence peddling, and federal investigators circling. He ultimately pled guilty to conspiracy charges in connection with bribing local officials and cooperated with prosecutors, but still served time. His empire? Gone.

You don't need to be a kingpin to catch a case. You just need to not react fast enough when your business starts slipping into the gray---or worse, red---zone. And here's the thing: there's no manual titled How to Run a Strip Club Without Losing Your Mind or Your License. You learn on the fly. You trust your instincts. Some dancers are polished, all business---sharp as razors with boundaries like barbed wire. Others? They see rules as soft suggestions, especially when the money's right.

And the customers? Jesus. Some of them couldn't tell the difference between fantasy and consent if it walked up and slapped them with a subpoena. I've had to escort more than a few out, mid-zipper, mid-stupidity. No, we didn't offer to help 'em tuck it back in. But every time something like that happened, my heart skipped. Because all it takes is one. One dumb decision. One repeat offense.

And the feds come knocking with handcuffs and a RICO playbook. Suddenly, you're not running a club---you're running for your life. That's the game. High risk. High reward. And one wrong move from losing it all.

But here's the thing---clubs like mine served a purpose. For some guys, it was an escape hatch. A fantasyland. A smoke-filled dream where no one judged and nothing from the outside world could sneak in. Just adults playing make-believe behind blackout curtains and bad decisions---guilt-free.

Sure, not all of them understood it was just an act. But that wasn't our responsibility.

Men have been doing dumb shit for sex since the first cave painting. All we did was give them a sandbox to play in---with rules, security, and a nightly cash-out. And here's a fun little absurdity: you can make prostitution legal... by filming it. Voilà---it's art. Porn turns felonies into feature films and makes Hollywood look like a church bake sale in comparison. Capitalism at its freakiest.

At the end of the day, I've always seen prostitution for what it is: a transaction. Supply. Demand. Raw commerce. Some men pay for sex because they have to. Some women sell it because they can. As long as everyone's in on the terms, who the hell are we to judge? Morality's been weaponized since the beginning of time. Me? I'll take honesty over hypocrisy any day. Let people live. Mind your business.

And don't confuse fantasy for consent---because that's where the line lives.

Not everyone was thrilled with our new venture. Practically overnight, the club became a magnet for law enforcement, code enforcement, and every other official with a clipboard and a badge, all keeping a watchful eye on our every move. But I ran a clean operation---no drugs, no shady deals, and strict rules that everyone had to follow. Hands off the dancers, no grinding, and absolutely no funny business. Funny business. Yeah, that's a term that gets thrown around a lot. But let's be real: growing a street strip club is a damn oxymoron. It's a recipe for chaos---straight-up debauchery. You get every stereotype you could imagine: dancers, patrons, and don't forget the occasional cop who stumbles in to "check things out." Funny business covers anything you can't put a real name to---stuff that's either too weird or just flat-out part of the job description.

Let's face it, fellas don't throw cash for a dance just to feel a little soft, sensual rub. Nah, they want to feel the heat---literally and figuratively. And the grind? That's the name of the game. I mean, it's a constant grind. And I don't just mean the lap dance. Sometimes, it's literally grinding until a guy's sweating bullets, struggling to hold on, or trying to express himself in ways you didn't know were possible.

And the funny business? I've seen it all. Like the guy who thought poking fun at vaginas meant, well... poking them. And I'm not talking about a joke here; he was really poking. Or the guy who regressed so hard he was out there trying to latch on to a nipple like he was a baby. The only thing he was sucking on, though, was disappointment. And, of course, there was no milk in sight. But trust me, that wasn't the real goal.

The challenges, however, never stopped. Fake IDs, dancers breaking rules, and plumbing disasters courtesy of condoms flushed down the urinals---it was a never-ending battle. But despite the chaos, Scarlett's Secrets thrived, proving that with grit, determination, and a sense of humor, even the wildest ventures can pay off.

We weren't just a "titty bar"---we were a business. And while the phrase "gentlemen's club" might be one of the biggest oxymorons in history, I was determined to keep things as professional as possible in this decidedly unprofessional world.

Looking back, the transformation of Scarlett's Secrets was nothing short of miraculous. What started as a last-ditch effort to save my business turned into a life-changing success. Sure, it was messy, chaotic, and full of unexpected hurdles, but it was also exhilarating, rewarding, and just crazy enough to work.

Chapter 4

The Fugly Lights

Mama Told me not to Come
Performed by: **Three Dog Night**
Written by: **Randy Newman**

Like the song *Mama Told Me Not to Come*---my mother saw the club as a Demon's Den. It had no place in her belief system and wanted no part of it. Years later, her so-called peers---disrespectful and cruel---mocked her as the *Porn Queen of Galaxy Beach*. We were all mortified. Heartbroken, even. That moment hit me hard. A real Gotcha moment. Because damn---Mom was right.

Allow me to clear up a big myth about owning a gentlemen's club: It's not the endless party or money-printing machine you've seen in movies, or maybe that eluded to in the last chapter. Far from it. In reality, plunking your name on that club license paints a huge target on your back---everyone from local bureaucrats to the rumor mill stands ready with pitchforks. One day, you're the new business in town; the next, you're a "public menace" and the scapegoat for every moral panic under the sun.

So there I was, owner of Scarlett's Secrets---my shiny new business---freshly crowned as the local outcast. Getting here was no walk in the park, and I quickly discovered I'd just stepped onto a political minefield. Gentlemen's clubs have always been an easy piñata for power-hungry officials, and our little county was no exception. Politicians used us like pawns in a twisted game of "Who's The Toughest on Adult Entertainment?" Meanwhile, the media loved painting us as drug-infested, prostitution-riddled dens of iniquity. Fun times, right?

Enter Commissioner Pullman---my personal archnemesis. Picture a politician with a

Grin so wide you just know it's fake. One of those politician smiles--- the kind that hides a knife behind it. Pullman claimed he could "protect" my existing clubs from a brutal new ordinance. What he really meant was: play ball, or get steamrolled. The ordinance was designed to shove us out of sight---banish us to some neon-gutted red-light district where we'd be forced to cannibalize each other just to survive. Classic political sleight-of-hand: pretend it's about morality, but really, it's about power, control, and who gets to eat at the top of the food chain.

He dangled "grandfathering" as bait---promising he'd lock my clubs into their current locations if I backed off my plans to open a third club. In his precious little district. It was a threat dressed as a favor. And like any hustler who's been around long enough, I smelled the rot, but the fear of losing it all is a hell of a motivator. After a lot of pacing, cursing, and chewing on the bitter end of a cigar, I said yes.

Spoiler: he sold me out faster than a hot dog vendor on the Fourth of July.

That's politics. Smile, shake hands, and stab you in the kidneys when the cameras are off. I should've known better. But desperation makes you gamble on liars when they sound like the only lifeline in a sinking ship.

After that, I swore I'd never be that vulnerable again.

I started learning other trades---not out of passion, but survival. That fear never left me. The constant threat that one clueless employee or one politician with a Bible in one hand and a vote in the other could legislate me into oblivion. One bad judgment call, and I could wake up to find my entire livelihood buried in legalese and city council bullshit.

Like any good pilot, I always have an alternate route. You don't fly into storms without a plan to get out. I wasn't gonna be a one-trick pony. I learned how to pivot. Fast. From running clubs to fixing cars, to aviation, to transportation---I trained myself to survive whatever flavor of nonsense came down the pipe next.

Because here's the truth, most people won't say out loud: you can work your ass off, play by the rules, and still get flattened by somebody who's never had skin in the game. Some paper-pushing lifer making $48,000 a year with zero clue about the real world, who gets off on checking boxes and issuing citations like it's power porn.

And that's just local government.

Washington? A whole other beast. It's a circus. A padded-room full of overpaid sociopaths playing Monopoly with people's futures. These guys make six figures, insider trade their way into generational wealth, make disastrous decisions daily, and somehow we keep reelecting them. Why? Because they show up in campaign ads kissing babies and saying "God bless America" with their hand on a pickup truck.

The system's rigged, not in some tinfoil hat way---but in the painfully obvious way that slaps you across the face when you've lived through it. They regulate industries they don't understand. They slap "moral" labels on things they secretly enjoy after hours. It's not just frustrating---it's flat-out dangerous. It's an oversight with no insight. Authority without consequence.

So, when the county commission finally met to vote on the ordinance, I showed up, ready for war. I brought a small army of my most loyal patrons---guys who practically had reserved seats at Scarlett's Secrets. You'd think that would count for something.

Wrong.

By Tuesday night, these same guys were suddenly sitting in pews next to some fire-and-brimstone Baptist pastor, nodding along while he condemned the same dancers they'd been motorboating 48 hours earlier. One even shouted "Amen!" like he hadn't spent Saturday night with glitter in places he'd need a priest to cleanse.

Loyalty in this business? Let's just say it comes with an expiration date and a dash of hypocrisy. And as if Pullman wasn't enough, I also had to deal with Commissioner Ryan O'Mally. Poster boy for bullshit. Known drunk. Wife-beater, if you believe the whispers---and I do. Yet somehow he was the face of "community morals," sitting there casting votes on what's decent and what's not. That's politics in a nutshell: the wolves writing the rules for the sheep.

So yeah, the ordinance passed. Big regulatory haymaker. Stripped down what we could show, where we could be, and how we could operate. But, silver lining? It locked in the value of clubs like mine---if you were licensed within six months, you were golden. The scarcity made us worth more. Great, right? Wrong.

Because in the process, I'd been forced to kill my plans for the third club---one that would've brought in tens of millions. All flushed down the drain because I trusted a grinning snake in a cheap suit named Pullman.

So when people ask me why I'm cynical---why I don't trust the system, the handshake, or the speech---I tell them this story. Because I lived it. And I've still got the scars.

Of course, the fiasco didn't stop there. My life started feeling like a low-budget spy flick---wiretaps, undercover agents, bogus sting operations over "straddle dancing." That's right, straddle dancing, prostitution's cousin. You'd think we were smuggling uranium, not showcasing women in stilettos working their hustle.

Some dancers were solid---sharp, focused, came in to make their money and go home. But let's not sugarcoat it: a lot of them came with baggage. Broken homes, addictions, records, no diploma, no backup plan. The club was their lifeline and their powder keg, all rolled into one. And when you mixed that with ego, dope, and the kind of jealousy only women with rent due and stilettos on can brew---you got a pressure cooker that could blow on any night of the week.

Then there were the whispers, the deals in the parking lot, the pills passed under cocktail napkins. We tried to keep it clean, but the club scene always walks the line. It's a beautiful disaster by design---loud, chaotic, impossible to micromanage. And then---ah, yes, taxes.

The government wanted a cut. Of course they did. They always do. But how exactly do you track cash that's stuffed into a G-string one crumpled bill at a time? Theoretically, dancers were "independent contractors," paying the house for stage time and keeping their tips. On paper, it made sense. In practice, it was a Wild West cash economy fueled by rum and bad decisions. Good luck getting an accurate ledger out of that circus.

The IRS? They knew. They've always known. But the truth is, they'd need a small army to properly audit the strip club industry---and they're not sending boots on the ground to shake down every dancer in six-inch heels. So they mostly looked the other way.

Millions in unclaimed income, flushed down the fiscal drain every year---and the real kicker? A huge percentage of these same dancers were collecting welfare, unemployment, or some other government assistance while raking in cash under black lights. If that makes you cringe, good. It should. And yeah, I see the irony. I'm no angel, but I was running a business---trying to keep the lights on, keep the girls safe, and keep the Feds off my back. Meanwhile, the system that claims to care about order and fairness was busy choking on its own hypocrisy.

They want to police morality, regulate fantasy, and tax the hell out of anything that breathes---but only if it doesn't take too much effort. Because let's be real: even the IRS knows, you don't audit the circus while you're sitting ringside.

I was meticulous. Every damn penny accounted for. Every return filed. Every tax obligation was met to the letter. If there was one agency I refused to play chicken with, it was the IRS---I knew better than to tempt that particular demon. I played it straight with the state of Georgia, too,

especially on sales tax. I crossed my t's, dotted every soul-sucking and still-
--I got dragged into it.

The Georgia Department of Revenue came knocking for an audit. Standard procedure, nothing shady. During the process, we found I had underpaid around $15,000 in taxes over the course of several years. Not by skimming or evading, but by not rounding up on literal pennies. An honest mistake. But I owned it. I didn't run. Didn't deflect.

The auditor, to his credit, saw that. He knew I wasn't gaming the system. He agreed to settle for just the amount due---waiving the crushing penalties and interest that would've ballooned it to over $50,000. We scheduled a final meeting---me, my accountant, my attorney, and him---to wrap it all up. That meeting never happened. The night before, while trying to sell his car, the auditor met with what he thought was a buyer. Instead, the man pulled a gun, carjacked him, and murdered him in cold blood. No warning. No reason. Just gone.

We were stunned. Blindsided. It was the kind of twist you don't see coming---one minute you're prepping paperwork, the next minute you're reading about a state employee you knew being shot dead in a parking lot.

Thankfully, the state honored the deal. They stuck to what the auditor had agreed to before he was killed. But that moment burned into me. It was a cold, brutal reminder: it doesn't matter how careful you are. One random act, one left turn from the universe, and your whole world can flip on its head.

And through it all, I tried to play it clean. I covered more skin when the city told me to. Revoked VIP passes when guys crossed lines. I bought a stretch limo to class up the experience, only to realize the optics made me look like some wannabe kingpin. So I split it off, made it a separate business, just to keep the whispers at bay. But no matter what I did, it was never enough. To the outside world, I was still the villain. Still the "strip club guy." Still public enemy number one in a world full of private sins.

People acted like I was running a cartel. Like I had offshore accounts and secret bunkers. Jesus. You'd think I was laundering money for a foreign government, not running a club that served vodka and fantasies. Don't think my family escaped it either. I had twins---a boy and a girl, both in daycare. One morning, after I dropped them off, I ran into a familiar face. A guy I knew. A regular. He'd been to Scarlett's Secrets more times than I could count. Dropped big money. Knew the girls by name. Smiled, shook my hand like everything was fine.

Ten minutes later, daycare calls. The same guy walked straight in and told the director he'd yank his kid unless mine were removed. Why? Because I owned a gentlemen's club. The same club he'd just visited that weekend. The hypocrisy made me sick. He could drink the booze, tip the dancers, enjoy the escape---but I wasn't fit to have my kids in the same building as his? That was the line he drew? I was good enough to take his money, but suddenly not good enough to be a father?

Fortunately, the daycare saw through the bull. They stood up for us. Said that if someone was leaving, it would be him. For once, we dodged the fallout. For once, the judgment didn't win. But it was a rare victory in a war I never asked to fight. Because here's the truth nobody wants to say out loud: when you run a business that society secretly craves but publicly condemns, you live with a bullseye on your back. Every. Stinking. Day.

My mother, God rest her soul, was the one who hated the idea of Scarlett's Secrets before it even existed. She caught nothing but ridicule for it, not just from her peers, but even from the doctors she worked with---who should've known better. In the end, because my mom was dubbed the "Porn Queen" of Galaxy Beach, my dad? Well, they crowned him the "Porn King of Galaxy Beach." Of course, dad wore it like a badge of honor, but to mom, it was humiliating, unnecessary, and downright disrespectful. No one deserved to be treated like that, especially not her.

The politicians, the bureaucrats, the clipboard cowboys, the pearl-clutching PTA parents---they all line up to point fingers and pass judgment. And half of them were in the front row of Scarlett's Secrets the weekend before, tipping like they were trying to buy redemption by the dollar.

I played by the rules. Filed the paperwork. Paid the taxes. Followed the law to the letter, even when it was written by people who couldn't spell "industry" without a lobbyist whispering in their ear. I did what they said we were supposed to do. Yet, they still came for me. Still looked at me like I was poison. Not because I did something wrong---But because I dared to make a living off the truth they're too cowardly to face.

They want the escape. They want the fantasy. They want the release. But God forbid someone profit off delivering it. The same men who moan about "protecting community values" were the first in line for the champagne room---and the first to call for your head when their wife started asking questions.

Despite making a damn good living, I wasn't just in it for myself. I've always had a big heart---and yeah, I tried to give back. Tried to help. But apparently, generosity becomes radioactive when it comes from someone in my line of work. I offered donations. Real money. To real causes. And got shut down across the board.

Not because the money wasn't needed.

Because I was the one offering it.

They couldn't separate the man from the marquee. They couldn't see past the neon. And it wasn't just money we tried to give---we offered our time. My wife, Regina, and I, both of us, hands-on, ready to help. And even that was denied. It didn't matter what we could contribute. Only who they believed we were.

It's the kind of judgment that cuts deeper than any tax audit or city ordinance. It doesn't just attack your business. It attacks your identity. Your family.

Speaking of irony---if you've ever stepped foot into a strip club, you know the hustle. Personally, I'd rather throw on a little porn and get the job done than be teased, milked, and worked over by a dancer who's running the long con for what's in your wallet. But some guys don't see it. Or worse, they do---and still fall for it.

Then there's the DUI trap. Every night, law enforcement sits like fishermen by the curb, waiting to reel in some poor bastard who had one too many and thinks he's okay to drive. Hook, line, and $10,000 gone--- not to mention the job, the license, sometimes the life. I've seen it more times than I can count---patrons walking out broke and broken, thinking they were in control, when in reality they'd just been bled dry by a woman who never once cared about anything other than tips.

And some guys? They go darker. Convinced they can flip the script, they lace a dancer's drink---thinking they'll gain the upper hand. It's sick. It's criminal. And it never ends well. Nine times out of ten, it's them in handcuffs and the dancer in an ambulance.

We knew the EMTs by name. No joke. We probably should've just put up a damn "Ambulances Only" parking sign out back. And sadly, it happened more often than people want to believe. That's the cost of doing business in an industry built on illusion---sometimes, people forget the boundaries are real.

That's why I covered my ass. Cameras everywhere. Front to back, top to bottom---more than Photoshop. Even the dressing rooms were monitored---fully disclosed, of course. Not because I wanted to spy on anyone, but because we had to. Too much liability. Too many drugs. Too many whispered deals and blurred lines.

And yeah, there were perks. Girls will be girls, and the teasing? Part of the show. You learn to take it in stride---laugh, keep it professional, and move on.

Owning a gentlemen's club can be wildly profitable---no doubt about that. But behind the velvet ropes and the fantasy, there's a battlefield. You're juggling legal landmines, moral crusaders, and the kind of political drama that would make D.C. blush. All it takes is one rumor. One offended church group. One jealous wife whispering in the ear of the wrong commissioner. Suddenly, you're not a businessman---you're a target.

One flimsy complaint. One code inspector with an ax to grind. One politician who needs a new headline. And just like that, your whole world can unravel.

But if you can stomach the roller coaster---if you've got thick skin, a quick mind, and enough grit to chew through the hypocrisy---then maybe, just maybe, you survive long enough to enjoy the ride. Or at the very least, you get one hell of a story to tell at dinner parties.

And as for the Fugly Lights?

That's what we called the house lights when they flipped on at closing time---when the fantasy ended, and reality kicked in. The smoke cleared, the music stopped, the glitter faded, and suddenly the cracks showed. The makeup couldn't hide everything. The darkness couldn't protect the illusion anymore. The money was gone, and all that was left was truth. Trust me---truth isn't always pretty. But it's always there. Waiting under the light.

Chapter 5

Under the Table and Over the Top.

Fantasy
Performed by: **Earth, Wind, and Fire**
Written by: Maurice White, Eduardo del Barrio, and Verdine White

Like the song *Fantasy, Scarlett's Secrets* didn't just turn men into mush --- it played them like a slot machine, flashing lights and promises that were never meant to pay out. They opened their hearts, cracked open their wallets, and chased a jackpot that was rigged from the start. Sad? Maybe. Predictable? Always. But while they burned through their chips, I was stacking mine --- right alongside the dancer dealing out the dream. And believe me, this was just the first hand. The real action was still ahead.

Look, it wasn't all doom and gloom. I mean, how many guys can say they've seen six thousand pairs of tits --- up close, sweating, and sometimes even got the ol' Florida orange juice squeeze... maybe even a little taste if luck (and a few dollars) were on their side? Not many --- unless they were in the game, or worked for me. And in Galaxy Beach, damn near everyone worth their salt started under my roof before moving on. Sure, you had to wade through a swamp of cigarette smoke and all the usual scumbaggery, but if you could hold your breath and keep your sense of humor, there were plenty of twisted, crazy, laugh-your-ass-off moments hiding under all that grime. You just had to have the stomach --- and the stones --- to find 'em.

Every month, we dragged in some new kind of sideshow --- everything from porn-star midgets to snake tamers. And not just the cold-blooded reptiles either. We had other "snake tamers" too --- human ones, like Ron Jeremy, slithering across our stage.

Inside our ten-thousand-square-foot meat grinder of a building, we had a spot set aside for these "special" acts. One night stamped itself into my memory harder than the rest --- a performer who rolled up carrying a twenty-foot boa constrictor. She gave me --- the owner --- a private show behind the locked door of our green room, and let's just say, it wasn't something you scrub out of your mind later.

I hate snakes. Always have. They're the monsters that coil up inside my dreams. So sitting just a few feet from a twenty-foot-long, foot-thick beast --- alive, hissing, heavy enough to crush the air right out of a man --- was like flirting with death while grinning through it. But the snake was just the opening act.

That woman had talents you don't put on a résumé. I watched her queef out a song --- full-on musical notes --- and fire ping-pong balls across the room like a sniper at a carnival. Then there were her 120-triple-Z breasts, rolling through the club's door like battering rams built for sin. It was grotesque. It was magnificent. It was everything Galaxy Beach never deserved but somehow got anyway.

Say what you want --- it made this forgotten little stretch of Georgia famous for a hot minute, and we wore that badge like warriors who survived the filth and came out grinning.

Then there was Ron Jeremy. Or whatever hollowed-out version of him still existed back then --- before the lawsuits, the scandals, the shame.

He was greasy, bloated, halfway rotted, but still dragging a loyal parade of gorgeous women behind him --- like some twisted Pied Piper of perversion. He was a legend, not because he deserved it, but because some myths are too dirty for the truth to kill.

When I picked him up from the airport, he staggered out with a black fifty-gallon trash bag slung over his shoulder and tossed it into the frunk of my Ferrari like it was yesterday's garbage.

I glared at him, more worried about my car than my conscience, and barked, "What the hell's in the bag?"

He just grunted, "My luggage."

I shook my head, asked why a guy with his kind of cash traveled like a vagrant.

He shrugged without missing a beat: "I'm Jewish."

And just like that, he closed the conversation --- like centuries of history somehow justified dragging a garbage bag full of God-knows-what through my Italian suede.

It was madness. It was genius. It was the business.

Before we hit a scheduled radio show in Atlanta, we stopped for lunch. I'd never broken bread with a guy as infamous as Ron Jeremy before, and let me tell you --- it was a scene straight out of a freak show. The second we walked in, the place changed. Staff, customers --- hell, even the busboy --- started whispering, pointing, and inching closer like we were carrying some contagious celebrity disease. A few had the balls to come right up, shake his hand, and mumble about how they'd "seen his work." No shit, Sherlock. The whole thing was surreal. But hey, I was having lunch with a legend --- if you can call him that --- and for a few hours, I got a front-row seat into the wild, weird, surprisingly nice guy that was Ron.

Turns out, he wasn't just a walking porno --- he fancied himself a comedian, had stories for days, both on and off the set, and could actually make you laugh when he wasn't grossing you out.

During his stay at Scarlett's Secret, his little traveling circus of groupies found their way to our place in the sun. On more than one occasion, I walked into the green room to find Ron kicked back on one side, and a team of anaconda tamers working him over on the other. Taming the snake, so to speak. Compared to Ron, I was built like a lawn gnome, but even so, he was pulling crowds --- and tricks --- that made my best nights look like amateur hour.

Believe it or not, one of the biggest draws we ever had at Scarlett's Secret wasn't Ron, or even the girls --- it was the little people (midget strippers). And no, we didn't toss them. These women were full-throttle performers, legends in their own right, and the crowds packed in shoulder to shoulder just to see the show. We couldn't sling drinks fast enough. The place was a madhouse --- loud, sweaty, chaotic --- and it printed money like a broken ATM.

If I learned anything in this business, it's this: the stranger it is, the harder it sells.

Most people say, "I don't like to take my work home."

Me? I dragged it inside, soaked it in gasoline, and torched it like a man who'd already stopped caring about the ashes.

My house didn't throw parties --- it swallowed people whole.

The nights started like fantasies --- me in a smoking jacket, drink in one hand, a swarm of lingerie-draped bodies orbiting me like dying stars.

That's when it hit me --- clear as the sweat dripping off the walls --

I finally knew who Hugh Hefner really was. Not the grinning man in the magazine, but the legend behind the smile --- the one too deep in his own dream to ever crawl back out.

My guest list? It read like a confession letter to everything society claims to hate: cops, lawyers, doctors, schoolteachers --- all of them clawing their way through the dark to live out the filth they swore they were above.

And me? I fed them every last rotten bite they begged for.

It wasn't a party. It was a bloodletting.

Bartenders hosed the crowd with top-shelf liquor like firefighters trying to put out a blaze already out of control. DJs pounded sound into the walls until the windows shook. The whole house --- my house --- shook under the weight of everything beautiful, broken, and doomed that we dragged inside with us.

The kids? Long gone, tucked away at the grandparents, hidden from the wreckage I built with my own two hands. The neighbors? Half cursed my name, the other half slipped into costume and came crawling to my doorstep like moths to a flame they knew would burn them. And when the sun finally cracked the horizon, panties floated in the pool skimmer like forgotten battle flags --- proof that nothing stayed clean, nothing stayed whole, and nothing --- not even the ones who came smiling --- walked away untouched.

To survive in the adult entertainment business, you needed more than a steady stream of customers --- you needed protection. Real protection. A handful of us club owners figured that out early. We formed an unofficial coalition --- a kind of "fighting brigade" --- to keep the commissioners, state officials, and the IRS off our necks. Hundreds of thousands of dollars bled into lawyers' pockets, all just to keep our doors open and the wolves at bay. But like any good war, alliances formed. We built our own inner circle --- a tight, weathered brotherhood of Gentlemen's Club owners who understood the blood-and-guts reality of surviving in a business the public loved to hate.

Every year, we gathered in Vegas for the Gentlemen's Club Owners Association conference --- a private summit for the sinners keeping the lights on.

We listened to industry legends like Larry Flynt --- a man who didn't just walk the line for free speech, he bulldozed it. God rest his soul.

Having that network wasn't a luxury --- it was a lifeline.

When you're in a business where the rules are written to break you, knowing there were others in the trenches --- fighting the same battles, facing the same storms --- was the only thing that kept some of us from slipping under.

We swapped ideas, shared money-making tricks, and found the kind of comfort only the damned can give each other.

And speaking of comfort...

Let's talk about one of the best perks of owning a gentlemen's club: access.

But first, a little context.

Almost everyone dreams or has dreamed of being on the big stage, or maybe even big screen---the fame, the money, the adoration. It's intoxicating. People want to believe they're special, destined to change the world, and that their talents will leave an indelible mark. Yet, for the lucky few who actually make it, fame can be a double-edged sword. Some bask in the limelight, while others crumble under the weight of all that attention. And let's not forget, a few take a sharp left turn into Weirdsville.

Take Michael Jackson. As a kid, he was it for me---the King of Pop, moonwalking straight through my imagination. But then things got...weird. He shifted from icon to enigma faster than you could say "Thriller." The nose jobs, the bizarre behavior, the sketchy sleepovers at Neverland---I had to draw a line somewhere. The man's artistry? Untouchable. His music still soundtracks moments I'll always cherish. But the rest? An unfortunate trainwreck.

These days, I look to Bruno Mars as the heir to that throne. Uber-talented, undefinable, grounded---or at least seems that way---and a born performer. He's got that same electric spark, that soul-lifting vibe. Plus, he belts out my all-time favorite song like he owns it. Well, he does. I admire his craft, his control, his cool.

And right behind him? Justin Timberlake, snapping at his heels with a mic in one hand and a smirk in the other. Whether he's owning a stage or a screen, the guy's got chops. And let's not pretend Dick in a Box sealed his comedic legacy. That's some legendary shit right there.

These days, if I had to name a hero, it's Howard Stern. Yeah, that's right---the self-proclaimed King of All Media. In my assessment, this guy who built an empire out of dick jokes, brutal honesty, and raw, unfiltered radio that made people squirm and laugh at the same time. While the world polished their public images and played it safe, Howard leaned into the chaos. He made a career out of saying what most people are too scared to even think out loud.

What I admire most isn't just the shock value---it's that he did it his way. Awkward, neurotic, self-deprecating as hell, and unapologetically him. The man put his flaws out there like scars he wore with pride. He didn't hide behind a brand or a curated persona. He made his therapy sessions public. He made his insecurity a character trait. And in doing that, he connected with millions of people who were just as fucked up, just as lost, just as weird. I certainly resemble that categorization.

In a world full of fake smiles and polished social media lives, Howard was the guy pulling back the curtain, lighting it on fire, and laughing while it burned. That takes guts. That takes grit. And that, to me, is what makes a real idol---someone who doesn't just succeed, but does it while flipping the middle finger to what everyone else thinks is the "right" way.

He didn't ask for permission. He just was. And for a guy like me--- someone who's lived in the shadows, the excess, the chaos---that kind of raw authenticity isn't just admirable. It's near fuckin sacred.

As a bonus, I got an education I didn't see coming---learning things I never knew about people I thought I had pegged. All thanks to Howard and his freakishly good interview skills. He doesn't just ask questions---he surgically peels people open, gets past the bullshit, and drags out their raw, unfiltered humanity. Nobody does it like him. Not in my lifetime. Not even close. And beyond the mic, the guy's a hell of a family man. The way he talks about his kids? Shit, he can go ahead and adopt me, too.

As for me, my "rockstar" status wasn't global, but it sure as hell mattered in my world. It was localized fame, the kind that sticks to your name like smoke in a strip club. I owned Scarlett's Secrets---and in that universe, I wasn't just a guy, I was the guy. The name behind the neon. The man who made the fantasy real.

People whispered when I walked in somewhere, eyes darting from across the bar or peeking over the rims of cocktail glasses. "That's the dude who owns Scarlett's." You could feel the ripple pass through a room like electricity. Cool or creepy? Depends who you asked---and how much they wanted in on the chaos.

Some looked at me like a legend, others like a cautionary tale in progress. Either way, they looked. I had attention. Influence. "Access." Power. I never had to chase the night---it waited for me, heels on, lips glossed, eyes hungry. That kind of recognition feeds your ego in ways that are hard to shake. And yeah, it comes at a cost---but back then, I was willing to pay it.

Fake friends? I had them in droves. Parasites in nice shoes. Smiling wide, laughing at every half-assed joke I told, clapping me on the back while they circled like sharks. But here's the truth---fake friends come with perks. You get invited everywhere. No waitlists, no velvet ropes. They'll blow smoke up your ass and pour your drink before you even sit down. They know your name, your club, your girls. They want to ride the wave, and while they're around, things stay lit.

But deep down, I knew most of them would disappear the second the music stopped. Loyalty wasn't part of the deal. They weren't there for me. They were there for the orbit, the access, the legend. The shine.

And when the lights dimmed and the hangover kicked in, I was often left with nothing but the echo of my own name---and a reminder that rockstar status, even the local kind, can be just as lonely as it is loud.

As in life and in business, I never hit the top in my trade---at least not from where I was standing. And that's not some self-esteem issue---it's just a fact. There was always someone with a slicker pitch, a sharper hook, a louder voice, or a face that drew more eyes. Always someone who grabbed the spotlight while I stayed grinding in the shadows. But maybe that's what kept me alive in it. I wasn't an overnight success. I was the one who kept showing up. And while the rockstars shot up fast and crashed even faster, I never climbed high enough to fall. I just kept moving forward.

My best buddy Tim was getting married---which was already mistake number one, considering the walking red flag he was hitching himself to. I was his best man and the ringleader for his last night of so-called freedom. And believe me, if you needed a good time back then, all it took was a giant brick of a cell phone and a couple of calls to the usual suspects. The late '80s, early '90s---pre-internet, pre-subtlety. So yeah, there were strippers. Of course, there were strippers. What kind of bachelor party doesn't come with glitter, heels, and questionable decisions?

I'd spent months planning this circus. We had a swanky hotel booked on the beach---two rooms: one for the party, one for me, because odds were high I wouldn't be crawling home to the wife that night, especially after what was about to go down. The whole thing was bankrolled by my no-limit, platinum American Express---because why not? Go big or go home, and I wasn't going home.

The evening kicked off at a restaurant. Ten guys deep in the back of my stretch limo, including Tim and our driver Jimmy---an old friend we all called Grandpa because, well, he looked like he should've been riding in a hearse, not driving a limo. Also in attendance were two Scarlett's Secret entertainers---solid twelves, no exaggeration. Outgoing as hell and even more into each other than they were into us. Chemistry like that? Let's just say the limo got a little warmer on the way over.

Dinner was exactly what you'd expect when you shove drunk degenerates and half-naked women into a family restaurant: loud, obnoxious, and about as subtle as a chainsaw through drywall. Apologies to the poor souls two tables over, just trying to enjoy their soup. We swung by Scarlett's Secrets for drinks and, if luck was on our side, to recruit a few more girls for the after-party. The moment the limo door swung open, it was like someone had fired the starting pistol at a frat house marathon---dudes bolting for the entrance like they were giving away free sins. I stayed behind, chatting up the dancers who'd already made a beeline for our limo. I gave them the usual spiel: If anyone gets handsy or makes you uncomfortable, come straight to me. I'll handle it. This wasn't just about fun; it was about respect. These were my girls tonight. They kissed me on the cheek, thanked me, and disappeared back inside.

Limo now quiet, I made the obligatory check-in call to my wife. Told her I was back at the club. Her response? "Who fucking cares?" Made me feel like dirt. But that was her M.O.---always quick to guilt, slow to gratitude. Never minded spending the money this lifestyle made, but God forbid I exist in the world that earned it. Sour hypocrite, through and through.

As I headed toward the club entrance, I noticed a security guard off to the side in the bushes, arms positioned like he was taking a piss. He looked over his shoulder at me, laughing like a cartoon goon. Sure enough, he was taking a piss---onto a guy laid out in the bushes, vomit streaking down his face like some horror show extra.

"What the hell, man?" I barked, completely fed up.

The guard turned to me, and while I don't think he had an actual speech issue, he spoke like he'd taken one too many hits to the head. Like a low-budget henchman from a bad action flick.

"I think he's having a diabetic seizure," he slurred.

"Then call the ambulance, dumbass!" I snapped, eyes wide in disbelief. I stormed off into the club, shaking my head, but not before catching the red glow of an ambulance pulling up. At least someone had the sense to do something. Still, the night was starting to wobble---like a drunk on a tightrope---and I wasn't sure if it was going to crash or somehow stick the landing.

Inside, things weren't much better. One of the dancers on stage was known to have some kind of neurological issue---strobe lights sometimes triggered seizures. Most of the regulars knew. The DJ knew. Security knew. Hell, the girl herself knew. But she'd found a way to turn it into a hustle---let people pay extra to watch her go into her little "episode." Morbid entertainment, right? I stood there watching, wondering if I should intervene or just pretend I didn't know any better. Welcome to one of the daily moral dilemmas at this club: step in or stay numb.

And just when I thought things couldn't get any weirder, one of the cocktail waitresses---who'd had a kid over a dozen years ago---was still somehow lactating. She thought it was hilarious to squirt breast milk into iced Jager, shake it like a martini, and serve it up in shot glasses. Guys ate it up. Tipped her like she was serving liquid gold. I wish I was kidding.

About an hour into the mayhem, I was mentally checked out---already fantasizing about that plush hotel suite upstairs, only miles away. So I rallied the troops and shoved everyone back into the limo, excluding Tim's dorky, buttoned-up brothers-in-law who had opted to follow us in their own car. Why they skipped the limo is beyond me. But in hindsight, it was a mistake. A big one.

Grabbing some stuff out of the cooler for the night's party, half-watching inventory, I caught sight of an incident report open on the desk.

It read: XXXX, one of our brilliant employees, pissed in a wine glass, stuck it in the fridge to chill, then tried to serve it to some asshole customer we all hated at Scarlett's Secrets.

As luck would have it, just before that sweet little revenge cocktail could reach its intended target, an underaged dancer swooped in, snatched it off the tray, and guzzled every last drop of that chilled piss like it was vintage Dom.

I stood there, horrified. And yeah, part of me thought---poetic justice would've been glorious. But not like that. Another day, another disaster I wasn't even there for but would've been on the hook for.

Looking back, it was a truly disgusting environment.

And believe me---I'm not talented enough to make this shit up. It wrote itself.

Oh, and lest we forget one more glamorous pit stop---the ever-prestigious guard shack out front. I trudged over to follow up on the patron who made his grand exit face-down in a pool of his own puke with piss on his clothes, chauffeured out by ambulance. I needed to make sure an incident report was filed---because around here, finding a clipboard was about as likely as finding a Harvard diploma stapled to a stripper pole.

I stepped inside expecting a bored guard sipping coffee. Instead, I walked straight into the Twilight Zone.

Inside were two employees---one, a day manager technically off duty, and the other, a security guard, also off duty. In the middle of the room, they had a dancer hogtied to a chair. No shit. Now, to be clear---she was of age, young, gorgeous (well, gorgeous with the lights on), a college student with brains, charm, and enough energy to light up a blackout. Total standout. But now? She looked half amused, half panicked. Then she turned to me, smiling like this was just another Tuesday, and said, "Wanna join the party?"

Before I could even get a word out, the manager---wearing nothing but a cowboy hat and boots---swaggered over and started banging her from behind like he was riding a Brahma bull at a rodeo. Meanwhile, the security guard---deaf, with a brutal speech impediment---was fumbling with a condom like it was a Rubik's Cube, frantically asking me to help him put it on so he could jump in too.

And I stood there thinking, I seriously need to reevaluate my hiring process. But in a town like this, the labor pool was laughably shallow. Hell, despite this circus act, both of these guys were loyal to the core. Always showed up, never stole, and only got freaky on their own time.

Decisions, decisions.

Back in the limousine a few miles down the road from the club, we were supposed to be headed to the hotel---but the girls had other plans. They stripped down right there in front of all of us, zero hesitation, and kicked off their own private dinner service---lipstick lesbian style. It was summer, which meant that unless the limo was moving, it turned into a damn sauna. And with two strippers putting on a live show and ten sweaty idiots packed in like cattle, the temperature shot up fast.

That's when I looked toward the front---and saw it. The divider was down.

There was Grandpa, chauffeur of the year, cranking his gear stick to the sight of it all.

No elegant way to say it: the old bastard was beating his meat like it owed him money.

At that exact moment, I knew---this day was going to be an absolute clown show.

And yep, it earned a chapter in this book. Right here. You're welcome.

On the way back to the hotel, we were caravanning when sirens lit up behind us. The brothers-in-law, brilliant tacticians that they were, got pulled over.

Turns out, what we didn't see was them in the backseat, friends of theirs chucking full beer cans at other cars like they were in some redneck Olympics.

When the cops asked if they had been drinking, the two clowns up front proudly confessed to fourteen shots, each.

Fourteen.

One guy even tried to math his way out of a DUI by explaining it averaged to "one an hour" because he "technically" started drinking the night before.

Yeah, even as I type this, it doesn't make a damn bit of sense.

But somehow, by the grace of every drunk saint in heaven, the cops let them go.

No proof.

No charges.

Just a warning and a miracle they didn't deserve. I've seen people get tackled and arrested for way less. When we finally got to the hotel, it was like unleashing a clown car at a circus. A parade of cars, half the bachelor party, three more strippers, and every random degenerate within a five-mile radius showed up. I didn't think it was physically possible to jam fifty people onto a tiny ninth-floor suite balcony overlooking the Atlantic, but somehow, we pulled it off. The place was wall-to-wall drunkenness, bad decisions, and enough bad cologne to peel the paint off the walls.

It was pure rockstar status---if the rockstars were broke, drunk, and had absolutely no shame.

Later, I started noticing there was more empty space in the hotel room. As it happened, these jackasses started throwing the furniture off the balcony. I couldn't believe my eyes, and by then, I couldn't believe the pain of my American Express bill growing quickly either. Could this meshuggah night get any worse?!

Fortunately, I was good friends with the hotel manager.

And yeah, he still had to pay us a visit after the complaints started rolling in.

Credit to him---he had the foresight to stick us in a corner of the hotel, away from the pools and families. If he hadn't, we would've made national news.

When he popped his head in the door, I promised him I'd get everything under control.

He just nodded, said his guys were already downstairs cleaning up whatever the hell had gone over the balcony. By then, the night was hitting me hard---the booze, the chaos, and that slow-burn guilt of knowing we'd turned my friend's hotel into a crime scene with a breakfast buffet. And somehow, it was about to get worse.

As the manager and I walked out together, whatever thin thread of decency the night had left snapped right in front of us. There he was--- some uninvited bottom-feeder---perched with his bare ass hanging over the ninth-floor balcony, pants tangled around his ankles, squeezing out a shit like it was a protest against civilization itself.

It was one of those moments where you don't even feel outrage---you just stand there, tired, hollowed out, wondering how the hell your life wound up orbiting this kind of human landfill. We asked him to leave, not because we gave a damn about him falling to his death, but because the idea of some family getting hit with an airborne turd on their vacation seemed a bridge too far---even for us. The manager didn't even argue.

We shook hands without a word. He was a good man, stuck doing triage on a party that had long since rotted from the inside out.

With barely any time to breathe before the next disaster introduced itself.

The bathroom lights were out, but there were voices inside---slurred, sloppy, too familiar. One of our friends, in his infinite wisdom, had decided that the blackout was the perfect setting for some backseat romance. I leaned in closer and caught the whisper:

"Hey, Sweet Brown... I'm hungry and ready to eat some chocolate..."

Jesus Christ. We had eaten dinner.

What he was hungry for now wasn't listed on any menu. I gave it a minute---curiosity, stupidity, whatever---and then flipped the lights back on. The scene that greeted me was straight out of a third-rate nightmare. There he was, face buried deep between a dancer's thighs, working her over like he was trying to win a trophy. If that wasn't enough to make a man give up on God entirely, there, tangled in another shower curtain, was another one of our so-called friends---pants half-down, working his own shaft like he was running the clock out on his last shred of dignity.

Apparently, the lighting had been dim enough for them to pretend they were alone---but just bright enough for him to enjoy the floor show. Or maybe they knew he was there. Maybe no one gave a damn anymore. That was the kind of night it had become: no shame, no boundaries, no brakes. Just bodies moving through the wreckage, too far gone to even realize they were part of it. I didn't say a word. Didn't even blink.

Just logged it somewhere deep in the back of my mind, another snapshot in a night so far past fucked it didn't even warrant outrage anymore. It was what it was.

And now, here it is, immortalized in these pages---because somehow, some way, this madness had to be accounted for. Around three in the morning, I was completely wrecked.

Done.

Tapped out.

I told everybody to GTFO---"Get the Fuck out," with my best, Eddie Murphy in Trading Places, impression, loudly, and with feeling.

As I stumbled back toward my own suite along the outside walkway, I noticed flashing blue lights downstairs. Figured I better go check it out---chances were good it was one of our little angels from the off-the-rails party. Sure enough, it was.

Our brilliant "fourteen-drinks-and-still-licensed-to-drive" friends, the same ones who'd narrowly dodged a DUI, were now brawling it out in the parking lot.

This time, the cops weren't feeling generous. They got cuffed, stuffed into cruisers, and sent off to jail to finish the night the way destiny clearly intended. Turns out, getting a free pass on conspiracy to hurling torpedoes wasn't enough to inspire gratitude. In case you're wondering---throwing full beer cans at other cars while drunk?

Yeah. That's a felony. Congratulations, boys. Real Mensa candidates.

By now, you've probably guessed this whole circus wasn't cheap.

By the time the sun came up, I was out over thirty grand---for food, booze, strippers, "entertainment," and, of course, replacing the hotel furniture that didn't survive the festivities. Rockstar life, right? All glory, no brains. Drained to the bone, I finally dragged myself back to my room, only to find my poor hotel manager friend had done me one last favor---he let three more girls into my suite. Yep. More strippers. Still dressed to party. Still wide awake. Still looking at me like I was the last man standing at the Alamo. One more drink, maybe three, and suddenly, I wasn't so tired anymore.

And before long, it was my turn to get caught with my pants around my ankles.

A couple of hours later, they were saying goodbye---and the rest, as they say, is history.

Or at least...it's somewhere between legend, regret, and whatever the hell this book is turning into.

Now, more than ready to go to sleshe adored ep, I got a knock on the door from my friend Piper, who was the first girl during my marriage who was able to talk me into sexual activity without saying a word. This kind of friend was one in a million. We could have deep conversations, get in a lot of laughs, travel together, have sex together, and then both go back to our separate lives. She told me that she saw the girls leave my room, and I told her that I was spent, and probably wouldn't be able to perform that night. In the morning, though, we managed to make up for the previous night. It was the perfect relationship scenario. But more on that to come...

And by the way---because it would be criminal not to mention it---Tim did get an appropriate send-off. Somewhere between the Jager-breastmilk shots and the moral collapse of humanity in the guard shack, two of his college (girl) "friends" showed up. Let's just say they weren't there for the shrimp cocktail.

Maybe they were nudged a little. Maybe someone who knew Tim needed something unforgettable---something jaw-dropping and marriage-questioning---sent a gentle suggestion their way. You know… someone like me. There he was, the groom-to-be, receiving a glorious 11th-hour farewell to bachelorhood in the form of a double-header blow job from two women who used to copy his homework and now seemed happy enough to polish his knob like they were up for extra credit.

Mission accomplished.

Soon, the sun was creeping toward the horizon, the room smelled like perfume, liquor, and regret, and Tim had that stupid grin that only a man about to ruin his life in a tuxedo could wear. The kind of grin that says, "I made it out alive… but just barely."

And me? I sat in the corner of the suite, looking out over the water, wondering what the hell had just happened. One part ringmaster, one part crisis manager, and full-time soul on fire. These nights---these chapters---they don't come with warning labels. They don't ask if you're ready. They just explode into existence and leave you with stories that sound too insane to be true… but are.

That night was excess in its purest form---raw, vulgar, human. The kind of chaos that doesn't just happen. You create it. You invite it. And if you're not careful, you become it. With that, we closed the chapter---one soaked in booze, blurred by bad decisions, and sealed with a head-nod to everything society pretends not to crave.

Onward.

Chapter 6

The Ties that Unbind

Sowing the Seeds of Love
Performed by: **Tears for Fears**
Written by: Roland **Orzabal and Curt Smith**

Looking back now, it's easy to chalk it all up to chaos for chaos' sake---wild nights, bad decisions, busted furniture, and bridges torched beyond repair. But under all that wreckage, something real was taking root. Every mistake, every trainwreck moment I should've seen coming but didn't… they were seeds. Whether I knew it or not, I was sowing. Sowing the seeds of love---not the Hallmark kind, but the kind you claw out of dirt and blood. The kind born from survival, from choosing real life over the lie.

That madness didn't destroy me. It planted something better. I just took a hell of a long time to see it.

Shaking up conventional thinking has been the running theme of my life---and this book---and this chapter's no exception.

There's a song that cracked my worldwide open.

It played through Piper's rattling Honda speakers the night she gave me the kind of "oral courage" no therapist on earth could've prepared me for.

Let's just say, if Bill Clinton had been in the backseat with us, my guess is, he'd have slow clapped, wept tears of pride, and handed me a Presidential Medal of Freedom.

That little act of mercy didn't just put a grin on my face---it blew up the last trace of loyalty I had left for a marriage that had already been buried six feet deep.

If you're trying to timeline the madness, this was a few months before the bachelor party from hell you barely survived reading about.

Now you know the spark that lit the fuse.

That night, parked behind the hangar, with Sowing the Seeds of Love bleeding out of that cracked stereo, Piper showed me how fast a man's life can shift. Not with words.

Not with promises. Not with the tired lies we tell ourselves just to keep breathing. But with something primal. Immediate. Undeniable.

Something that grabbed me by the throat and said, Wake the fuck up. The truth?

That night wasn't the beginning of my downfall. It was the start of my resurrection.

The first breath of something real.

Oh, Piper.

She brought "intriguing" to a whole new level. Sexy as hell---face of an angel, body built for sin, and a mind that made sure you knew it. Hanging with her was easy.

Fucking her? Electric. She wasn't just wild---she was weaponized pleasure, wrapped in smooth skin and unapologetic confidence. There was no one like her.

She said what she wanted, when she wanted---even if it was one of my friends.

Zero filter. Zero shame. And somehow, that made her even more dangerous.

But here's the twist---she was real. Solid. Trustworthy. The kind of woman you'd call if you hit the jackpot and didn't want to celebrate alone. Even now, if I hit the lottery, I'd reach out and buy her anything she wanted. No questions asked.

Set the scene:

Most wives would've fallen to their knees for a chauffeur-driven limo, a private airplane, a Ferrari in the garage, a mansion by the water, and a brand-new BMW wagon---the full "I've made it" starter pack. Mine? Regina. She left the keys on the kitchen table with a note that said, "Thanks, but no thanks," then stormed off to buy a new car like she was returning a defective toaster. At least she bought it from my dad.

Cold. Clinical. Final.

If Farrah Fawcett ditched the glam squad and spent her weekends handing out hymnals, you'd have Regina. Tall, quiet, terrified of flying and boats---two things that ran straight through the center of my DNA like a freight train. We weren't a love story.

We were two cardboard cutouts dressed up like a marriage. Just for the record---I wasn't exactly a prize either. At 125 pounds soaking wet, I looked like a stiff breeze could turn me into a weather balloon. No movie-star jawline, no million-dollar smile.

Just a stubborn, hungry, confused kid trying to fake it until he made it---and maybe even after he did.

I had money, status, the toys, the freedom...and a crater where my soul used to be.

Money doesn't fix the foundation---it just lets you build a nicer house on top of the same rotting wood. Our marriage became a slow, bloodless implosion---no screaming, no flying plates, just two exhausted strangers quietly sinking into different worlds.

It was only a matter of time before Hooters threw me a life raft. And yeah, I grabbed it. Not proud. Not apologizing either. Hooters was a breeding ground for Scarlett's Secrets on occasion. Orange shorts traded for stilettos, trading dreams for dollar signs. No judgment---I wasn't exactly standing outside the system looking in.

Enter Stacy---a casualty of my personal recruiting efforts at Hooters.

She never made it to Scarlett's Secrets, but she sure as hell made it onto my desk.

All thanks to Piper. Piper was the one who cracked the dam wide open.

With her, I finally had something close to a steady girlfriend---no strings, no obligations. She was deep in her own chaos, juggling a married man, and somehow still had space for me in her orbit of beautiful, controlled disaster.

We got close. Real close. But we understood the terms.

Boundaries. Unspoken rules. See you when I see you---that was our mantra.

Emboldened, I shifted my attention to Stacy. Beautiful. Reckless. Everything Regina wasn't. I was so smitten, I commissioned an artist to design her silhouette for the new Scarlett's Secrets sign---Stacy, front and center, immortalized in neon for every poor bastard who drove by.

She had a mark. A look. A fire I couldn't hide---and didn't try to. When Regina saw the sign, she demanded to know who the girl was. I didn't sugarcoat it.

I told her the truth---I'd crossed every line with Stacy. She didn't scream.

She didn't cry. She just looked me dead in the eyes and said: Get the hell out. And that was that.

One minute later, I was unpacking my life into a poolside villa run by a priest.

Yeah, a priest. He didn't love my line of work, but my rent checks seemed to help him sleep at night.

Let me be a gentleman here, for all Regina's flaws, she wasn't the villain here.

We were just two people built wrong for each other, stitched together by good intentions and bad timing.

Meanwhile, I was juggling Stacy, Piper, and a new flame---Tonya, and believe it or not, still having a little bump and grind with Regina. Tonya was stunning, a magazine cover come to life. For a millisecond, I thought maybe she was the one. Seemingly different, older than the other interests, and steady, without any other ties, that I knew of. Tonya was a new regular at the New Pool Villa.

Back at Regina's, the revolving door kept spinning. She hired a babysitter named Kate---a nearly 17-year-old with the wisdom (and mouth) of a woman twice her age.

Kate didn't just babysit; she policed. If she thought I'd had one too many beers, she didn't lecture me---she dumped them down the sink without blinking. Refreshing, if not mildly infuriating.

And Kate?

She adored Piper. And Piper adored Kate. Two women who probably should've never crossed paths---but when they did...Let's just say: there's more to come. And none of it's simple.

By now, Regina and I were officially over. She had a new boyfriend---and she made damn sure I knew it. First came the phone call, her voice casual, almost friendly, while in the background I heard the unmistakable soundtrack of someone else's body in hers. You don't need a vivid imagination to fill in the rest. Then came the second act: a visit to the house, him hiding just behind the front door, still inside her while she twisted the knife with the subtlety of a prison shank. Fresh breakups already cut deep, but witnessing the replacement in action? That was a whole different kind of agony---raw, humiliating, unforgettable.

Sure, I can hear the judgment already. No pity for me, right? I made my bed. Now lie in it. But before you rush to hang that verdict around my neck, take a breath and hear me out. I didn't step out because I wanted to set my life on fire. I stepped out because I was already choking on the smoke of a marriage that refused to let me breathe. Everything that made me me---the boats, the flying, the adrenaline, the need to chase something bigger than the daily grind---none of it fit in her world. With Regina, there was no space for who I truly was. So yeah, maybe stepping out wasn't about betrayal. Maybe it was about survival.

Still not convinced? Think I was just another selfish asshole playing victim? Fair enough. But keep reading. This story isn't wrapped in a neat little bow. Because I didn't just sit there licking my wounds---I retaliated the only way I knew how: by setting my own fires and watching the smoke rise high enough to reach wherever she was lying next. And wouldn't you know it---one afternoon, I got a call from a woman claiming to be my neighbor, who said she lived in a penthouse overlooking my pool villa. After a few pleasantries, she dropped a bombshell:

"Please promise me you'll never put curtains on your bedroom window."

Puzzled, I asked why.

"I've got a telescope," she admitted. "Watching you is better than porn. I get off on this daily."

Flattered? Embarrassed? Both. I wasn't sure whether to tell Regina, or some of the stars in this new porn role, such as Tonya, but I figured it was a clear victory in our ongoing game of one-upmanship.

In the middle of the absolute shitstorm my life had become, I decided what every sensible man juggling five women and a barely functioning existence would do--

Buy a new car. Or at least new tires. Naturally, I found myself at the Lamborghini dealership, because clearly, more horsepower was the missing piece of my collapsing empire. That's where I met Bridget. Confident. Magnetic. Dangerous in all the right ways. She locked eyes with my Ferrari, gave me a once-over, and said flat-out, "You don't look like someone who drives that." Fair point. I looked more like the guy who parked cars at the valet stand than the one who owned them.

But Bridget wasn't just shooting looks---there was heat between her and Ira, the dealership's GM, hot enough to melt the Pirellis off a showroom car. They had history. The kind you could smell. But hell, I wasn't exactly operating under a strict moral code at that point. I wasn't in a monogamous state of mind, a monogamous zip code, or a monogamous planet.

In case you're wondering---no, I never bought the Lamborghini. I'd waited years to drive one, ever since my dad's boss dangled his in front of me like a carrot in a suit. It represented everything I thought I wanted---speed, power, proof that I'd made it. But when the time came, I didn't pull the trigger. Instead, I walked away with something more reckless. I asked Bridget out. She didn't even blink. Said yes like she'd been waiting for me to catch up.

By then, I was balancing five women like spinning plates on a grease-slicked floor---Piper, Stacy, Tonya, Bridget, and, yeah, Regina still made the occasional guest appearance in my bed. On paper, it sounds impossible. In practice, it was chaos---raw, exhilarating, and completely unsustainable.

But that was just the core cast. Add in the waitresses looking for comfort, the dancers chasing something real in a fantasy world, and the strays who wandered into Scarlett's Secrets and never quite found their way back out. My life had turned into a carnival of flesh and fire---a hedonistic loop of bodies, sweat, and desperate connection. It wasn't just sex. It was a production. A power trip. A way to outrun the numbness.

And I didn't want to stop.

After my penthouse neighbor called to inform me she had front-row seats to the nightly debauchery, I should've felt shame. Regret. Something. Instead, I leaned into it like a method actor who'd finally found his role. I calibrated the lighting. Angled the mirrors. Positioned the bed like a stage.

I even timed the music to hit just right when the clothes hit the floor. I wasn't just screwing---I was orchestrating.

The threesomes were no longer shocking. They were routine. A sort of Tuesday night ritual, like poker or tacos, but louder and sweatier. I stopped pretending to be surprised when two women climbed into the pool topless and ended up in my bedroom. The blurred lines between fun and dysfunction disappeared. I lost count of how many names I never bothered to learn.

And yeah---I knew she was watching. That penthouse neighbor. She confessed to it outright, said she looked forward to my nights more than her subscription TV. The idea that I was being observed turned the whole thing up another notch. It gave it stakes. Meaning. Purpose, even. I wasn't just living recklessly---I was performing recklessly. Every moan, every climax, every headboard slamming into drywall---it was theater, and the applause was silent but understood.

Did I tell Regina? Did I confess to the fan club, the parties, the rotating cast list? Of course I did. I was tired of the limbo we were pretending wasn't hell. I laid it all out, hoping she'd snap, scream, pull the plug once and for all. I was done living in the shadows of a dead marriage. This time, I begged for it to be over.

In court, she showed no mercy. She painted me as the devil's little brother, humping his way through suburbia, corrupting innocence one pool party at a time. And in those days, courts didn't just lean toward mothers---they rolled out the damn red carpet.

Everyone told me the same thing: "Don't fight. Take your weekends. Fade into the background." But I couldn't. Divorce didn't scare me. Losing houses? Cars? Reputation? I could stomach all that. What I couldn't stomach was becoming a weekend dad in my kids' lives. Showing up with Happy Meals and hollow smiles twice a month while the real moments passed without me.

They wanted to surrender. They got war.

Regina's sister sat in the courtroom gallery, arms crossed, eyes full of venom. She always saw me as human garbage---an imposter in their perfectly curated world. Never mind the irony that her own husband turned out to be a damn bank robber. But hypocrisy never stopped her from staring daggers, like this whole thing was personal. Maybe it was. Maybe it burned her to see me fighting for something her husband never did---fatherhood.

When the judge entered, robe flowing, face unreadable, I felt the cold pinch of fear. My only shield was my lawyer---a woman who didn't flinch. She treated the courtroom like a battlefield and Regina like an enemy combatant.

Strike one: Regina fled the County with the kids, no court order, no warning. Her lawyer gave her the green light. The judge didn't appreciate the stunt.

Strike two: It wasn't hard to see her lawyer's attention was divided---more interested in Regina's cleavage than her custody case. Hard to argue for full rights when your counsel's pitching a tent under the table.

Despite the odds, the judge handed me a win. Temporary custody. Not the war, but a battle. Enough to plant my flag and scream: I'm not a part-time dad. Not a weekend ghost. I was here, flawed and bloodied, but fighting.

Even with that win, I knew what was right. It wasn't about winning or losing---it was about the kids. Two people bring them into the world, and nobody---not a judge, not a vengeful ex---should get to cut a parent out of their lives without damn good reason.

Still, as I sat there watching Regina cry, it hit me harder than I wanted to admit. The tears were real. Raw. Not courtroom theatrics, not manipulation---just pain, stripped down and pouring out. And it wrecked me a little, because even if the war she started had made her my enemy, she was still the woman I'd once built a life with. Still the mother of my kids.

But make no mistake---those tears didn't erase what she tried to do. She'd tried to erase me, like I was just some scribbled mistake on a marriage certificate. Acted like the kids were hers and hers alone, like I was nothing more than a sperm donor who'd overstayed his welcome. I wanted to believe it was just a broken heart lashing out, that beneath the venom was the same woman I once loved. But the poison she fed our children? The lies, the doubts, the whispered rewrites of our history---those things don't just evaporate. They root deep. They bloom in silence. And those walls she started building between me and my kids? I'd spend the next decade clawing at them with bloody hands, trying to tear them down brick by bitter brick. Trying to remind them that I was still their father, still in the fight, no matter how far away she tried to push me.

That night, after the courtroom emptied and the victory dust settled, the quiet came rushing in. The kids were asleep in their rooms, temporary peace wrapped in cartoon bedsheets and nightlights. And me? I was alone with the aftermath. That kind of loneliness doesn't scream. It seeps. A slow, invisible leak that drowns you without a sound. I called Bridget. I needed someone---anyone---to hear me breathe, to remind me I was still alive. Kate called too, asking how it went, her voice soft and careful like she was handling broken glass. They meant well. They always did. But nothing they could say would unring the bell that had been struck in that courtroom.

By midnight, it was just me, a half-empty bottle of whiskey, and a thousand broken thoughts clinking around in my head like loose change. I sat in the dark, replaying everything---what I gained, what I lost, what I'd never get back. I toasted to the win, because that's what you're supposed to do, right?

Then I drank twice as hard for everything that had bled out along the way.

Then, at 3 a.m., the phone rang.

"Cole, your bar is on fire. I'm not joking," Dean, my bar manager, said, his voice frantic.

"What? Is the fire department there?"

"Yeah, but if you wait too long, there'll be nothing left. One of the firefighters has already been taken to the hospital for smoke inhalation."

"Holy shit. I'm with my kids---I can't leave right now," I stammered.

"Dude, you need to get down here now."

I hung up and immediately called Bridget.

"Scarlett's Secrets is on fire," I said.

"Oh my God. What are you going to do?"

"I need to get down there. Can you come over to stay with the kids?"

"I'm on my way," she said without hesitation.

Ten minutes later, Bridget was at my front door. I kissed her goodbye and sped off.

Driving like a maniac, I reached the scene in record time. Red and blue lights illuminated the night, and the air reeked of smoke. The road was blocked off, but after a brief exchange with a deputy, I was escorted to the scene by Detective Jose Marko.

During our ride, he broke the news: "This wasn't an accident. It's arson."

My heart sank. "Arson? Do you think it could've been electrical? We just had the stage rewired."

"No, this was deliberate. Do you know a DJ named Thomas Karin?"

"Yeah, that's TK. Why?"

"Someone threw a Molotov cocktail into his bedroom while he and his girlfriend were sleeping."

"Are they okay?"

"They made it out, but they're in the hospital for smoke inhalation," he replied.

As the night wore on, the devastation became clearer. Scarlett's Secrets was gone. The new roof, the new carpets, the rewired lights---everything was reduced to charred rubble. The only things left standing were the concrete walls.

The next few days were a damn whirlwind. The insurance investigator came at me like I was the arsonist, drilling into my finances, my debts, my supposed "motive" to torch my own club. Every question felt like an accusation wrapped in a polite tone. Meanwhile, Detective Marko was busy chasing his own trail—Frank Miller. A walking red flag. Disgruntled, mean, and with a history that burned hotter than gasoline.

Miller had once worked for a construction company, and legend said he'd lit up a few of the homes he built—maybe for revenge, maybe just to watch them burn. But, as always in this town, when it came to restitution and Scarlett's Secrets, the system found a way to look the other way. Nothing ever stuck. He probably handed someone bigger to the feds, greased a few palms, and walked. Charges vanished like smoke in the wind. Some said he'd done time for arson in another state—but that's the thing about men like Frank Miller. The truth always burns just out of reach, and the system's too damn crooked to care.

Now, if I really was the arsonist, you can bet your ass they'd have come at me full throttle—no deals, no mercy, no wiggle room. But I wasn't, and somehow that made it worse. The game was rigged from the start. I wasn't asking for favors, just fairness. Instead, I got suspicion, double standards, and the quiet reminder that justice in this town only shows up when it's convenient.

As the dust settled, I started making plans to rebuild, despite the county ordinance that could potentially prevent me from doing so. The insurance payout would take months, if not longer, but I wasn't going to let Scarlett's Secrets die without a fight.

Still, the damage wasn't just physical. The fire had left scars---on my business, on my reputation, and on my sense of security. And as if that wasn't enough, a visit to the eye doctor revealed another potential nightmare.

"Mr. Walker, I need you to see a neurologist immediately. There's a chance this could be a brain tumor," the doctor said.

From the courthouse to the firehouse, to the doctor's office---it seemed my life was unraveling faster than I could hold it together.

Chapter 7

Bracing for Impact

Any Which Way You Can
Performed by: **Glen Campbell**
written by: **Snuff Garrett, Steve Dorff & Milton Brown.**

Like the song *Any Which Way You Can*, clandestine---if ever there were a word that perfectly captured my time with Kate, this was it. Every moment was wrapped in secrecy, a delicate balancing act of emotions and circumstances neither of us deserved, yet somehow, both of us craved.

The kids and I moved back into the old marital home---the same house I once shared with Regina. It was time to settle down and be the dad I'd fought like hell to become.

Didn't take long before Bridget's bags were on the front stoop and our driver's licenses listed the same address. From the outside, it looked like progress.

On the inside, it felt like I'd just invited the fuse into the powder keg.

Piper was still around, but drifting.

She saw what was happening---how Bridget was muscling everyone else out of the way, trying to plant her flag as "first chair" in my life---and it pissed her off. Rightfully so. Piper had been there through a lot. She knew the kids. She knew me.

Not just the curated version, but the raw, sleep-deprived, overstretched man underneath. She hated the way Bridget walked in like she owned the place, rewriting the script without earning the part. So we hit pause on the fucking to try and make sense of what we were doing. It wasn't some dramatic break---it was more like a mutual breath. A silent agreement to figure out what this was and whether we were just filling voids or actually meant to go the distance. Truth is, I respected Piper. Still do. She deserved more than being a side note in someone else's power struggle.

And deep down, I think we both knew we were better at understanding each other's damage than healing it.

Tonya, I had to let go.

I convinced myself she loved my lifestyle more than she ever loved me.

Maybe that was my ego talking. Maybe it was my battered self-esteem, too wrecked to believe anyone could love me without the flash and the toys. Truth is, Tonya didn't seem much interested in being a stepmom either. Later, I found out she was crushed after we split---so crushed she couldn't even bear to see my brother, because we looked too damn much alike. Funny how the truth hits heavier when it shows up late.

As for Regina--

She would've slit my throat if it had been legal, my guess. No more booty calls there.

All because I fought to be something she never expected or maybe never even wanted me to be---a real dad. And being a real dad? That meant being there---for the scraped knees, the tough mornings to get to school. The spelling bees, the heartbreaks, the graduations. The little things as much as the big wins. It didn't matter that I'd never had a real say before---on the hard stuff, the choices I had to live with, like the child we never got to meet. These beautiful kids---the ones standing in front of me---were my life. And they still are.

And Stacy? That was a different story. She was a fun chapter---brief, reckless, real in its own way. She beat the odds, too---skipped Scarlett's Secrets, blew off Hooters, and chased a PhD instead. I'm proud of her. Happy we had our time. Sometimes, things don't have to last forever to be good.

Kate: Now here comes the atomic bomb. Let me be extremely clear, now an adult, A Love That Was Never Simple. "It's Complicated" doesn't even begin to describe it. Here I was, technically knee deep in a relationship with Bridget, but completely and utterly in love with Kate. Not just an infatuation, this was the kind of love that grips you, shakes you to your core, and leaves you longing for more. It was the kind of love that lingers in your dreams, where waking up feels like a betrayal of the euphoria you experience while asleep.

This love didn't begin with Kate, though. Long before I met her, I dreamt of a girl I couldn't name. She'd visit me in the quiet hours of the night, filling my subconscious with warmth, connection, and an unshakable sense of belonging. I never understood it until I met Kate. Suddenly, the puzzle pieces clicked into place. She was the girl in my dream I'd unknowingly searched for all my life.

When I looked at Kate, I saw something I'd never encountered before---stability, simplicity, and a natural beauty that needed no embellishment. She had the lean, effortless grace of a track star and the kind of quiet confidence that didn't beg for attention. She was everything Regina and Bridget were not. She didn't crave material things or validation---she only wanted to be loved. And I wanted to be the one to give her that and more.

They say never quit a job without another one lined up.

Turns out, relationships operate on the same principle.

It was barely a blink after the ink dried on the divorce papers with Regina before things were consummated with Bridget. We married fast. Too fast. Call it selfish. Call it calculated. I call it contingency planning---pilot brain. You're always thinking ten steps ahead, running mental and physical checklists for every possible failure: an engine flameout, a bird strike, a drunk in the jumpseat at 38,000 feet losing his mind. Relationships, in that context? Just as volatile. Just as likely to take you down in seconds if you're not vigilant. Being in the right one---it isn't a luxury, it's a survival tactic. Because when you're in the wrong one, it's not just your heart on the line. It's your peace. Your trajectory. Your soul. If you've got kids? The stakes go nuclear. A bad partner doesn't just pull you down. They pull everything around you into the undertow---your ambition, your confidence, your children's sense of safety. The wrong relationship can make the world feel like it's closing in. The right one? That's oxygen.

With Bridget, it started like a spark. Maybe even a rescue. But soon enough, it was clear: we were fire without fuel. We had heat, sure. Passion. But depth? No sustenance. We cared, even loved in our own broken way---but we were dragging so much baggage behind us, it's a miracle we even made it down the aisle. I had just clawed my way out of a marriage built on pressure and pretense. Regina and I stayed long after the expiration date because we didn't want to fail our children. Or maybe we just didn't know how to leave without setting the whole house on fire.

So I entered the next one carrying that smoke---paranoid, protective, and unwilling to let anyone inside the bunker. Bridget wanted access. I couldn't give it. I needed distraction, ego-strokes, validation, and sex. She needed clarity, commitment, and maybe even redemption. What we gave each other was anesthesia.

But I'd be lying if I said I didn't chase it with both hands. Bridget--- God, she was magnetic. The kind of woman you don't meet, you survive. A walking contradiction wrapped in honey and fire. Half African, half British, born in a fog-covered village called Braylock, buried deep in the North Yorkshire moors---population six thousand and change. You'd never guess it by looking at her. She didn't wear her origins like a badge. She wore them like a loaded weapon.

Bridget was fully uncontainable. A category five hurricane in designer heels, sucking the oxygen out of every room she entered and leaving you gasping for meaning in her wake. She didn't just love---she detonated. She crashed into you with the force of every feeling she'd ever suppressed, her heart massive, radiant, and tragic. Titanic-sized. Beautiful and doomed if you didn't know how to hold it. And I didn't.

She was the kind of woman who made you forget your own name while saying hers like a prayer. And even as you drowned, you thanked her for the water.

Her presence was theater. She owned space like a queen in exile. Skin like bronze satin, curves built by equal parts rebellion and indulgence, and a voice that wove royalty with reckless abandon---Princess Catherine with a dash of Amy Winehouse. When she walked across the bedroom naked, the world just paused. And when she stepped out of the shower, hair exploding in every direction like an angry Chia Pet, it was absurdly disarming. A kind of beauty that didn't ask for permission---just barreled through the front door and made itself at home.

She wasn't cruel. She wasn't heartless. But she lived on the surface of things. Her emotions were loud but not always deep. Her presence was a performance, and maybe I was guilty of clapping along instead of asking her to take off the mask. Or maybe I never gave her the runway to land on in the first place. Either way, she wasn't mine. Not truly. And I wasn't hers.

She left a scar---one made of late-night screaming matches, wine-stained sheets, and a few moments of something real that flickered before they were crushed by timing and pride. We weren't good together. We burned bright but never warm. We knew how to ignite, but not how to sustain. It wasn't love. It wasn't hate. It was bad timing, bruised hearts, and an ego cocktail too potent to swallow without gagging.

Then came Kate.

No grand entrance. No dramatic monologue. She just showed up. Quietly. Consistently. Like gravity. While Bridget was fire---unpredictable, electrifying---Kate was grounding. She didn't try to dazzle me. She didn't have to. She was just there. Watching. Helping. Caring.

Kate had been my nanny. Just a kid when she started---seventeen, maybe. I was already drowning in custody battles and chaos, and she showed up like a pair of steady hands in a room full of shaking ones. By nineteen, she wasn't just part of our household, she was part of our family. She wasn't a fling. She wasn't a distraction. She was my kids' protector. My co-pilot through the wreckage.

I never looked at her that way. Not at first. She was too young. Too innocent. And I had too much respect for her role in our lives. But somewhere in the blur of sleepless nights and emotional triage, I started seeing her. Really seeing her. Not as the nanny. Not as a girl. But as a woman. A partner. Someone who gave without agenda and listened without judgment.

She didn't try to save me. She didn't need me to save her. She just showed up---again and again---and that kind of loyalty doesn't go unnoticed. While the world spun off its axis, Kate stood still. While others shouted, she whispered the truth. When I was drowning, she offered me breath without ever demanding I swim.

And still---I built walls. Massive ones. Unscalable. Because of optics. Because of headlines. Because of the age gap and the industry I was in. Because society doesn't care about nuance, just scandal. I didn't want to be another tabloid punchline. I didn't want my kids reading about me like I was a walking cliché.

In my head, I could already hear the headlines: Middle-aged club owner seduces teenage nanny. And it didn't matter that she was of age. It didn't matter that the relationship didn't start until well after the boundaries had been respectfully and firmly in place. The court of public opinion doesn't care about details.

All it would've taken was one person with a grudge, and suddenly, I'm Joey Buttafuoco 2.0---every past mistake repackaged into a cautionary tale. I saw it play out in my head like a B-movie on repeat: her as Alicia Silverstone in The Crush, me cast as the older man who should've known better. It wasn't real---but that didn't matter. In the minds of a judge, a jury, a PTA mom down the street---it didn't take facts. Just fear. Just a suggestion. One uncomfortable age gap and a background in adult entertainment, and suddenly you're everyone's villain.

So I held the line. Not because I wasn't tempted. God knows I was. But because I was terrified. Not of love---but of how it could be twisted.

Eventually, my walls began to buckle. Not from pressure. From trust. Not because I was weak. Because I was ready.

Kate wasn't a rebound. She wasn't a reaction. She was a revolution. The first person who didn't just tolerate my scars---she held them. She didn't flinch when I was ugly. She didn't bolt when I was broken. She stayed. And that scared the shit out of me more than anything.

Eventually, the relationship between Kate, Bridget, and I became… unconventional. Before long, I found myself in a full-blown Cole sandwich---naked between two women who genuinely cared about me. The sex was unreal. Like Olympic-level. And don't think for a second they weren't competing. Every touch, every whisper, every look across the sheets was a subtle bid for dominance. And me? I wasn't complaining. I was drunk on the attention, the validation, the chaos disguised as intimacy.

But that kind of triangle doesn't stay balanced forever.

Kate and I got reckless. Brazen. Midnight kitchen rendezvous, quick sessions in the laundry room, entire days lost in the guesthouse. Sometimes we were tangled together in bed---our bed---while Bridget slept inches away. It was silent. Sinful. Insane. And still, somehow, it felt like the most honest thing in my life.

We had permission, technically. Kate was practically our live-in girlfriend. It wasn't Big Love, but it damn sure felt like the after-hours director's cut. Smiles in daylight. Jealousy at dusk. By nightfall, you could cut the tension with a steak knife.

I tried to keep the worlds separate. Scarlett's Secrets in one box. Domestic normalcy in another. Kate in the shadows. Bridget in the light. But life doesn't work that way. The boxes leaked. The compartments cracked. And once you start compartmentalizing love, you've already lost it.

Bridget noticed. Of course she did. She didn't need a smoking gun. She had intuition. She felt the shift in the way Kate and I moved. In the way we looked at each other when we thought no one else was watching. You can't hide a connection---not real connection. And we had it.

Kate wasn't just the girl in the guesthouse. She was the girl in my bones.

As Bridget and I slowly unraveled, Kate kept showing up. Not with fireworks, but with steadiness. With peace. She reminded me that love didn't have to be theatrical to be true. That sometimes the loudest kind of devotion is the one that stands still when everyone else is running. She never made demands. Never gave ultimatums. She just kept being there. And in a life that had been built on performances, her presence felt like a curtain finally falling.

Looking back now, Regina, Bridget---even Piper---they were chapters. Volatile. Necessary. But chapters. Each one taught me something about love, about pain, about where I'd been and what I couldn't survive again. But Kate? She wasn't a chapter. She was the plot twist.

With her, it wasn't about lust or ego or escape. It was about finally choosing what was real over what was reckless. It was about being seen, not consumed. Loved, not used. She wasn't a fix. She was a mirror. A match. And a second chance, I didn't think someone like me ever got.

It wasn't easy. There was shame. Secrecy. Judgment. The weight of everyone else's opinions. But Kate never wavered. She stayed grounded even when I lost mine. And for the first time in my chaotic, bullet-riddled journey---I wasn't falling.

I was landing.

Chapter 8

The Boogeyman

I always feel like somebody's watchin' me
Performed by: **Rockwell and Michael Jackson**
Written by; **Kennedy "Rockwell" Gordy**

Like the song Somebody's Watching Me, it wasn't paranoia---it was survival instinct. I wasn't losing my mind, I was being hunted. Watched. Every move dissected by a shadow in the system---the Boogeyman. I never saw, but always felt breathing down my neck. My privacy wasn't just invaded---it was shattered. And while I was screaming truth into a void, the same law enforcement I counted on branded me the criminal. They thought I was the threat. Meanwhile, the real one stayed in the shadows, smiling.

Fire doesn't just take your building. It strips you bare. Steals your air, your memories, your damn dignity. One minute, you're standing on top of everything you built---the next, you're drowning in ash, lungs full of what you couldn't hold on to. It doesn't just burn the walls. It burns the years. The sacrifices. The long nights. The stupid dreams you dared to believe in. Gone in a flash of orange and sirens.

We spent days---long, filthy, soul-grinding days---dragging the charred bones of our place into dumpsters. Each haul was a funeral. Blackened drywall, melted fixtures, barstools that looked like twisted skeletons. We peeled back layers of soot like bandages from a wound that refused to close. Every wall ripped down. Every ceiling tile stomped into powder under our boots.

That smell---Jesus, that smell. No matter how many gallons of bleach, how many coats of Kilz primer we threw at it, that stench of burnt dreams hung in the air like a curse. It was in the wiring, in the floorboards, in our lungs. A mix of melted insulation, scorched liquor, and something darker---regret, maybe. Or rage.

But we didn't quit. We rebuilt. One hammer swing at a time. One breath at a time. We didn't wait for a miracle. We became the miracle. Blood, sweat, spite, and stubbornness---we poured it into every nail we drove and every screw we twisted back into place. Then one day, the smoke was gone. The soot was gone. The wreckage---mostly---cleared

What remained was the sharp bite of fresh paint. The clean scratch of new carpet under steel-toe boots. For the first time in a long time, the air that didn't taste like failure. No cigarette smoke yet. No spilled whiskey. Not yet. But give it time. Because this wasn't just about reopening the doors. This was resurrection. And we weren't coming back quiet. We were kicking the damn doors open and daring the world to try us again.

A redneck comic with bourbon-soaked swagger—to my eyes, he appeared drunker than a priest on payday and twice as loud—hosted the damn circus. And that's exactly what it felt like: a full-blown, alcohol-fueled, no-safety-net spectacle. The man stumbled on stage like he owned the joint, mic in one hand, bourbon in the other, firing off punchlines and profanities like he was trying to outshout the fire codes. The house was packed tighter than a coffin at a mob funeral. The fire marshal showed up, took one look, and probably pissed himself while pretending to scribble something useful on his clipboard. Then he just stood there---arms crossed, dead inside---watching the madness unfold while calculating whether his pension was worth shutting it all down. It wasn't.

The line outside wrapped around the building three full times, snaking through the parking lot and down the block. People were pressed up against the glass like starving animals at the zoo, trying to catch even a sliver of what was happening inside. Most of them didn't stand a chance. We were already over capacity, sweating whiskey and adrenaline under fresh lights and even fresher wounds.

Inside, the air was thick---booze, perfume, sweat, and that electric scent of rebirth. It wasn't just a reopening. It was a resurrection with bass and neon. My club, rebuilt from the charred bones of its former self, wasn't just open for business---it was screaming, I'm back, right in the face of every bastard who doubted I could do it. Every city official who wanted me buried. Every competitor who tried to cash in on my funeral.

It gleamed---loud, proud, and unapologetic. A polished middle finger to every bank, every ex, every demon that ever said I wouldn't make it. We didn't come back humbled. We came back meaner, slicker, and bulletproof. That night, the walls didn't hold sound. They threw it back. The floor didn't support a crowd. It pulsed with them. And for one savage, glorious night, we didn't just survive---we owned the moment.

Thank God for small mercies---because I had two babies on the way.

Oh, did I forget to mention that part? Yeah, just a minor detail. That whole Cole-sandwich situation I'd stumbled into---wedged between Bridget and Kate---turned into something a hell of a lot more permanent. Two pregnancies. Two women. Same timeline. No pause. No breath. Just boom---a double-barreled, life-altering gut punch that knocked the wind out of everything I thought I was controlling.

Kate had her alibi sharpened like a switchblade and ready to carve through reality. To Bridget, she spun this carefully curated fairytale: the father of her child was some elusive military guy she had "sort of" dated. Supposedly stationed somewhere far, conveniently classified, conveniently unreachable. No address. No social. No digital footprint. Not a single friend who'd ever met him. Just a name. A blurry outline. A rumor with breath. Let's be clear, though---he was real. A guy she once crossed paths with.. We'll call him John Doe, because that's all he ever was---an empty uniform with a backstory no one could verify.

Now, Kate's version of the story to me? That was even more delicate. She swore up and down that she and John had never actually slept together. Claimed it was some borderline platonic slip, a one-off that never crossed into bedroom territory. In her words, the pregnancy had to be mine. But if Bridget ever came sniffing around---it was John. John in camo. John with the vague orders. John, the convenient scapegoat.

Here's the twisted part--Bridget actually considered it. Not because it added up, but because I'd always used protection around her. Made a show of it, too. Magnum every time, like I was trying to impress somebody. Alright, fine. Call me out. The two-inch punisher, which goes like a hummingbird, but never needed a Magnum. That was pure ego, a lie wrapped in latex and brand labels. For a second, I got caught up in my own fantasy---swaggering through life like I had some kind of divine right to be irresponsible. But let's bring it back to earth: no one outside our warped little ménage-à-trois was buying this John Doe fantasy. It was laughable. Thin as tissue paper in a thunderstorm. Yet, we clung to it. Especially Kate. She held onto that lie like it was the only thing keeping her afloat---clutching it with white knuckles, refusing to let go, even as the truth circled like sharks in bloody water.

Weirdly, I played along. Not because I believed it, but because I had come up with it. I gave her that story. Handcrafted the alibi. Delivered it like some twisted form of comfort, a security blanket for her conscience and a smokescreen for mine. It was easier than the truth. Less painful than honesty.

Because when the baby daddy's a myth, no one shows up with court orders or DNA kits. No awkward stares across Thanksgiving dinner. No "so how'd you two meet?" No baby shower invites from out-of-town relatives. Just silence. Cold, clean, and convenient. No mess---at least not one you couldn't bury under a stack of well-rehearsed lies. That silence? It became our oxygen. Our camouflage. A story told so many times, with such straight faces, it started to feel... true, and close enough to survive on. We didn't just tell the lie---we lived inside it. Wore it like armor. A dad named John Doe became the shield that kept everything from falling apart.

We were all expected to nod. Smile. Act like this invisible soldier existed. Refer to him as "dad" like we were reading from a script nobody dared rewrite. But let's call it what it was---he was a shadow. A stitched-together illusion born of fear, shame, and desperation. Nothing more. No face, no voice, just a blurry sketch of convenience.

Deep down, we all knew. Especially Bridget. She wasn't stupid. She could do the math. She knew the timeline. She felt the tension. She knew the truth---our truth. But instead of lighting a match to the whole circus, she bit down on the betrayal like it was a bullet and swallowed it dry. Smiled through her teeth. Pretended the numbers lined up and the logic made sense. Because what the hell else could she do? Admit it and lose everything? Rip apart her own life because of mine? She was already knee-deep in the wreckage, so she did what survivors do---she kept moving. Silent. Controlled. Tightly wound. She swallowed the hurt like a shot of rotgut whiskey. Bitter. Burning. But strong enough to keep her upright. Together, we played house like everything was just fine. It wasn't. But we pretended. It was a beautiful, reckless mess. I was the architect.

Let's not pretty it up---I wasn't exactly a role model for fatherhood. Especially not with how casually I treated where I parked my rocket. But apparently that little bastard had a mission and a map. Heat-seeking, target-locked, zero hesitation. Undefeated. No gloves. No warning. Just boom---legacy incoming. The wildest part? I wasn't even trying. I wasn't out chasing headlines or angling for drama. I was just doing what I'd always done---living loud, moving fast, making dumb decisions dressed in charm. I was young. Cocky. Flush with cash and just famous enough in a town that worshipped billboards and blurred lines. When your name's on a marquee or a dancer's inner thigh, you don't need a resume. You are the fantasy.

But I didn't tiptoe into that fantasy---I slammed into it full-speed, no brakes, no helmet. And it wasn't some sleek, polished, Hollywood daydream. This was raw. Sticky. Chaotic. It had claws and teeth and consequences that didn't wait politely at the door. And I should've known better. Maybe it was dumb luck. Maybe it was karma cashing in a long-overdue tab. Or maybe I just couldn't keep my pants zipped long enough to figure out what kind of man I was supposed to be.

Of course, every perk came with a price. That's the unspoken contract when you build a kingdom out of neon, vice, and whispers. The women, the money, the local clout---it was intoxicating. But like any good drug, there was a comedown, and mine came with flashing lights and legal pads. Fake friends were easy. You can see 'em coming. Hungry eyes, too many compliments, always circling---never landing---just waiting to leech onto something solid. I learned to spot them the same way you clock a hustler at a poker table---too smooth, too rehearsed. But what you can't always spot is the storm brewing behind the velvet curtain.

The drug scene? That was the snake in the garden. It was everywhere, and I mean everywhere. Coke in bathroom stalls. Molly tucked in bras and G-strings. Pills wrapped in crumpled twenties. Rich frat boys looking to numb daddy issues. Washed-up dealers trying to reinvent themselves. Promoters pushing the product like it was part of the VIP package. Me? I was the one guy who couldn't afford to play. I knew my wiring---once I was in, I wasn't coming out clean. I wasn't built for moderation. So I steered clear. Said all the right things. Kept my distance. But in that world, proximity was guilt. Just standing next to the wrong person could bury you. Trouble didn't tap me on the shoulder. It kicked the door in.

Two cops from the local narcotics task force took a special interest in me. They weren't just watching---they were hovering. Day and night. I could feel it when I drove home, when I unlocked the back office, when I walked into the club's restroom and caught a glimpse of myself in the mirror---eyes darting, breath shallow. They were in my head. Watching, waiting, circling.

One of them---real name Ken, though the smart ones never used it--- I called The Boogeyman. And he wore that title like a second skin. I never stood in the same room as him, but I felt him---always one step behind me, or maybe one step ahead. He was the creak in the floorboards, the static on the line, the reason people stopped talking when I entered the room. You don't see guys like him. You sense them. In whispers. In redacted reports. In the pit of your stomach, right before your life starts circling the drain.

Ken came after the truth—or at least his version of it—and I believe he thought he was doing it honestly. But his tactics were unconventional, and the pressure he applied was relentless. Ken didn't just chase justice—he chased headlines. He was out for truth, but also for blood that would look good on the front page. To me, it often felt like facts were optional. All he seemed to need was a whiff of smoke, a crooked shadow, a silhouette in the fog he could cast into a monster. His tools weren't subpoenas and statutes in my eyes—they were fear, pressure, and a voice that could rattle your spine. And if those didn't break you, it felt like he'd squeeze your desperation until they did. He didn't build cases—he engineered implosions. And me? I was a gift-wrapped target. Loud. Flashy. Unapologetic. Everything he hated. Everything he could use. Maybe that's why he came after me like a man possessed. Or maybe, when you peel it back, he was just doing his job—with a little extra venom.

Then came the bridge girl.

They found her curled under an overpass like a broken doll---skin gray, eyes vacant, soul already halfway gone. Young. Real young. No ID. No purse. Just a fading tattoo and a whisper that she might've worked for me. That's all it took. One maybe. One flimsy thread. Suddenly, I wasn't a businessman---I was a suspect. A predator. A name with weight behind it, now soaked in scandal.

The truth? She'd never stepped foot on my stage. Never auditioned. Hell, I didn't even recognize her. But it didn't matter. Nobody was listening. Because the truth is slow. Scandal? Scandal's a bullet train.

Reporters circled like sharks. Cameras flashed. Headlines screamed: Club Owner Linked to Overpass Tragedy. But no one gave a damn about the girl---not really. She was just a prop, a cold body to pin a narrative on.

And I? I was the perfect villain. Easy to hate. Easier to sell.

In the end, it went nowhere. A dead-end from the start. Once the media realized they had a noose with no neck to fit it, the story died---quietly, without apology---of cold indifference. Tragic, yes. But also predictable. Expensive as hell, too. The kind of witch hunt reserved for guys like me---anyone tied to the adult world by reputation, rumor, or rumor dressed as reputation. It was almost cliché, the stink that clings to men in this business. Guilty until profitable. Then forgotten.

Then came the setup.

One of my dancers---troubled, magnetic, all hips and hard trauma---got herself tangled in a robbery straight out of a bad student film. Her boyfriend, a low-rent idiot with more testosterone than brains, pulled the job. Cheap ski masks, a stolen sedan, a dye pack that blew in his lap before he made it a block. Classic rookie hour. He panicked. Ran. Got caught red-handed---literally. Stained, sweating, and stupid. She went down with him. Didn't argue. Didn't cry. Just stood there, quiet and coiled, like she'd been waiting on this moment her whole life.

What she didn't expect was the deal.

The Boogeymanslid it across the table like a poisoned gift. No jail. No record. No trial. All she had to do was give them a story. Just one. Didn't matter if it was true. Hell, it didn't even have to be believable---just *believable enough*. All she had to do was say my name.

Say I was the bankroll behind the robbery. That I was washing drug money through the club. That I was the puppet master, pulling strings from the shadows while girls danced under lights I supposedly bought with blood money. They didn't need proof. They needed optics. They needed someone to crucify in the court of public opinion.

She paused. You could see the flicker of guilt. For a second, she almost held the line. Almost. But pressure is a brutal thing. It warps the spine and scrambles loyalties. And when your freedom's on the table---freedom or the rest of your life rotting in a cell---loyalty becomes a luxury most can't afford.

Survival turns saints into snitches.

So she gave them what they wanted. Spun her lies with a side of mascara tears and trembling hands. She played the victim. Said I corrupted her. Said I knew everything and turned a blind eye. And just like that, the narrative shifted. My name hit the reports again, got stamped on files, whispered in back rooms, headlined in articles written by hacks who never once stepped foot inside my business but knew exactly how to vilify it.

My life got sliced into headlines and dissected on late-night news panels. Again. My business---bled out in public like a stuck pig.

But this time, it didn't stick.

Thanks to a viciously competent lawyer, a few favors called in, and a phone call straight to the DA's desk, the entire mess was scrubbed from the surface faster than a cancerous mole. The girl's credibility cracked under cross-examination. Her story started to unravel the moment someone asked her the same question twice. Her boyfriend flipped, too---turns out, freedom talks louder than loyalty for him, too.

Still, the damage was done.

Because even when the ink fades, the stain remains. Once your name's been dragged through that kind of filth, innocence doesn't matter. You're marked. Tainted. People remember the smoke, not the fact that there was no fire.

As for the dancer and her idiot boyfriend? They each got twenty years. Deserved every minute. And I promise you this---neither one ever got a visit, a letter, or even a damn postcard from me.

And that's exactly what The Boogeymancounted on.

But here's the real gut-punch: me and The Boogeyman? We shared more than bad blood.

We shared a woman.

Not at the same time, but close enough. Close enough to matter. Close enough for ego and jealousy to muddy the water. I didn't know it then--- but I'd learn. Too late to fix anything. She'd been running both of us--- whispering one thing into my ear, then turning around and feeding him another version of the same lie. Maybe it was manipulation. Maybe survival. Maybe she just liked the game. But in the end, she played us both. And I never saw it coming.

The Boogeymandidn't just want to break me. He wanted to own my destruction. He wanted to make me doubt my own reflection. To feel my grip slip inch by inch while the whole damn world watched and clapped. And I gave him exactly what he wanted.

Small towns have long memories and short fuses. And everyone's in everyone's business, whether they admit it or not. So yeah, maybe it wasn't just about justice. Maybe it was personal. Maybe it always had been.

But I digress.

The truth is, paranoia became my second skin. I stopped trusting people. Kept my circle tighter than ever. Security cameras everywhere. Burn phones. Background checks on anyone who got too close. I wasn't running a club anymore---I was running for my life in slow motion. Just trying to keep it all from caving in. That's the part they don't tell you about success. The higher you climb, the more hands reach up to pull you down. Some wear badges. Some wear G-strings. And some just smile and wait for the right moment to twist the knife.

Eventually, The Boogeyman faded into the background. His little crusade lost steam, and word got around that his "tour of booty" behind bars had finally come to an end. Poetic, really. The hunter never caged his prey. And when the dust finally settled, something wild happened---after all his attempts to paint me as the villain, the truth came to light: I wasn't some underworld kingpin. I was just a stand-up guy who happened to run a controversial business. Boring, even---at least by criminal standards.

Maybe a little too flashy, too loud, but not dirty. Not crooked.

Apparently, his bosses figured that out too. Word must've filtered up the chain, because suddenly I wasn't Public Enemy #1 anymore. I was shaking hands with guys in uniform. Getting called "Cole" instead of "Sir." Invitations to barbecues. Friendly nods in parking lots. Suddenly, I had friends in law enforcement---lots of friends.

And that, ironically, became its own problem.

They started showing up like regulars. Off-duty deputies posted up at the bar, buying drinks for dancers, getting a little too cozy with the staff. It got to the point where they felt more like bouncers than customers. Comfortable? Way too. They were drawing their guns when minor scuffles broke out---acting like Scarlett's Secret was their own personal jurisdiction. Problem was, they were drunk. Off-duty. Armed. And on camera.

That didn't sit well with the Sheriff.

Turns out, it also didn't look great when county cruisers started doubling as motel rooms in the back lot. More than a few squad cars were caught on surveillance, rocking ever so slightly while a deputy inside was---let's just say---showing his badge off on her, not to her. Some even used the club like a drive-thru love shack, one-hour romance included. I didn't run a church, but come on.

It didn't take long before I got "the call."

A quiet meeting was set up at a steakhouse---neutral ground. Just me, the Sheriff, and a plate of ribs cooling between us while he wiped his forehead with a napkin and begged me, *begged me*, to help avoid a full-blown public affairs disaster. The department was under fire already, and the last thing he needed was a leaked video of Deputy Lovehammer going full porno in his patrol car outside a strip club.

Who was I to say no?

Compliant business owner that I was, I agreed to tone it down. Asked the staff to politely decline service to the more "enthusiastic" law enforcement regulars. I was nervous about the fallout---about telling badge-carrying drinkers that the welcome mat was suddenly rolled up---but I didn't have to worry.

Surveillance footage had already sealed their fate.

The deputies in question were caught bush-handed, pants down, guns holstered sideways, and they were fired before I even had time to worry. Sheriff cleaned house before the press could. Quietly. No drama. Just another mess behind me.

At least that one didn't have my name on it.

But order doesn't last long in a world built on tequila shots, secrets, and stiletto heels. Cleaning up one mess only gave the others room to grow teeth. With the deputies gone, a vacuum opened up---and nature abhors a vacuum, especially when it's laced with cash, power, and girls who knew how to make a man forget his wedding ring and his common sense.

Soon, new faces started showing up. Guys, I didn't know, flashing cash like it had an expiration date. Supposed "businessmen" who ordered top-shelf liquor and whispered like they were auditioning for a Scorsese film. Out-of-town "investors" wanting to get in on the club action, sniffing around the books, offering favors with smiles that didn't reach their eyes. I'd seen the type before. Parasites in tailored suits. They don't ask for permission. They circle, wait for weakness, and dig in.

Meanwhile, the girls were restless. The regulars felt the shift in energy, and so did the dancers. One got arrested in a DUI wearing nothing but body glitter and a pair of heels. Another stabbed her ex in a Walgreens parking lot with a cocktail straw. I found one crying backstage because some high-roller promised to take her to Miami and instead left her in a Waffle House parking lot with a broken phone and an unpaid bar tab. It was a rolling avalanche of bad choices and worse timing.

Security was cracking. Fights became weekly. One guy got thrown through the front *door*---literally *through* the door. Not out. Through. Broke the hinges. Bouncer ended up with a fractured wrist. Lawsuit followed. Of course it did. And it didn't help that half the chaos was caught on surveillance footage that the local news would've paid *real money* to get their hands on.

And I wasn't sleeping.

Nights blurred into mornings. Coffee turned into whiskey. My phone buzzed around the clock---staff quitting, cops calling, girls crying, attorneys reminding me I was still on thin ice from the last round of accusations. I'd built an empire on fantasy, but the reality was starting to eat it from the inside out.

I stopped going home. Started crashing in my office---door locked, blinds drawn. I'd sit there, watching the cameras, drinking cheap scotch from a souvenir mug while the walls closed in. My face aged ten years in six months. My name became a question mark. A liability. A warning. Through it all, the crowds kept coming. That was the sickest part.

Business boomed. Nothing draws curiosity like chaos. People wanted a peek behind the curtain---to brush up against the scandal. Lines out the door. Lap dances turning to therapy sessions. Girls turning mild tricks in the champagne room and pretending not to cry about it afterward. The smell of desperation and cologne mixed with dollar bills and fake promises. Scarlett's Secret was no longer just a club. It was a burning cathedral and I was its high priest, choking on the incense and trying like hell not to get swallowed by the fire.

Now, here are my worst fears coming true. During the rebuild, another fire started kindling. One in particular came with a side of betrayal. A former manager---someone I'd once trusted to lock up the place and count cash without supervision---got salty when he wasn't invited back for the grand reopening. Apparently, his ego didn't take rejection well. Instead of moving on like a grown ass man, he decided to reinvent himself as a whistleblower. Ran straight to the IRS like a jilted lover, tossing around words like tax evasion and illicit activity like confetti. None of it was true. But the truth doesn't always matter to people looking for a headline or a vendetta.

Contrary to the cliché of the "sleazy strip club owner skimming cash off the top," I ran a tight ship. Every dollar was tracked. My accountants were sharks in suits---brilliant, precise, and ruthless with the numbers. I had nothing to hide. I didn't need to cut corners---I was already making more money than I could reasonably spend without looking like a cartel boss. But let's not hang a halo on my head just yet.

While I was putting out business fires and dodging tax grenades, my personal life was a wrecking ball in motion. I tried---*tried*---to juggle my responsibilities as a father and a husband. But Kate was becoming an issue being pregnant. True, we crossed every line man could draw and then some. Emotionally. Physically. Repeatedly.

In one of the most twisted chapters of my life, I somehow managed to convince both Bridget and Kate---*both pregnant with my children*---to join me in what I can only describe as a three-way experiment in blurred boundaries and delusion. A "bonding experience," if we're dressing it up for polite company. One night. All three of us. A cocktail of hormones, lust, and denial.

It was surreal. Erotic. Unhinged. And ultimately, a colossal mistake.

During this act---somewhere between trying to keep it together and totally losing control---I made a comment. Just a few words. But it was enough. A slip. A tell. Something I said made it very clear just how well I knew Kate… too well. A flash of familiarity that couldn't be chalked up to casual encounters we've all enjoyed together. That's when Pandora's box flew wide open. Bridget's eyes cut through the room like a blade. The questions came fast, frantic, and full of venom.

"Whose baby is that?"

"It's John's," I muttered, trying to hang onto the lie we'd all agreed to.

"Who the hell is John?"

"I don't know. I've never met him."

"Then how do you know it's not yours?"

Bridget exploded. "I never should have done this!" she shouted, scrambling to cover herself---physically and emotionally. The air turned thick, like the aftermath of a detonation. Rage, confusion, betrayal---it all spilled into the room like gasoline on tile. Bridget stormed off, and Kate broke down. That perfect illusion I had somehow kept spinning in midair for months? It shattered in a single night. I stood there---naked, literally and metaphorically---I realized I was the architect of my own collapse.

Adding to the mental spectacle I was already starring in, the noose around my neck came in the form of my mortgage. The lender? A barely functioning alcoholic with a talent for chaos and a bad habit of waving power around like a loaded gun. He held what's called an *on-demand note*---which is just a polite, legal way of saying he could pull the rug out from under me anytime he felt like it. No warning. No grace. Just gone.

It wasn't just a financial weight---it was a constant threat, looming over me like a piano suspended by frayed string. And given the circus of my life and now IRS pressure, baby mama drama, and managerial betrayals I was navigating, this was one fire I desperately needed to snuff out.

Enter the lifeline---or so I thought.

I got an offer from two so-called seasoned operators who wanted to buy out the mortgage, get rid of the drunk lender, and hand me a check hefty enough to stabilize things and breathe for a minute. There was a catch, of course. There's always a catch. I'd be bringing in new partners---unfamiliar faces, unfamiliar motives. Not ideal, but compared to the alternative---financial collapse---it was a devil I could live with.

Meet my new business partners: Fiona and Claire.

Two lesbians who'd run a handful of clubs before---mostly the glitter-and-glam type, with drag shows, rainbow flags, and enough sass to fill a Pride parade. On paper, they were exactly what I needed. Sharp. Experienced. Strategic. The kind of operators who knew how to work the margins and squeeze every dollar from a slow Tuesday. But beneath the smiles and bulletproof résumés, I had my doubts. Not because of their background. Because of their *appetite*. The kind of hunger that didn't stop at profits or payroll. The kind that made me wonder how long before they started treating Scarlett's Secrets like their own personal buffet---financially, socially, and everything in between.

If they could stay focused on the bottom line and keep the drama out of the books, we'd be fine. *Big* if.

At first, it all looked clean. The lender got paid off. The ink dried. For one brief, golden moment, the pressure lifted. I could breathe without checking over my shoulder or sleeping with one eye open. The deal even included escrow funds earmarked to cover any lingering tax liabilities---on the *club's* side, not mine personally. That alone felt like a rare win. But in my world, peace is never permanent. It's rented by the hour. And the lease was about to run out.

The cracks came slow. Subtle. A bounced check here. A missed vendor payment there. Hairline fractures in their business ethics that widened into gaping chasms. Turns out, Fiona and Claire weren't just club owners---they were full-blown embezzlers. They had a majority stake in another club across town, and instead of running it clean, they were siphoning it dry. Quiet skimming, shady wire transfers, cooked books. And while their partner was kept in the dark, they were trying to buy me out on the sly---violating a non-compete clause and dragging Scarlett's into their mess without blinking.

I didn't see it at first. They were slick. Calculated. And when the walls started to crumble, their secrets spilled like gasoline into my lap.

Suddenly, vendors from their other club were calling me, looking for payment. My name started popping up in lawsuits I didn't recognize. Their house of cards was collapsing in public, and I was standing dead center in the blast zone. I should've cut ties. Pulled the ripcord. But I thought I could wall it off---keep their disaster quarantined. My books were clean. My systems were airtight. I wasn't laundering cash or skimming from the till. I figured Scarlett's could weather the storm.

Until he showed up.

Enter Joseph. Nickname: *Guido*. I don't need to paint the picture---you already know the type. Slicked-back hair, a gold chain thicker than a garden hose, and a track suit tight enough to show the outline of his Glock. He smelled like cologne and consequences. Found me in the parking lot one night, just standing there like it was his place.

No small talk. No pleasantries. Just a quick jacket lift to flash the heat and a line I won't forget:

"You're gonna fix this. Or it gets fixed *for you.*"

And just like that, my stomach dropped.

This wasn't business anymore. This was street-level enforcement. No subpoenas. No court dates. Just pressure. The kind that ends with duct tape and unmarked vans. Guido didn't give a damn about paperwork. He was there on behalf of someone who'd been burned--$50,000 bad check burned. Written from Fiona and Claire's other club. He had a legitimate grievance, and unfortunately for me, a very direct method of expressing it.

I called a meeting with my partners that night.

No pleasantries. No cocktails. I laid it out: *We're wiring that money today. And we're laying ground rules moving forward. No more surprise debts. No more shady side deals. We clean this shit up, or I'm out.*

They agreed---nervously. Smiles thin as paper. I could see the panic bubbling behind their eyes.

But I knew better than to think this was over.

Next, I had to survive a full-blown IRS audit. They'd already threatened jail time in our first meeting, just to make sure I knew they were serious. And while I kept every receipt, every report, every dollar accounted for, the stress was like being waterboarded with red tape.

Somehow, I stayed afloat.

And through all of it, there was one bright spot on the horizon---a break from the madness. Tickets to see Michael Jackson's reunion tour with his brothers in New York City, September 7–10, 2001. A moment of escape. Music, nostalgia, and maybe a night where I didn't have to watch my back or take a phone call that could blow up my world.

Life was chaotic. Beautifully, horrifically chaotic. I was juggling more flaming swords than a carnival act. Rebuilding Scarlett's. Dodging Boogeyman's shadows. Deflecting Guido's threats. Appeasing the IRS. Managing my new partners---chicks with big dicks and bigger drama. And somehow, I kept it all from crashing. Just barely.

"The windshield is larger than the rearview mirror for a reason: focus on moving forward, with just an occasional glance at the unchangeable past." ---Cole Walker

My rearview mirror held bodies, lies, and burn marks---more than enough for a bestseller. But my eyes? My eyes were on the road. The future was still wide open---full of landmines, sure, but also full of opportunity. And if I was lucky, maybe, just maybe, I'd figure out how to make it all work.

Or fake it well enough to keep driving.

Chapter 9

Just Beat It!

Heal the World Heal
Performed and written by: **Michael Jackson**

This chapter seems like the right place for this discussion, especially in light of recent events. "Heal the World" is a nice sentiment---wishful thinking, at best. With all the bears the U.S. continues to poke---some justifiably, others not---it's no surprise we've become a target for radical ideologies and those determined to strip away the freedoms our country once knew. Take, for example, the heightened security checkpoints that now stretch well beyond airport gates. It's a response to the world we've created, and it's a reality we'll never escape.

Unfortunately, events like the one that set all of this into motion have happened before and will happen again. That singular event shattered the world's sense of stability, and its effects still echo through our lives today. We see it in the security lines we now stand in at every turn---lines that, sadly, have become a necessity. It's a direct response to the success of terrorism that day. But the scars run deeper. We see the aftermath in the ongoing acts of terror---attacks in schools and public spaces---that have birthed a new wave of domestic terrorists. And this is just the beginning.

After a soul-crushing day of blackjack and slot machine betrayal, I sat slumped in a Vegas casino lounge, nursing a bruised ego and blood pressure high enough to set off TSA alarms. Around me, a gathering of fellow losers---let's call them The Fellowship of Regret---sat with that same hollow stare, casualties of this adult amusement park disguised as a high-roller fantasy. And me? I wanted to punch myself in the face. Hard. I'd broken my own cardinal rule---etched somewhere deep in the cracked marble of my personal Ten Commandments: *Stop gambling, asshole.* That inner voice had been screaming all day. But like every idiot who thinks the next hand is the one, I let it ride. And then I let it ride again. And again. Now I was dipping into money I'd earmarked for our New York City trip---the one I'd promised would be special, something romantic, something redeeming. Something I wasn't supposed to blow chasing three cherries on a neon-lit slot machine with a soundtrack of failure.

Furious at myself, I called Delta, desperate to change our return flight, to salvage something by leaving Vegas early and cutting hotel costs. As I was rebooking, Bridget strolled over like a smug prophet, hands full of $100 chips, practically glowing with victory. "You're such a loser," she said, her voice soaked in satisfaction, the kind of jab that cuts deeper because it's true. "Yeah? We'll see," I muttered, flipping her off as I hit confirm---rebooking our flights out of Vegas and locking in our tickets to New York.

Fast forward ten days. We're packed for NYC, and I'm high on redemption fumes, holding two Michael Jackson 30th Anniversary concert tickets I'd scored on eBay for $1,500. Floor seats, front section. I figured that'd buy me back some dignity. Bridget, of course, remained unimpressed, still carrying the stench of Vegas disappointment. "Do you have the cash and cards?" she asked, giving me that look, like she was evaluating whether I could be trusted with a lunch order, let alone our finances. I checked my wallet. One crisp $100 bill, a couple of credit cards, and my prized possession---a 1934 $500 bill I'd carried for five years like a financial talisman. Most people thought it was fake, but it was real, and it was mine, and it was worth about $750 to the right person. That bill had outlived failed business deals, botched vacations, and one near-divorce.

Then came the hiccup. Julio, my go-to limo driver, called. Flat tire. No backup car. His voice, drenched in Puerto Rican fury, was a stream of rapid-fire curses that covered every known deity and automotive brand. "No problem," I said as I tossed the phone down and got behind the wheel of my own car, waving as we passed him on the roadside, sweat-soaked and kicking his shredded tire.

New York hit different. The air had bite, the kind that wakes you up. The city buzzed with that signature chaos, until we hit the cab line at LaGuardia---longer than a Vegas buffet on payday. "Let's grab a limo," Bridget said with a shit-eating grin. "Oh sure," I fired back. "Because we're flush with cash after my Vegas masterclass in financial ruin." She grinned wider, throwing up the "L" on her forehead like a teenage troll. "Loser."

We landed a room at a hotel that boasted "budget-friendly charm," which turned out to be code for gay-themed boutique. From the hot pink elevator glow to the statues with enough anatomical confidence to make Michelangelo blush, it was clear we were in for a fabulous stay. Bridget and I exchanged that eyebrow raise---equal parts open-minded amusement and "Well, this should be interesting." The room was large, clean, and unapologetically flamboyant. Honestly, it was probably the most memorable we'd had in years.

That night, we geared up for the concert. It was pouring rain, but nothing was stopping me. I strutted to the Madison Square Garden entrance like a man who finally got something right. I handed the valet our golden tickets. He glanced at them, then looked up at me with pity in his eyes. "Sir... these tickets are for Friday's show." My soul left my body. It was Monday. Bridget's stare could've melted steel. "You dumbass," she hissed, her voice like a razor across my confidence. My plan to be thrifty had just detonated in my face. I'd saved a few bucks flying early and lost a small fortune in dignity.

But I wasn't giving up. Not tonight. Not after all that. I was in full redemption mode. With only $100 cash and my prized $500 bill, I hit the scalper circuit like a man on fire. One guy offered two tickets for $900. I gave him the whole sob story, flashed my 1934 bill, swore on my dead uncle's soul it was real and worth more than he could Google. He called a buddy. They verified it. Finally, he nodded. Deal. I handed over my lucky bill like a man giving away his dog before a long prison sentence---equal parts pride, pain, and pathetic desperation.

And you know what? Michael delivered. That man moonwalked like it was 1984, and the energy in that arena could've powered half of Manhattan. Celebrities were everywhere. I remember catching a glimpse of Usher riding on top of a limo---I didn't even know who he was at the time, just another guy waving to the crowd like he owned the place. We grabbed hot dogs after the show, wandered the city like we were in our twenties, and somehow ended the night at a gentleman's club---for "business research," of course.

I lost in Vegas. I screwed up the tickets. I gave away my prized possession. And yet... somehow, I walked away feeling like I'd won something bigger. Experience. Street cred. Or at the very least, one hell of a story. For the record---Vegas didn't break my wallet, just my psyche. I punish myself on purpose. It's a reminder that gambling isn't a thrill--- it's a trap. It doesn't just empty your pockets. It empties your sanity. I've seen it ruin lives. I've seen it eat people whole.

Then came the morning after. My phone wouldn't stop ringing. I ignored it, groggy and hungover, until Bridget picked up. The hotel clerk was on the line. He said our stay had been extended, on the house. "You haven't seen the news?" he asked. I turned on the TV. The Twin Towers had collapsed. The World Trade Center Marriott---our original hotel--- was gone. Gone. Bridget and I just stared at the screen. "If we hadn't lost in Vegas..." I muttered, knowing damn well how close we'd come to being there.

The rest of that day was pure chaos. New York City became a cage. The air felt thinner, the buildings taller, the exits fewer. The whole city was drowning in sirens, confusion, and fear. Payphone lines stretched down blocks. Cell service was next to useless. Police were everywhere. Emergency vehicles ran red lights like the laws had been erased. The silence between sirens was the loudest thing I've ever heard. But the worst part wasn't the logistics---it was the fear etched into everyone's face. A fear that mutated into suspicion. Middle Eastern people---hell, even people who just looked Middle Eastern---were suddenly targets. Not individuals. Not neighbors. Just suspects. That shift in the air, that ugliness---it spread fast.

We couldn't fly. Bridges were shut down. We were stuck---until we found a car dealership that had a base-model Honda Accord for sale. Twenty-one grand, loaded with markup. It didn't even take a phone for American Express to approve the charge, signed the papers, and we drove that overpriced sedan all the way to Georgia, passing nothing but chaos and silence. Another grand slam to the idea of a "money-saving" trip.

That night, we made it to North Carolina---the first place with a hotel and a vacancy. We took dozens of snapshots on disposable cameras, tried to process what had happened. We even drove to D.C. to see the Pentagon. When the film was developed later, every shot of the Pentagon's damaged side was blacked out. Not blurry. Not overexposed. Just black. To this day, I don't know what that was, but it creeped me out more than I like to admit.

Looking back, the whole trip was a mess of bad luck, dumb decisions, near-death timing, and weird cosmic nudges that kept us just out of reach of disaster. Vegas may have emptied my pride, but it probably saved my life.

Chapter 10

Pocket Notes

It Don't Matter to Me
Performed by **Bread**
written by **David Gates**

I've always loved the song *It Don't Matter to Me*---the single version remake. It hits different when you're trying to play the big man, pretending you're cool with letting someone go. Like it's no big deal to watch her walk away and end up in someone else's arms. But when it's not what either of you really want---when the love is still there but the situation is completely fucked---that song starts cutting deep. Saying I was okay with it? Total bullshit. It tore me up. Still does, if I'm honest. But sometimes, even when your heart's still in it, a decision has to be made. And so I made it---knowing full well it would hurt like hell.

It's been years now since the tangled beginning of my love affair with Kate and my marriage to Bridget. Time has passed, but nothing about it feels distant. Kate is still in my life, still in my dreams, still not in my bed at night. The feelings haven't faded---they've grown deeper, sharper, more soul-shaking than ever. I'm still in love with her in the kind of way that doesn't go away. It just sits there, quietly wrecking you, every damn day.

Now we have a daughter together. Julia. A beautiful, perfect baby girl. Her arrival should've been one of the happiest moments of my life, but the truth is, I wasn't even there when she was born. That reality still tears me apart. It haunts me in a quiet, merciless way. Kate's parents---still clinging to the idea of her fantasy boyfriend, this legend they'd built in their heads, by us, still weren't convinced I wasn't the father. While they played pretend, I was neck-deep in my own reality. Seven kids already.

Bridget had just given birth to Jordan---our daughter---another tiny heartbeat I'd fallen for the moment I laid eyes on her. Julia made nine. Nine kids. Nine lives I was responsible for. And somewhere in the chaos of diapers, secrets, and half-truths, everything started to buckle.

Julia changed Kate. Something in her shifted. She reached her breaking point. Years of hiding, years of sneaking around and pouring love into the spaces between what we could have and what we weren't allowed to hold---she was done. It all came to a head the day she slipped me a note, handwritten, shaky but final. It said Julia needed her father. And Kate was finished hiding. Finished pretending. She wanted our daughter to grow up in truth, not shadows. If I couldn't step up, she would walk away---forever.

That moment hit like a brick wall at full speed. Everything we'd built---quiet conversations behind closed doors, stolen weekends, the ache of missing each other even when we were five feet apart---all of it crumbled in one decisive blow. The fantasy died, and the consequences rolled in, unforgiving and fast. The genie was out of the bottle, and she wasn't going back in.

It started unraveling the night Kate's note surfaced from the abyss of my pants pocket, crumpled and never seen by me, just minutes from getting tossed into the washing machine. Bridget found it. Her face went pale, then red, then something else entirely---betrayal mixed with confirmation, rage doused in heartbreak. The screaming began before I could think, before I could lie, before I could run. She demanded answers in clipped, furious bursts, holding the note like a murder weapon she hadn't expected to find.

We ended up in the parking lot of Scarlett's Secrets, the club where Kate had been working nights while juggling college classes, the club that had become our halfway house, our neutral zone, the only place our lives consistently crossed without judgment. That night, it turned into a war zone.

Bridget didn't hesitate. She made a beeline for Kate the moment she caught sight of her stepping out of the employee entrance, face drawn and shoulders slumped from another soul-sucking shift. Bridget's voice---crisp, clipped, and full of venom---slashed through the night air, her British accent turning every accusation into a razor's edge. Kate held her ground---until she didn't have to.

What started as words turned to wreckage in seconds. The argument ignited, fast and feral, the kind of scene that gets seared into your memory whether you want it there or not. Bridget struck first---wild, messy, heartbreak masquerading as rage. Kate didn't swing back. She could have. She had the training to end it in one clean move---drop Bridget like a bad habit and walk away. But she didn't lift a finger. She stood there, took it. Out of guilt? Maybe. Out of some warped sense of justice or grace? Maybe that too. Or maybe she just knew that the second she fought back, it wouldn't be a confrontation anymore---it'd be a catastrophe. And neither of them would walk away clean.

Two sheriff's deputies had been sitting nearby in their cruiser, probably half-asleep, before the screams pulled them from their boredom. They stepped in just as Bridget was winding up again, pulled her off Kate, and cuffed her right there in front of the neon-lit club sign. Watching her in handcuffs did something to me I still can't explain. It didn't hurt because I thought she didn't deserve it. It hurt because I knew the blood was on my hands. This whole damn disaster had been set in motion by me---my choices, my lies, my cowardice. Despite years of working with local law enforcement, it still took more begging than I care to admit to get her released with a simple notice to appear instead of an overnight stay in the county.

The aftermath was surreal. Unbelievably, almost insultingly surreal. Somewhere between the tears and the twisted remains of that parking lot showdown, the two of them embraced. Not a warm, mutual hug, but one of those strange, broken understandings that happen when two people realize they've both been drowning in the same wreck. Then, in one of the most bizarre and emotionally disorienting moments of my life, the two of them led me---without words, without explanation---to a nearby hotel room. What followed wasn't romance. It wasn't closure. It was desperation in silk sheets. It was silence and sadness pretending to be intimacy. It was the last time the three of us would ever be in the same room like that again. Bridget wasn't giving forgiveness. She was reclaiming territory, marking the ending on her terms. That night didn't fix anything. It only shattered me further. Because for me, it just deepened everything I already felt for Kate. Losing her wasn't something I could process. It was like being asked to cut off a limb and then smile like it didn't hurt.

The fallout came fast and came hard. Bridget turned every memory of Kate into a weapon, sharp and deliberate, launching them like grenades in every argument we had from that night on. There was no line she wouldn't cross, no piece of our history too sacred to twist. Kate's name became poison in our house---unspoken but always present, hanging in the air like smoke after a fire. Gifts I'd given her were turned into props for fury. Engagement rings thrown in the trash. Dresses and shoes dropped off at Goodwill with receipts still in the boxes. Framed photos that used to sit quietly on shelves disappeared without a trace, as if erasing the evidence could somehow undo the betrayal. It was scorched earth. Bridget didn't just want to hurt me---she wanted to leave no trace that Kate had ever existed in my life. I didn't fight her on it. I had no defense. I had lit the match that burned it all down.

Through all the fury and drama and pitiful attempts to keep the peace, I couldn't stop thinking about Kate. Her silence hit harder than Bridget's rage ever could. The absence of her voice, her laugh, her warmth---it carved into me. That kind of loss doesn't fade. It festers. I let her go. I told myself it was the right move, the grown-up choice, the responsible decision. I convinced myself I was doing it for the kids, that I was preserving some version of stability for their sake. That's the lie I leaned on to sleep at night. But children are sharp. They read between the lines. They feel the tension. They see the way your eyes wander when someone mentions a name you're not supposed to react to. They know when you're smiling through the ache. They're the wisest souls in the room, and I was the idiot thinking I could fool them.

The other truth---the one I don't say out loud in polite company---is this: I didn't want to get financially gutted in divorce court again. I didn't want to lose another million in equity or add another strike to my marriage record. I was already deep into my own Hall of Fame of poor choices. I stayed out of fear. I stayed out of cowardice. I stayed because I didn't want to feel the full weight of my failures. I stayed because it was easier to suffer than to start over. So yes, I let Kate go for the wrong reasons. All the wrong reasons. It wasn't noble. It wasn't selfless. It was survival dressed up as sacrifice, and I've had to live with that ever since. Because some losses don't just hurt, they rot you from the inside out.

What Bridget and I had was never clean. It was a chaotic, torrid storm of passion, lies, and constant third-party interference. There was always someone else in the picture---always an extra shadow in the bedroom. Sometimes it was my girlfriend. Sometimes hers. It was never about loyalty. It was about control, about heat, about the illusion of freedom in a relationship built on quicksand.

Kate was the first "official" girlfriend we brought in together, if that's what you want to call it. But the irony is, Kate and I had already been sleeping together for years behind Bridget's back. So when I suggested a threesome, it wasn't some bold leap into sexual exploration. It was a strategic act of damage control. I figured that if Bridget ever found out, it might sting a little less if she felt like she'd been in on it all along. A twisted kind of illusion. A workaround to avoid complete implosion.

It might sound wild, but the jealousy wasn't always about what I saw. It was about what I didn't. It was the idea of my partner connecting with someone else behind closed doors, sharing laughter I wasn't a part of, touching emotions I didn't have access to. That haunted me more than any physical act. So I dragged Bridget into the room. Figured if she saw it for herself—if she witnessed the mess—it might cool the fire burning because of Kate. Maybe she'd call it even. Maybe we could smother betrayal under some half-assed version of honesty. That was the plan---or the illusion of one.

Was it selfish? Without a doubt. Strategic? Absolutely. Let's not dress it up as something noble or enlightened. I orchestrated that moment because I was in too deep and too scared to be honest. I wanted Kate. I didn't want to lose Bridget. I thought I could have both. That's not polyamory. That's delusion.

When Kate finally stepped away from our circus of dysfunction, more women stepped in without missing a beat. Like a casting call had gone out and the universe had just filled the vacancies. These weren't random one-night stands. These were regulars. Rotating fixtures over the years. This wasn't a phase. It was a pattern. A behavior loop I kept walking, pretending it was a coincidence.

I'm not a therapist, but I'm not blind either. When the same shit keeps happening, it's not bad luck---it's a pattern. A cycle. A twisted script you keep signing your name to, like you don't already know how it ends. Bridget used to say I got "dragged" into threesomes, like she was some poor victim swept up in the tidal wave of someone else's fantasy, like she was an innocent bystander. But that's complete bullshit. I wasn't kicking and screaming either. I wasn't protesting. Half the time, I was holding the door open and lighting the candles.

I wasn't the puppet, sure---but I sure as hell wasn't cutting the strings either. I didn't always lead the charge. I didn't always send the first message or book the hotel, but I wasn't slamming on the brakes either. I let it happen. I gave it oxygen. I watched the fire grow, stood there like some wide-eyed fool, and when it finally roared out of control, I had the audacity to act surprised. I wasn't some passive passenger in this wreck. Maybe I wasn't driving the train, but I laid the tracks. Every derailment, every twisted pile of wreckage, every emotional collision that left someone bleeding---it all followed a blueprint I helped design. It was the result of choices I made, red flags I ignored, lines I crossed, and boundaries I refused to draw.

That's the brutal truth I live with now. I wasn't manipulated. I wasn't dragged. I wasn't the misunderstood antihero stumbling through life trying to do the right thing. I was the architect. I sketched the chaos with my own pen. I mixed the concrete, built the playground, and left the gate wide open while the wolves circled. I handed out matches like party favors and dared the storm to blow through. I played with fire, got scorched, and still acted confused when everything around me turned to ash. There's no sympathy in that. No redemption arc waiting in the wings. Just consequences. Hard, unforgiving, long-haul consequences that don't care about your intentions, only your impact.

That's what guts you. Not the crash, not the burn, not the dramatic freefall everyone warns you about---it's the moment you stop making excuses, stop pointing fingers, stop narrating your life like someone else wrote it. It's when you finally stand still long enough to stare down the wreckage. When you stop lying to yourself about what happened and see it for what it is. You weren't betrayed---you just didn't pay attention. You weren't tricked---you went in with your eyes open. You weren't ambushed or blindsided or sucker-punched. You walked right into it. You weren't the casualty---you were the cause. That's the part no one prepares you for. That's the ride home when the music's off and the adrenaline's gone and it's just you and your guilt in the dark. That's the aftertaste that doesn't wash out with whiskey or therapy or time. You don't get to play the victim when you're the one who pulled the pin and walked away like the grenade wasn't going to explode in your own damn living room.

Meanwhile, the skeletons weren't in the closet---they were knocking with bills in hand. Regina was legally in my rearview, but the damage she left behind kept showing up on my doorstep. Our custody battle ended in a negotiated compromise---shared time with the kids instead of the scorched-earth fight she was aiming for. I wrote her a $500,000 check, not so much to settle up as to settle her down. A payoff, plain and simple. Half a million to close a chapter that refused to stay closed. I thought that would be the end of it. I was wrong.

Before the ink dried, the IRS knocked on my door like a thug with a clipboard. A $400,000 audit bill, out of nowhere, right in the teeth. Months of back and forth, blood pressure through the roof, and lawyers draining me dry. Eventually, the dust settled around $100,000. Still a brutal hit. Still another scar. What triggered it? A horse. One single horse I'd donated to a charity for at-risk kids. That was the red flag. Not the cash businesses. Not the shady write-offs. Not the nightlife expenses labeled "research." Nope---a Friggin horse. The auditors latched onto it like bloodhounds. By the time I finished defending myself, I could've bought a dozen horses, built a barn, and had enough left over to name one after the IRS agent who hounded me.

Here's the punchline. Not one eyebrow was raised over the seven sets of breast implants I'd deducted under "promotional enhancements." Seven pairs. Zero questions. But a horse? That launched a six-month investigation. I wish I was making this up. I don't know whether to laugh or smash something.

And just when I thought I could see daylight, it got dumber. I wrote a $20,000 check on the spot, agreed to pay the rest in 30 days. When I went back to pay the balance, they couldn't find the debt. I stood there, ready to hand over the money, and they had nothing to apply it to. The account had disappeared into some bureaucratic black hole called a "non-master file." Apparently, even the IRS can lose its own damn paperwork. Close enough for government work, I guess.

But all that chaos---the audits, the settlements, the financial gut punches---they were nothing compared to what was happening inside my own house. Compared to Kate walking away. Compared to the empty seat at the table, the silence on the other end of the phone, the brutal finality of a love I couldn't hold onto. Her leaving didn't resolve anything. It exposed everything. It ripped the cover off my life and showed me what I really was---weak, indecisive, wrecked. I didn't stop loving her. I couldn't. Losing her didn't bring peace, it brought obsession. It made me reckless. It made me vulnerable. It made me Bridget's favorite target.

Bridget didn't fight fair. She was smarter than that. She went for the soft tissue, every time. Emotional shrapnel, expertly aimed. She knew exactly where the bruises were and pressed on them daily. Some days it felt like a war, other days it felt like penance. I took the hits because part of me believed I deserved every single one. That's what shame does. It makes you sit quietly in your own punishment, too tired to protest, too guilty to leave.

Looking back on all of it, it doesn't feel like real life. It reads like something pulled from a bad novel---too wild, too dramatic, too messed up to be believable. The kind of story you'd skim at the airport bookstore, scoff at halfway through, and leave behind on the plane. But I didn't just read it. I lived every messy, brutal, beautiful, stupid, gut-wrenching second of it. I lived the highs that felt like flying, and the lows that felt like falling face-first into pavement. I lived the love that made my chest ache, the cheating that made my stomach turn, the shouting matches that echoed into the walls like war, and the quiet lies whispered in the dark corners of back seats. I lived the truth when it finally clawed its way out, loud and undeniable, shouted across front yards and hotel rooms, text threads and courtrooms. I lived the looks from people who thought they knew. I lived the shame. I lived the implosion. I lived the parts no one wants to write down.

There weren't any clean exits. No graceful bows, no fade-to-black moments. Just jagged endings, sharp as glass and twice as dangerous. Life didn't give me closure---it gave me wreckage. It gave me silence in the places where laughter used to echo. It gave me the cold hum of a refrigerator late at night, and no one to talk to. It gave me questions with no answers, choices with no do-overs, and the slow, crushing realization that the future I thought I was building had already collapsed behind me, and I was too busy lying to myself to hear it fall. That's where the truth lives. Not in some feel-good redemption arc. Not in some Hallmark epiphany. It lives in the wreckage. In the debris you crawl through when the party's over and the lights are on. It lives in the silence you try to fill with noise. It lives in the walk---barefoot, bleeding---across the mess you created, just trying to keep moving.

Because sometimes survival isn't brave. It isn't noble. It's not some cinematic comeback. Sometimes, survival is waking up, breathing in the stale air of your own consequences, and trying not to fuck it up worse than you did yesterday.

Kate moved on. That's what people do when they're tired of waiting for you to grow up. She found someone new. Moved in with him while he was still technically married, which was rich in irony, but none of us were exactly saints. I guess the lesson flew right over both our heads. The needle stayed on repeat, and the same song kept playing. The real complication, though, was Julia---our daughter. My daughter. A little girl who deserved more than the mess she was born into. I tried to be part of her life. I tried to step in. I tried to make good on the promises I never spoke but always felt. But Bridget shut it down like flipping a switch. She forbade it, threw down the ultimatum like a gavel, and I folded like I always did when she brought the fire. Another spineless decision in a long history of them. Another moment I wish I could yank back and do differently.

Then came the lawsuit. Kate took legal action---she had to. Julia needed support, and Kate wasn't wrong for coming after it. I did what I always did when cornered: put on a strong face, hired an overpriced lawyer, and told myself I was doing it to protect my home life. Truth is, I was just trying to please Bridget. I fought Kate in court, not because I didn't believe in supporting our daughter, but because I was afraid to piss off the woman who had me by the throat emotionally and financially. Deep down, I knew I should've taken the original ultimatum---walked away from the chaos, embraced fatherhood, rebuilt my life around something real. But I didn't. I hesitated. I played both sides. I tried to walk the line. And in the end, I paid the money, signed the paperwork, and watched as I was slowly cut out of my daughter's life---not by Kate, but by Bridget, who wielded control like a scalpel and made damn sure I never got to be the father Julia deserved.

That's the part that doesn't leave you. Not the checks, not the court dates, not the arguments. It's the silence. It's knowing your child is out there, growing up without your stories, without your voice, without your presence. It's knowing you chose comfort over courage. It's knowing you didn't fight hard enough when it actually mattered. That's the kind of regret that doesn't fade. It settles in your bones. It doesn't scream. It whispers. Every damn day.

Chapter 11

Pillows, Pills, and Partners

Rockstar
Performed by **Nickelback**
written by:**Daniel Adair, Mike Kroeger, Ryan Peake & Chad sKroeger**

"Living vicariously through you"---I heard that line from friends more times than I can count. I had access, options, opportunity---and yeah, I indulged. I didn't hold back. *Never drugs, though.* But let's be clear---I wasn't some rockstar or movie star crashing Bentleys into swimming pools. I wasn't famous, just fortunate. Still, I had a front-row view of that kind of flameout. I can imagine the pressure real rockstars face---the weight of being idolized. It breaks people. When everyone's looking up to you and there's no one left for you to look up to, things get dark. That's when the drugs come in---not for fun, not to party, but to escape. To kill the noise. More often than not, they don't just kill the noise. They kill you. Usually young.

It was late Wednesday afternoon, and I'd been counting down the months to this New Year's weekend blowout. The destination? A mystery. And Bridget and I? We weren't exactly seasoned in mingling with this crowd---next-level rich, power players in every circle, the kind of open-minded elite who had everything on tap. This is the way real rock stars and celebrities lived, not us. Yet there we were, stepping into our six-year-old, financed limousine like we belonged. I cracked open a beer. Bridget sipped her favorite white wine, a bowl of strawberries within reach. Julio---our friend turned part-time chauffeur---navigated us toward a gated slice of paradise in Galaxy Beach. The kind of neighborhood we could only afford in our dreams. Between kids, an ex-wife, child support, and life's relentless overhead, discretionary income a bit more estranged these days in the Walker household.

As we pulled up to the gate, a uniformed, armed guard stepped forward. The divider was down, so I heard him ask Julio for ID, then approach our window. I scrambled over to roll it down and let Bridget take in the view. The guard eyed us, then nodded and returned with instructions: "Mr. and Mrs. Walker, take a left after the bridge. Sixth gate on the right. Have your driver ring the bell." Inside, the place was obscene in its perfection. Every inch sculpted, manicured, and screaming, "You don't belong here." Julio eased past a brand-new Rolls-Royce Phantom and a stretch Escalade with glowing neon opera lights. Bridget leaned in and whispered, "Hooollyyy shit." I matched her awe: "Un-freaking-real."

As we arrived, Julio's phone rang. He answered, distracted, while I stepped out and helped Bridget from the car. My full attention snapped to her sultry black dress---elegant, but dangerous. As she stepped out, I couldn't help myself. "A little flash of those panties?" She smirked. "You're out of luck, baby. I'm not wearing any." Then, with a wicked grin, she parted her legs just enough to reveal a freshly groomed landing strip. "You like that, don't cha'?" "Hell yeah," I growled, pulling her close.

Hand in hand, we walked toward the oceanfront mansion. The twenty-foot wrought-iron doors loomed ahead like the gates to another dimension. Before we could even touch the bell, they parted with a mechanical whisper. Alan and Alexandria Diamond stood waiting---flawless, glowing, ridiculously welcoming. We were met with hugs... then Alan kissed Bridget full on the lips, with tongue, and Alex kissed me in the same manner. Bridget and I shared a quick *what the hell is happening* glance---but we rolled with it.

We'd dipped a toe into this world months earlier, on a trip to Atlanta. A couple of Swingers Clubs. Just voyeur stuff, maybe some playful touching. Nothing serious. But once the door cracked open, it was hard to close. The intrigue---the rush---was real. One of those nights, we'd bumped into the Diamonds. Back then, it was small talk and shared drinks. Business chat. Discreet laughs and an unspoken pact: In a town like Galaxy Beach, where whispers travel faster than Wi-Fi, silence was golden.

The Diamonds were big players. They owned a national medical supply company, lived extravagantly, and moved in circles far beyond our reach. Along with them were Dr. Rick Manetti, a well-known local urologist, buff, confident, and Italian, and his wife, Carla, as hot as you would expect and many years his junior. They often had a "fifth wheel" in tow---this time, a guy named Jay. I recognized him instantly as someone who had been kicked out of Scarlett's Secrets for selling drugs. That alone put me on high alert.

Jay was an entrepreneur---the kind drug dealers like to think they are. In his late 20s, good-looking, overflowing with charisma, and sporting a raspy smoker's voice, he was the quintessential "I Gotta Guy" guy for the weekend. But just wait---Jay didn't just hover on the edges of my world. He infiltrated my life in ways that will make you shake your head. Standby.

Atlanta became our secret getaway---a judgment-free zone miles away from prying eyes. The clubs were a world of their own: dance floors, meet-and-greet bars, and private rooms lined with mattresses. There were big, mirrored spaces for the exhibitionists and smaller, dimly lit nooks for more private encounters. While Bridget and I mostly stuck to watching, we couldn't help but notice the brazen disregard for safety, with strangers engaging in unprotected acts as if STDs didn't exist. Add in the omnipresent drugs---marijuana, cocaine, ecstasy---and it was clear that for many, the high wasn't just about the sex.

Back to the present: The Diamonds' mansion was everything you'd expect from people who owned a private island. After some pleasantries, Alan suggested we head to their third-floor master suite. As we rode the glass elevator, he teased, "Did you bring clothes for a couple of days?" Bridget nodded. "Where are we going?"

"Vegas, baby!" Alan announced. "We'll break in our new G 4 Jet."

Bridget's jaw dropped. I was just as stunned, but my love for airplanes quickly overshadowed everything else. I rushed to retrieve our bags, leaving her in the hands of Alex and their other guests. Screw the formalities---I wanted to meet this jet.

Downstairs, I helped Julio load our luggage into the Escalade limo. "Where's the jet parked?" I asked Alan's driver, Mark. "Savanah," he replied, confirming the night's surreal trajectory. As we wrapped up, I took a moment to reconnect with Mark, an old acquaintance from my limo service days. Life had come full circle in the strangest of ways.

When I returned upstairs, the scene had shifted---drastically. Bridget was sprawled on the bathroom counter, her landing strip being shaved off by Alex. Maria and Jay were doing lines of coke, and Alan was feeding Bridget ecstasy with his tongue. I froze. This wasn't what we'd discussed. Swinging was supposed to be mutual---consensual, respectful, communicative. Drugs were never part of the deal. Watching Bridget cross that line felt like betrayal. We had just arrived.

Maria---gorgeous and impossibly young---was barely twenty, a random waitress with a body built for sin. We'd picked her up at a club in Atlanta, part of a bet I made with Alan. I told him he couldn't pull her based on charm alone. Secretly, I wanted her in the mix. Alan failed, predictably. But once she heard we traveled by jet and limo, she was all in. As for the bet? A gentleman's wager. Winning the girl should've been enough. Maybe it wasn't.

I asked Bridget what the hell was going on. "Relax, baby," she said, casual as ever. "Have a beer and enjoy the night."

Alan chimed in, offering me everything from ecstasy to coke. I declined. Stuck with my beer. Though for a second, I wondered what was in it. The party ramped up fast. Bridget drifted---mentally, emotionally--- off into some haze that I wasn't invited into. This wasn't what we came for. Was she chasing freedom now? Or just running from something neither of us could name?

Finally, it was time to board the jet. I peeled away from the chaos and walked straight into aviation heaven---introduced myself to the pilots, ran my hands over the switches, soaked in the cockpit's futuristic glow. But even surrounded by all that beauty, something felt off. Bridget's choices. My silence. This entire ride---it was a gamble. And we were already at altitude.

The engines hummed with a deep, co"fort'ng thrust as the flat panels flickered to life. It felt like stepping into a video game---only the stakes were real. As we hit takeoff speed, the nose lifted, gear up, and we climbed into the darkness en route to Vegas. About twenty minutes in, the Captain cracked the intercom: "Folks, feel free to stretch your legs and move around the cabin---but save some fun for us working stiffs up here." I could only imagine what he'd seen.

That's when I felt a tap on my shoulder. "Hi. I'm Dakota. You ready to serve His Majesty, Alan?" she asked with a grin.

"You mean to be the hostess, Dakota?" I laughed.

"Exactly," she said, smirking. "Lord Farquaad has spoken."

I shrugged. "How about you take the orders, and I'll make the drinks? I own a bar, after all."

Dakota lit up. "Sounds great! You gonna take me to your bar sometime?"

"Hell yeah," I said, smiling.

She was gorgeous---girl-next-door hot, with zero flash, probably no makeup, and a body that didn't need filters. More than that, she radiated warmth. Real warmth. We'd just met, and already, I liked her better than half the people on board.

I made my way over to the galley and checked in with the pilots, offering soda, water, or juice. They asked me to swing back in twenty, so I got to work---prepping mixers, slicing fruit, chilling beer. Didn't take long before I was ready.

"Okay, my biatch, fix my drinks," Dakota teased.

"Biatch? Nah, you're my biatch," I shot back.

"Nope," she laughed. "You're mine. I'm the boss here."

I looked around. "Holy shii-at. This plane is full of hot girls---with boyfriends and husbands five feet away. Talk about open-minded."

"So why aren't you back there partaking in the festivities? How'd you get roped into this?" I asked.

"I don't use drugs," she said, her tone shifting. "My ex-husband forced me to. He was a piece of shit. I hate drugs, I hate that world---it eats at me."

I swallowed hard. Not the time to push. But damn---Dakota was the real deal. No drugs. No bullshit. Just heart. I was starting to seriously rethink Maria.

"You're with Jack, right?" I asked. "You guys married? Does he partake?"

She nodded toward the cabin. "Look at that son of a bitch." Jack was doing a line with Alex. "He promised me he wouldn't. If he wants to marry me, he'd better get his shit together."

So that was Jack---a transplant surgeon in his late 50s. Distinguished, polished, loaded. And Dakota? Late 20s, a teacher with a master's in special needs education. With every word, she kept climbing the ladder of real.

As we wrapped up the first round of drinks, she said, "Cole, there are pre-made sandwiches, salads, chips, and condiments in the fridge."

"Where is it?" I asked, scanning the galley.

She pointed. "One of those cabinets."

"Jackpot," I said, swinging it open. "Anyone hungry?"

Dakota grinned. "Hold on a sec." She slid the curtain open, and just like that, the cabin transformed. No Coke. No sex. Just your average flight again.

She leaned in and whispered, "Eevee's here. Everyone's cleaning up their act. She has no idea what's going on, and Alan wants to keep it that way."

"How can she not know?" I asked. "They were just snorting lines."

"They're good at hiding it. She doesn't live in Galaxy Beach, so she's clueless," Dakota said. "Just not picking up the signs."

I shook my head. "This is insane. But I'm staying out of it."

As I handed out food and drinks, I felt a shift in pressure. "What's the cabin altitude?" I asked.

"Automatic system says about sixty-five hundred feet," Kevin, one of the pilots, replied.

"I think you're putting everyone to sleep," I joked. "Can you bump it up a little?"

Kevin grinned and tweaked the dial. "There you go. Should liven things up."

Private jets. Even the air does what you want.

Then Kevin looked at me. "Cole, want some stick time? Mike's gotta hit the head."

I hesitated. "I've had a few drinks. No way I'm touching those controls---not right now."

Kevin nodded. "I commend you. Not everyone has that kind of integrity."

"Appreciate it. I've known guys who'd take a shot of whiskey ten minutes before takeoff. I don't step on a plane unless I know the pilot's sober. Same rule for me. Twelve hours---bottle to throttle... or in this case, bottle to thrust."

Back in the galley, Dakota and I started cleaning up. She bent over the sink in those tight jeans, and I couldn't help but admire the view---perfect. I wished she was into this lifestyle, but even if she was, I wouldn't cross that line. Respect still mattered---even in a world built on blurred ones.

With a grin, I asked, "So, Dakota… how did you and Jack end up together? You seem disturbed by his antics, and there's like a generation and a half between you."

She laughed. "I'll be thirty soon, and Jack reminds me of the father I never had. He's a great listener, my best friend, and he treats me like a queen. But yeah… he's childish. His issue is the drugs. They're part of the swinging scene, and he lives for it. But when he's sober? He's someone else entirely."

"That's heavy," I said, letting it sink in. "It's like the swinging only works when everyone's messed up."

"Exactly. It's messed up," she said. "Drugs were always a band-aid for us. Covered the cracks---but the cracks just kept spreading. I even fell for someone else while we were swinging. It got super dangerous."

Her honesty forced me inward.

"I cheated on Bridget years ago," I said. "Sometimes I think we're both just waiting for the other to be the one to leave. Our marriage isn't solid. And we both know it."

Dakota gave me a slow, knowing nod. "Swinging doesn't fix anything. It's just a temporary escape."

Her words hit harder than I expected. Maybe this whole world was a house of mirrors---distorting everything, showing us only what we wanted to see while hiding the truth behind the reflection.

That's when Jack strolled up from the back of the plane. He winked. "Alan says you two are quite the item."

"Jealous, baby?" Dakota teased, brushing up against him.

Jack laughed and pulled her into a kiss. "Just came to steal you away. You two can finish this little bonding session later---at the hotel."

I wiped down the counter and made my way to the back of the plane. Figured I'd check on Bridget, try to reconnect---but she was already asleep. So was everyone else. The drinks, the drugs, the altitude---it all added up. Vegas wasn't going to wait, though. I could only hope the party kicked back to life once we hit the ground.

About twenty minutes out, Kevin's voice crackled through the intercom: "Prepare for landing at McCarran International Airport."

I looked out the window as we descended---rows of private jets stretching across the runway, every size, shape, and color. Wealth shimmered like heat off the tarmac. We pulled up in the Rolls-Royce of jets---literally, powered by Rolls-Royce engines---and I couldn't help but think, I'd take any one of these if I could just afford it.

The cabin stirred. People are groggy, but slowly coming back to life. I leaned toward Bridget. "Did you sleep well, honey?"

"Yes, baby," she said softly, her voice lined with something rare---vulnerability. "I know you're probably upset with me. I broke all the rules. Can we talk about it and not let it ruin the weekend?"

Before I could respond, she bolted for the restroom, brushing past the others gathering their bags.

I followed, standing by the door as I heard her retching. A woman I hadn't met before approached and introduced herself. "I'm Evee, Alan's sister. I'm here for a clothing show---great excuse to travel in style." She gave a sardonic twirl, gesturing at the jet's plush interior. Big Brothers have their benefits.

The toilet flushed, and Bridget emerged, pale but composed. "Do I look okay?" she asked.

"You look beautiful," I reassured her.

"Sometimes I forget how great you are," she said, kissing my cheek. Thankfully, she'd drowned herself in mouthwash. The bathroom's marble floors, gold fixtures, and spacious design---fit for royalty---were a far cry from any commercial airline lavatory.

As the jet's stairs folded down to meet the red carpet, 2 stretch limos awaited us. Ground staff loaded bags into a van behind it. With tens of thousands of dollars in Louis Vuitton luggage onboard, I silently hoped everything made it to the hotel; Bridget would never let me hear the end of it otherwise.

We arrived at the Wynn Hotel, a masterpiece of opulence. Alan and Jack argued over whose Black AmEx would cover the limo tab. Jack won, as Alan had footed the bill for the jet. At this stage in my life, I keep my Black Card hidden. Too much previous abuse, though, once supported by a lot more disposable income.

Bridget leaned over and whispered, "Did you just agree to split the New Year's table with Dr. Rick?"

"Yes, why?"

"That table costs $12,000," she hissed, calling me a "ratard" as she made a mocking "L" on her forehead. My stomach churned. Obviously, she's feeling better.

Later, as we relaxed in the suite, I couldn't hold back any longer. "Bridget, what were you thinking using drugs without talking to me first? This isn't a one-time thing anymore."

She shot back, "You have no room to talk. You're the one who slept with our babysitter and had a baby with her."

"That was years ago. I've done everything to make amends."

"I can't let it go," she said. "Sometimes I've got to do things just to get under your skin as pure retaliation."

Her voice escalated as she ripped off her wedding ring and hurled it at the armoire. The impact loosened the diamond. "You ungrateful bitch," I muttered, under my voice quivering.

Taking a deep breath, I tried to defuse the situation. "Bridget, let's take a hot shower and reset. We're in Vegas, for God's sake. I can unring that bell, and remind you that you bared witness to it all." This reality didn't help.

She broke down, tears streaming. "I know you've tried, but the pain's still there."

"I'm worried about you," I said. "Drugs aren't the answer. Can we move forward?"

"I'll stop after this weekend," she promised.

Later, Bridget emerged in pink lingerie, looking stunning. We poured drinks and admired the view from the 30th floor. The moment was interrupted when Jack and Dakota entered, adding their own energy to the suite. Dakota whispered in my ear, "I want you tonight." That was a clear message on her stance about everything. No wondering.

We sat for drinks. Dakota wore a monogrammed robe, the kind that made her look like royalty on vacation. Jack, of course, showed up in a smoking jacket, channeling Hugh Hefner. I've seen this look before, in the mirror. Me? I looked like the outsider. Too many clothes, too much tension in my shoulders, not enough chemical numbness to blend in. I wasn't proud of my body like the rest of them. Maybe it was insecurity. Maybe it was years of damage. Or maybe it was just that I wasn't doped up enough to float through the night like they were.

Except for Dakota. She was the anomaly. Clear eyes, sharp wit, and a grounded energy that cut through the haze like a spotlight. She didn't need Coke to feel alive. She didn't need Molly to connect. She was all heat and honesty---and it showed.

The conversation started light---life, kids, the usual icebreakers of adults pretending this was all normal. But it didn't take long to slide sideways. The talk turned to sex. Wild stories. Bucket list fantasies. Trade-offs and trade-ups. Everyone had something to say. Everyone laughed like we were sharing recipes.

Eventually, Bridget and Jack slipped off into the kitchen, bodies too close, eyes too dialed in. Their laughter bounced off the tile and spilled back into the room like smoke. I heard it. I felt it. And yeah, it fucked with me.

Dakota and I stayed on the couch, our bodies inching closer by the second. Her leg brushed mine. Her hand lingered when she passed the tequila. Her voice dipped into low, deliberate tones that sent a different kind of signal. She didn't need to say it out loud---I already knew.

Still, part of me was stuck. Torn between the spell Dakota was casting and the storm brewing in the kitchen. Bridget and Jack. That image burned at the edges of my mind, clawing for attention. And yet... Dakota's presence grounded me. Calmed me. Made me feel seen in a way I hadn't in years.

This wasn't just a party anymore. This wasn't just swapping and smiling and pretending nothing meant anything. This felt different. This was the night the line got crossed, and there was no walking it back.

With this moment, with these choices, there was no question---we'd be painted with the swinger's brush. No denying it. No, unseeing it.

But I didn't care.

Because Dakota's heat was pulling me in, and whatever was happening behind that kitchen door? That was someone else's mess. I needed something for me. A pressure release. A happiness band-aid. Something to help me sort out the noise in my head. I didn't know where this was going, but for the first time in a long time, I was finally choosing myself.

Dakota moved in with zero hesitation and kissed me---deep, wet, and full of unfiltered heat. It was the kind of kiss that doesn't ask for permission and sure as hell doesn't apologize afterward. It wasn't cute or sweet---it was need. Urgent and unashamed. And it hit me like a defibrillator. I hadn't felt that kind of raw passion since Kate, and that was saying something. My pulse spiked, my hands gripped her hips instinctively, and in that moment, I wasn't thinking about anything but her.

She tasted like trouble---the good kind, the addictive kind---and I was already all in. Before long, she was voicing her only real concern: I was wearing too many damn clothes. The way she stripped me down wasn't seductive---it was surgical. Like every layer she peeled back brought her closer to something she craved. And when her hands reached the last of the fabric clinging to my body and discovered just how turned on I was, she gave me a grin that said, *Yeah, I know what I'm doing.*

She dropped down on me like a memory from a better past---moving with the same grace and skill Piper once had back when I was married and still believed in fairy tales. But this wasn't sentimental. This was focused, intense, calculated pleasure. She worked me like an artist with a favorite brush, bringing me right to the edge---and just when I thought I was seconds away from the promised land, she slammed on the anti-lock brakes, popped up like she'd come up for air after a deep dive, and whispered, "Not so fast. We've got more business."

Then she stood. Slowly. Intentionally. Letting her curves unravel in front of me like a striptease designed by God Himself. It was hypnotic--- every step, every sway of her hips. Her skin caught the low cabin light just enough to make her look almost unreal. And I've seen a lot of curves in my day---some reckless, some dangerous, some that left scars. But this? This was perfection. The kind of body sculpted not for vanity, but for pleasure, and soul, I might add.

She laid me out on the sofa like I was the canvas and she was ready to paint. And when she straddled my face, I knew exactly what she needed-

--and I didn't hesitate. I got to work with every ounce of hunger I had in me, and I didn't stop until the noise she made could've echoed all the way to the Vegas Strip. I was in the zone, locked in. She tasted like a secret and a promise all at once. Every reaction she gave me was fuel, and I was burning hot.

But that was just the beginning.

Next came reverse cowgirl. And let me tell you---if there's a better seat in the house, I haven't found it. Watching her move, back arched, rhythm locked, moaning like the world outside that suite didn't exist---it was a show, and I had a front-row ticket. But just as we were hitting the next level, I realized something important. My little man didn't have his party hat. And given my track record, that wasn't just a minor oversight---it was a red flag waving in the wind.

I tried to play it cool, tried to pump the brakes and shift to responsible adult mode. The 8-second rodeo came to an abrupt halt, and I made a half-assed attempt to dismount like a guilty cowboy. But Dakota? She wasn't buying it.

She grabbed me by the jaw, looked me square in the eyes, and said with a smirk, "I want Maxwell House coffee—you know, that *good to the last drop* ' line from the ads." That was it. No more talking. No more thinking. This was just round one.

Rounds two and three followed like they had a score to settle. The kind of rounds where bodies glisten, bedsheets get ruined, and you forget your own damn name. She took everything I had and asked for more. And I gave it. Happily. Recklessly. I was in the deep end and didn't want a lifeline. I just kept ringing the bell again and again, like I didn't care who heard it.

By the time we collapsed, sweat-soaked and breathless, the world outside that suite didn't just feel far away---it felt irrelevant. Vegas, the lights, the noise, the madness---none of it mattered. All that existed in that moment was her skin on mine, the scent of sex in the air, and the pounding silence that followed release.

That night carved itself into my brain like graffiti on a bathroom wall. Raw. Messy. Permanent. The kind of memory you don't brag about, but you never forget. Loud, dirty, chaotic---a fever dream that played like a highlight reel of everything I wasn't supposed to want but couldn't stay away from.

It ended the same way it began---with a kiss. Slow, heavy, full of passion and surrender. That look in her eyes said it all. She did care. This wasn't just another notch on a bedpost for her. There was something unspoken between us---a pull, a current. Something real. And maybe that's what made it even harder. Because as much as she cared, she still walked out. Not because she didn't want to stay, but because she knew I wasn't hers. Not really.

And just like that, I was alone.

Naked. Spent. Lying in a cold soak of sweat and confusion.

That's when the weight of everything slammed into me. The guilt. The fear. The what-ifs. Beneath the post-coital fog was a sharp, gnawing dread about what the next nine months might look like. Dakota hadn't mentioned birth control. I hadn't asked. Jack, for all his smooth talk and bravado, was sterile---a fact he made known more than once. That left one possible outcome if nature took its course.

And if I'd been confused about my marriage before? I had just driven a titanium stake straight through the middle of it---shattered what little foundation was left and buried the remains under a pile of selfish choices and blurred lines.

I stared at the ceiling, heart still racing, wondering how the hell I'd explain any of this to myself come morning. And deep down, I already knew---there was no going back from this.

Hours later, Bridget came back---slightly kerfuffled, but with that smile. Wide. Seductive. Satisfied. I knew the look. A guy always does. You don't need to ask questions when the answer's smeared across her face like lipstick after a secret. So I logged it. Quietly. That's what we do---we clock it, file it somewhere behind the ribs, and pretend we didn't. We don't always speak it, but we never unsee it.

To this day, there's no proof. Nothing you could print or point to. Just the weight of a look that never left---and the silence that confirmed everything it didn't say.

When she walked in, I gave her the quick-and-dirty on what went down while she was gone—reminding her we were officially swingers now. This wasn't just threesomes anymore.

Her first question wasn't about names or details—it was, "Were you safe? You just breathe on women and next thing you know…"

"I tried to be."

Her eyes narrowed. "What the hell does that mean?"

"It means… I tried to pull out, but she locked her legs like a wrestler going for the pin and wouldn't let go."

"You're kidding me?" she snapped. "You don't have enough kids? You should've taken Dr. J's free vasectomy years ago."

"I told you—it's like carrying a .45 with no bullets."

"You're the biggest asshole."

Before the argument could properly detonate, Bridget crumbled like a house of cards---collapsing without warning, her body going limp. Unresponsive. I panicked. Just as I was about to bolt for help, Alan came strolling into our room holding a water bottle.

"Did you drink out of this?" he asked, holding it up.

"No," I said, confused. "It's just water. What's the big deal?"

"It's GHB," he said bluntly. "Did she drink from it?"

"I don't know---I was *literally* coming to get help. Look at her, man. Shallow breathing, no response. She's limp. Do you think---?"

"Yes," Alan snapped, cutting me off. His voice was clipped and cold, like we were talking about a dead battery, not a human being. "Obviously, she's had something."

"Fucking fantastic," I shot back, heart pounding like a jackhammer in my chest. "So what---do I call an ambulance? Because she's not breathing right, Alan. She's barely fucking responsive. You want to keep playing host, or you want to handle this like a Friggin adult?"

Alan's eyes went wide, pupils pinned like he'd just realized the cops were hiding behind the curtains. "Are you *fucking crazy?* You want cops showing up here? Lights? Sirens? Reports? You want them combing through this place? We'd be toast. Royally fucked. No cops. No medics. Just stay with her. Watch her until she comes out of it."

My pulse hammered in my ears. "And if she *doesn't?*"

Alan shrugged like he was talking about a spilled drink. "I'll have Dr. Rick check her," he muttered, already halfway out the door like this was just another cleanup in his twisted carnival. "Just don't let her stop breathing."

Just like that, the night took a hard left. No more glitz. No more pleasure cruise. The indulgence train derailed into a long, brutal waiting game. Me and Bridget, turning slowly like a rotisserie chicken---her body twitching every few minutes like some kind of cruel clock reset. It wasn't fun anymore. Wasn't sexy. No more music. No more bodies in motion. Just silence, panic, and the sick weight of watching someone you love fade in and out without a safety net.

Dr. Rick finally showed up, casual as a Sunday visit, walking in like a sitcom dad with a golf tee time. Gave her a glance. Maybe two fingers to the neck. Nodded like it was no big deal. "Just watch her," he said. Just like that. Like she had a hangover, and a nap would fix it.

She didn't have a hangover. She had GHB in her system from a mislabeled fucking bottle, and Alan stood there acting like this wasn't his circus. Like he hadn't handed out the tickets, built the tent, and hired the freaks.

So I sat with her. All night. Eyes locked on her chest, counting breaths. Checking her pulse. Whispering her name. Torn between calling 911 and praying to a God I hadn't talked to in a long damn time. The suite felt like a tomb. Every minute dragged like an hour. I was cold, wired, and furious.

Furious at Alan. Alan the Ringleader. Alan, the smiling devil, who built this playground of ego and pills. The same Alan they all called "One-Pump Chump," which, honestly, I hadn't seen the proof of yet, but I didn't doubt it for a second. A man like that? He didn't perform---he posed.

And while I sat there holding Bridget's hand, that clown was back out front playing host, pouring drinks, laughing too loud, pretending none of this was happening. I wanted to smash a bottle across his face. I wanted to drag him in there and scream, "Look what you did!"

But I didn't. I didn't puff my chest. Didn't let my ego take the wheel. Because none of that mattered.

What mattered was Bridget. Her breath. Her pulse. Her making it to daylight.

And she did.

When the sun finally cut through the curtains and her eyes fluttered open, groggy and glassy but alive, it felt like a Friggin miracle. She looked at me with that soft, vulnerable look she used to give me when we first fell in love and said, "Cole… I love you. Thank you for staying with me. Let's not fight anymore. Let's make today count."

That hit harder than anything all night.

I couldn't even speak. I just nodded and walked her to the kitchen, arm in arm, both of us shaken. Still wobbly. Still processing.

And Alan? First thing out of his mouth?

"Well, look who's awake?"

Like this was all part of the ride. Like last night hadn't damn near ended in a body bag.

That's when it finally snapped into place. Last night? That was the warm-up. That was the night shift.

The real circus started in daylight.

Steroid shots to the arm before breakfast. Tequila or beer by lunch. Coke lines carved with hotel keys. Then came the molly. Then more Coke. More Molly. Designer pills that looked like candy and drinks in every damn color. And when it was time to crash? GHB to shut it all down. Rinse. Repeat.

That was the routine. Every. Single. Day.

These weren't lost college kids or party tourists. These were doctors. Lawyers. Executives. People who signed million-dollar deals by day and snorted their souls away by night. And not one of them---not a single one---checked on Bridget. No texts. No knocks. No guilt.

They just slipped back into their designer robes and carried on like nothing happened. Like they were gods.

Me? I'd have traded the jet, the suite, the champagne showers, and the private chef for none of it. I wanted out. Out of this padded madhouse masquerading as freedom.

And then came the final insult.

Dr. Rick announces he's got a medical conference in town. Important, of course. Required. Carla, his wife? Not on the invite list.

And the second that door clicked behind him, Alan, Alex, and Carla darted off like kids sneaking into a liquor cabinet. Racing to the nearest bedroom. Laughing. Stripping. No shame. No hesitation.

I stood frozen, watching it happen.

Alan caught my eye mid-stumble and pressed a finger to his lips. Shhh. Be cool.

Be cool? Be quiet? This---this *cheating?*---was what we were supposed to keep quiet?

In a house where GHB is handed out like breath mints and strangers fuck like it's a live-streamed sport, this was the secret?

It hit me like a freight train.

This wasn't open-mindedness. It wasn't exploration or freedom or any of that utopian bullshit. This was rot in disguise. Hypocrisy wrapped in silk sheets. A slow-motion implosion hiding behind tailored suits and smug smirks.

And me?

I was standing in the rubble, trying to figure out if I was still one of them---or already buried beneath the wreckage. The aftermath wasn't just physical. It was psychic. Emotional. A slow rot working its way through my chest. Everything smelled like smoke, even though nothing had burned. Not literally anyway.

Bridget was at the kitchen table, sipping coffee like she hadn't almost flatlined a few hours ago. Her eyes were distant but steady, that familiar mask back on her face. And then Dakota walked in---barefoot, glowing, calm. The kind of calm that only comes from being fully at peace with your choices. She looked right at Bridget, then glanced at me, and with a sly, casual smile said, "You taught Cole well. He knows how to treat a lady."

Bridget didn't miss a beat. "I didn't teach that cheating asshole anything. He's a manwhore."

Just like that, the air thickened. The temperature shifted. Everything bloomed back into chaos mode. A detonation without warning.

Dakota, standing there in one of Jack's monogrammed shirts, looking completely natural, radiant even---first thing in the morning and somehow still stunning. She had that effortless confidence that makes women dangerous and unforgettable. The kind of look that says, No regrets.

Me? I looked like a guy who'd just woken up in the wrong movie. A hangover made of guilt, confusion, and a little leftover tequila. I tried to play it cool, but inside, the switch had been flipped, and the feelings were flooding in faster than I could box them up.

That's the real danger of this lifestyle. Not the STDs. Not the rumors. Not even the soul decay. It's that you might feel something when you're not supposed to. That one unexpected connection---a spark in the middle of a dumpster fire.

My thoughts weren't just spinning, they were glitching. Looping. Did I just stumble into a one-off moment with Dakota---a night of passion, no strings, just sweat and noise? Or was this something else? Something that might circle back? In swinger life, did I just hit my peak---my final curtain call? Was that it for me?

This was the strangest feeling. An emotional hangover in a room full of people pretending feelings don't exist. Dakota belonged to Jack. Publicly, fully. No confusion there. And Jack? He's the golden boy. A transplant surgeon who saves lives before breakfast. A guy who wears a smoking jacket and somehow pulls it off.

Me? I'm a sleaze peddler with decent hair and a working zipper. I serve cocktails, sell lies, and ruin marriages. If this was a scoreboard?

Jack: 100. Cole: 0.

That was the math. Cold. Brutal. And probably true.

But then she looked at me again---just a flick of the eye, a whisper of a smile---and I didn't feel like zero. Not for that second.

And that might've been the most dangerous part of all.

Chapter 12

Invisible Strings

Die With A Smile
Performed by: **Lady Gaga and Bruno Mars**
Written by: **Lady Gaga, Bruno Mars, Dernst "D'Mile" Emile II, Andrew Watt, and James Fauntleroy**

That night, in the middle of all the chaos---piles of blow, booze flowing like tap water, and a buffet of naked women within arm's reach---I couldn't stop thinking about Kate. She was the tension in the room, the truth grinding under the noise. If that one song had existed back then, the kind that guts you with clarity, it would've hit me square in the chest. Because even surrounded by everything men are supposed to want, she was the only thing that ever felt real. The one I wanted holding me when the lights finally go out.

We hadn't spoken in a while, but we still had our ways---quiet signals, unspoken codes. How to reach out without drawing attention. Without triggering the press. Without blowing up what little peace we each had left.

The main event, the New Year's table, loomed large---a $12,000 reservation at one of Vegas' most exclusive hotels. This group was prepped for another night of extravagant celebration, another round of indulgence disguised as sophistication. Yet beneath the sequins and excess, I felt the familiar weight---unresolved emotions, fractured trust, and the rotting truth behind our designer veneers. Bridget and I had weathered yet another storm, but even as I stood beside her, I couldn't shake the question: how many more hits could we take before the foundation fell into the earth like a Florida sinkhole.

The table itself turned out to be a bust. The high-profile guest---the heiress of a hotel dynasty, famous for being famously chic---was supposed to join us. Make the whole night sparkle. Turn common folk into something just by proximity. But she never showed. Maybe she got wind of the circus she'd be stepping into. The table fee? Never collected. Or at least not that I saw. Alan threw down his black card like it was just another Tuesday. Dr. Rick and I were off the hook, financially speaking.

Still, the air was flat. Deflated. The hype fizzled before it could light. We didn't even make it to midnight before the group slithered back to the suite. Not without first downing their typical pharmaceutical cocktail--- uppers, downers, tequila, coke, a tab of Molly. The moment we stepped through the suite doors, clothes hit the floor like a choreographed strip routine. Naked bodies sprawled across makeshift bedding. Blankets covered the carpet in a patchwork of barely controlled chaos. It was the same circus, different night---except now it had a holiday theme.

The room swirled with naked limbs and powdered highs. Beautiful women lounged like art installations, glazed eyes and perfect skin. A few men---mostly the usual crew---moved through it all like they owned the place. For a moment, I stood frozen. Not unsure, not ashamed---just taking it all in. Where the hell do you even begin in a scene like this?

Bridget, to her credit---or concern---wasn't fully spun. She'd built up a tolerance, and while she was loose, she wasn't gone. At least not yet. Small wins in this arena. The two waitresses who followed us up looked shell-shocked at first. Even by Vegas standards, this was a level up. But peer pressure is a hell of a thing. It didn't take long before a rolled-up bill hit their nostrils, and they were giggling like they'd just gotten away with something.

Their handler---Dakota---gravitated toward Bridget, Alex, and Alan. The three of them had formed their own drug-drenched triangle, laughing too loudly about nothing at all. I scanned the room---no Maria in sight. Evee had been sent back to her room. Jay was off with his newest conquest. Fine by me. Fewer liabilities to juggle.

Feeling like a fifth wheel in my own circus, I wandered over to the Coke lounge the waitresses had set up on a low table.

"Want some?" one of them offered, holding out a perfect little white runway.

"No, thanks," I said, trying to keep my tone firm but cool.

"You're Cole, right?" the other one asked.

"Yeah," I nodded. "How'd you know?"

"We met your hot wife. She told us about your club in Galaxy Beach. Think we'd make money there?"

I laughed. "You two are stunning. You'd probably steal all my dancers' tips. Sorry---not sorry."

"That's sweet," the first one said. "I'm Cindy. This is Tonya."

I shook both their hands, then kissed each one lightly. Couldn't resist. "Pleasure to meet you."

"Wanna party with us?" Cindy asked, her tone dipping into playful.

"I don't do drugs," I reminded them.

"No," Tonya giggled, brushing her hand over my chest. "We mean party."

Before I could overthink it, they pulled me down onto a pile of cushions. Clothes came off quick---like this wasn't their first time treating chaos like a stage. Cindy and Tonya kissed each other, hands roaming, eyes flicking toward me as if daring me to dive in.

Cindy turned and grinned. "If you want this," she said, tugging at her panties, "you'll need to use your teeth, only. No hands."

Challenge accepted.

I knelt down like I'd just dropped to prayer, my mouth working delicately, teasing each edge until the fabric gave. The second her skin hit the air, her hips bucked slightly, and a moan slipped free. I took my time---slow, deliberate, like I was trying to win a competition.

Just as I turned to Tonya, she was already massaging me through my pants---bold, fast, like she had something to prove. My dick reacted before my brain could catch up, standing at full attention like it had a shift to cover and zero fucks to give.

Without hesitation, she yanked my pants down and looked up with a wicked grin. "I know you don't do drugs," she purred, "but mind if I use your cock to snort a line?"

I blinked. That line should've made me pause. Instead, I shrugged like it was just another Tuesday. Fuck it.

She lined it up---confident, clinical---and took a deep inhale, her nose gliding along me with practiced intent. The cold, tingling burn of powder and the heat of her breath hit all at once. The sensation was surreal. Filthy. Electric.

Meanwhile, Cindy pulled me back to her like I was a song she couldn't stop singing. I buried myself between her legs, devouring her like I was starved for it. Her breath turned ragged, her thighs started shaking, and her nails dug so deep into the cushions they might've hit the springs.

Then it was Tonya's turn.

She straddled me like a woman clocked in for battle---riding me hard, kissing Cindy in a slow, sensual rhythm that made time blur. Their bodies tangled, moans overlapping like layers in a dirty symphony. I let go. Fully. No clocks. No guilt. Just sweat, skin, and a soundtrack of sins I'd never confess.

Somewhere between round two and whatever came after, I collapsed back on the couch, trying to catch my breath. Tonya stood, wiped her nose with a giggle, then crouched down between my legs again.

"You gave us all that," she whispered, "Now it's our turn."

Cindy joined her. The two of them took their time---like they were unwrapping something expensive. Mouths, hands, tongues---working in rhythm. They teased, edged, and dragged it out, taking turns devouring me with the same hunger I'd shown them. No rush. Just payback. Real, tangible return fire.

Cindy whispered filth while Tonya kept eye contact and made a mess of me. It wasn't love---it was power. A perfect, chaotic exchange. In that moment, I wasn't just being pleasured, I was being worshipped. And I soaked in every Friggin second.

Eventually, when I exploded, it wasn't quiet. It wasn't clean. It was volcanic.

Both of them laughed, kissed, and collapsed beside me, spent and glowing. I lay there, wrecked in the best way possible, staring at the ceiling like I'd just seen God---if God wore heels and had coke on her gums.

Shortly after, they gathered their stuff like nothing ever happened. No goodbyes to anyone else, just two slow, lingering kisses on my lips---then silence. They disappeared into the night like smoke.

Then came Maria.

She stepped out of the bathroom, mascara smudged and eyes red. Her phone slammed shut as she muttered, "Fuck you."

"What's wrong, baby girl?" I asked, half-dressed and still sweating.

"My boyfriend's being an asshole," she said, voice brittle. "He's pissed I'm here."

I laughed, low and dark. "I'd be pissed too if my girl was partying with this crew."

"He doesn't know," she added, like saying it made it true.

I put my arm around her, and just like that, she kissed me---no buildup, no hesitation. She took my hand, led me to one of the bedrooms, and shut the door behind us.

In Jack and Dakota's room, she ripped my shirt off, biting my chest with playful aggression. Clothes hit the floor fast. I reached for protection---no chances, not tonight. Maria was young, wild, gorgeous, but caution wasn't in her vocabulary.

The sex? Unreal. She was raw but eager, not jaded yet---every touch, every move had energy. But just as I was about to finish, she pulled off the condom and locked her legs around me.

"What the hell are you doing?" I gasped. "Are you on the pill? Counting days?"

"Neither," she said, eyes shining. "I wanted the full experience with you."

"You're out of your mind," I snapped.

"If something happens, you'll never hear from me," she whispered. "I'll just blame it on my boyfriend."

Great. That made me feel real secure.

Before I could untangle myself or my thoughts, the door blew open. Bridget. No knock. No warning. Just her, eyes blazing.

"We need to talk. Now."

I grabbed my clothes, heart pounding, and followed her out.

"It's over," she said coldly.

"What's over?"

"You and me, Cole. You came here just to sleep with that baby, and now you got your wish."

"You serious?" I shot back. "You've been God-knows-where, doing God-knows-who, and you're mad at me?"

"This isn't what I signed up for," she snapped. "Our whole marriage has been about you chasing pussy. You screwed the babysitter and had a baby with her---I'll never be okay with that."

Her words hit like a body blow.

"I didn't create this chaos alone," I said. "We opened the door together. We shared people, remember? Don't hang it all on me."

But she was already packing. Tossing shit into a suitcase like she was trying to erase me with every zip. I notice Carla is witnessing all that was being said.

"I'm done," she said. "When we get home, we're done."

And just like that, she stormed out.

An hour later---just as I'm sitting in the quiet wreckage she left behind---Bridget walks back in like nothing happened. She kisses me. Smiles. "Where's Maria?"

"In her room," I say, cautiously.

She grabs my hand, leads me straight to the room, opens the door without knocking. Maria looks up, wide-eyed.

Bridget smiles. "Let's have some fun."

I never told Maria what Bridget said earlier. Never told her about the bags, the threats, the mess. I ghosted her after round one without a word, but I had a hunch she was still more worried about her boyfriend's freak-outs than anything I could say.

The night ended with a wild, twisted three-way---bizarre, satisfying, but with a thick cloud of tension still hanging between Bridget and me. I knew it. This lifestyle had run its course. It had taken more than it gave, and if we had any shot at surviving, we needed to walk away. Burn the map. Start over.

By now, everyone had scattered to their overpriced suites like wreckage after impact. Bridget crashed in ours, passed out in her dress, one shoe still on, like some half-finished thought. I hadn't seen Dakota all night, which said everything. Whatever we had---however fragile or reckless or hypnotic---had been swallowed whole by the chaos. It didn't survive the noise, the games, or the liquor.

Still, I couldn't lie to myself. I was enthralled. Dakota had that kind of gravity. But I knew the damn rules. Nights like this weren't built for second chances. This wasn't some rinse-and-repeat romantic spiral. This was one night, one explosion, and too much smoke left in the air to find anyone on the other side.

Maria had vanished, too. No text. No goodbye. Just gone. The whole place felt hollow without her hurricane energy. The living room had turned into a graveyard of red Solo cups and rumpled blankets. So I drifted into the kitchen---not for water, not for food. I needed silence. I needed to remember who the hell I was beneath all this glitter and noise.

It was 4 a.m., and Kate was there again---lodged in my head like a splinter under the skin. Some memories you don't forget because they're beautiful. Others, because they haunt you. Kate was both.

I grabbed my phone. Sent the code. Three digits that said everything and nothing at once. She answered instantly. No names. No formalities. Just that familiar voice---low, guarded, unmistakably her.

We talked like we always did, toeing the line of confessions. We laughed like people who hadn't lost everything. We didn't bring up the man asleep in her bed. We didn't talk about the wife passed out beside me. We didn't need to. The silence around those details was louder than any admission. We were in love---just buried under the wrong roofs, in the wrong sheets, living the wrong lives.

Our voices dropped. We slipped into that slow-burn space we knew too well. Breath to breath, word to word, we built the heat back up. And before long, I was bracing against a kitchen counter, whispering her name under my breath like a prayer I knew wouldn't be answered. It was like running a long-distance race on a treadmill---nowhere to go, but all the same rush. Fifth checkered flag of the day, Richard Petty-style. Unreal, considering I was barefoot in a stranger's rental kitchen surrounded by passed-out bodies and bad decisions. But I didn't care. Most of these people had already seen me naked---physically, emotionally, or both. There weren't many secrets left.

Afterward, we made plans. Not the kind you make just to feel something---but real ones. We were done starving for each other. Done pretending we didn't exist. Despite the debris of our lives---marriages, affairs, expectations---we meant it this time. Or at least I thought we did.

Then reality punched through the moment like a wrecking ball. My phone rang. I almost didn't answer. Wish I hadn't.

It was the Galaxy Beach Sheriff's Department.

Scarlett's had been hit. A break-in. Not some amateur smash-and-grab---this was surgical. One of our own employees. A guy I'd once trusted enough to lock up the damn bar. He'd found a weak spot in the rebuild---where I thought we'd poured solid concrete, turns out it was only cinder block. He took a sledgehammer to it. Cut a hole big enough to drive regrets through.

Chained the safe to his truck. Yanked it across the floor like it was nothing, even though it had been bolted down. Dragged twelve grand in cash, tip-out, and reserves straight through the wall and disappeared into the night.

Caught red-handed on camera. Crystal-clear footage. But it didn't matter.

Because he had intel on a federal suspect, they cut him a deal. Slap on the wrist. Walked out smiling. Never served a day. Never paid Scarlett's back. Just vanished like a bad dream and left me with a busted wall, a gutted bar, and a bank account bleeding out. And that, right there, is the kind of bullshit you can't make up. But I didn't need to.

Back to this moment, by noon, Maria was the first one up, already dressed, already moving like the night hadn't even happened. She asked if I wanted to go to the mall with her.

I told her I had to check with Bridget.

I nudged Bridget gently. She didn't even flinch, just mumbled, "No problem," like it was any other day. Like my soul hadn't been filleted and left out on the tile between a stolen safe and a whispered orgasm.

Somehow, it all just kept going.

And so did I.

And off we went.

It didn't take long before Maria and I stumbled into one of those high-end designer shoe boutiques---the kind of place where the air smells like overpriced regret and the sales associates size you up like a credit report before faking a smile. I'm not dropping names, since nobody's paying me for product placement, but let's just say the brand sounds like it might be manufactured in China... though I'm sure they're not. Choo on that for a second. The whole store had the feel of a luxury train---silent, polished, and full of people pretending not to notice you don't belong. No price tags in sight. Just sleek track lighting, velvet benches, and stilettos perched on glass shelves like they were rare fossils. It wasn't built for people like us. Truth be told, even we didn't know what the hell we were doing there.

Maria was a part-time waitress, busting ass between college classes and graveyard shifts slinging whiskey to creeps. Me? I had some cash, yeah--- but most of it had already been claimed by lawyers, child support, bills, and the ever-growing tab of my past mistakes. Still, for some reason--- maybe because we were punch-drunk from the night before, maybe because the world had been chewing on us for too long---we walked in like we owned the place. Like the universe owed us a win for surviving this far without snapping.

She zeroed in on a pair of stilettos with the kind of hunger that had nothing to do with shoes. Black leather, razor-thin straps, a heel that looked more like a weapon than footwear. Twelve hundred bucks. I knew it because I flipped the price tag over before the sales guy could tell me not to. She slipped them on like they'd been molded for her. Instantly, her legs transformed---longer, stronger, damn near deadly. She gave me that look. Not the sweet-girl smile. The other one. The one that said you know exactly what these shoes are going to do to you later.

And she was right.

She twirled, checked herself out in the mirror, and posed like she'd been born on a runway. It wasn't just about the shoes. It was what they did to her spine, to her smirk, to her aura. Those heels weren't shoes--- they were sex, status, defiance. She could've walked into a courtroom, a nightclub, or a war zone, and nobody would've questioned a damn thing. For a split second, the boutique felt like her personal stage. And everyone- --customers, clerks, me---was just background noise.

While she debated recklessness, admiring herself like a goddess on a high thread-count cloud, I caught a voice behind me. Familiar. Warm. Loaded with that effortless star quality that doesn't need a damn spotlight.

I turned.

And there she was. Cameron Diaz.

Yeah---that Cameron Diaz. Looking like California sunshine in a ponytail and gray sweatpants that probably cost more than my first car. She had that glow that didn't come from lighting---it came from legacy. For a heartbeat, I was back in '94, sitting in that dark theater, watching The Mask for the first time and thinking no one on earth could touch her beauty.

She smiled, real easy, like we were old friends or co-stars in some movie neither of us auditioned for. Her eyes dropped to Maria's feet.

"Those are gorgeous on you," she said, then flicked her gaze to me with a smirk that could start fires. "You'd better buy those for your beautiful lady."

We weren't exactly flying under the radar. We'd walked in hand-in- hand, still buzzing from a morning that had left nail marks on my back and perfume on my collar. We looked like the aftermath of something sweaty and sinful. That kind of glow doesn't come from yoga or good moisturizer. That's the glow of just-fucked and unapologetic.

I didn't flinch. Didn't think. Reached into my jacket and pulled out a wad of cash I'd stashed for the blackjack tables and a string of other stupid decisions. Thick roll---mostly hundreds. The kind of money that makes clerks straighten up and watch your hands. Maria's eyes widened like I'd just turned water into whiskey. There was awe there. And something else. Like maybe, for the first time in a while, someone had said you deserve this---and meant it.

"Wrap 'em up," I told the clerk, keeping my eyes locked on Cameron like we were sharing some unspoken truth. Then I nodded at her, slow and deliberate. "Thanks for the advice."

She grinned, that signature Hollywood mischief lighting up her face. "You're welcome."

And just like that, she vanished---drifted back into the rows of designer nonsense like a dream that knows when to exit before it gets questioned.

Maria stepped closer, still wearing the heels, still radiating heat. "Did that just happen?"

"Yeah," I said. "And we're gonna walk outta here like it happens every damn day."

Because sometimes, the only way to outrun your past is to lean all the way into the lie---and wear it like it costs twelve hundred bucks plus tax.

And just like that, Cinderella walked out with her new glass slippers--- only this time, she wore them with a short skirt, no curfew, and absolutely no intention of going home at midnight.

As we stepped out into the daylight, Maria leaned in close and whispered again, "Did that just really happen?"

I smiled. "Yeah. But don't get used to it."

Because even in fantasy moments like that---when you're dropping grand-level money on a girl you barely know, with Cameron Diaz giving relationship advice---you still wake up to real life. Still got to answer to yourself. And I was starting to feel the weight again. Not guilt. Just the awareness that this story, whatever it was, had an expiration date.

But for now? She looked lethal in those heels. Legs for miles, the kind of strut that could stop traffic---and for one sliver of time, I wasn't ready to end the fairytale. It was indulgent. It was reckless. But damn, it felt good. Felt earned. And then---like most fairytales---it ended. Not with a glass slipper, but with a pregnancy test.

So let's not waste time with suspense---Dakota ended up pregnant after that weekend. That's the headline. But here's the subtext: I'm told I was the first---but not the last---so who the hell knows. Could be mine. Could be another man's. Odds say maybe. Vegas wouldn't touch it. Hell, there's a chance I've got a eleventh kid walking around out there, rocking my jawline and cursing my bloodline. Stranger things have happened.

Oh, and in case you're keeping score---Maria? Pregnant too.

Dakota married Jack. They're raising their child together, playing house, doing the PTA thing like model parents. But facts are facts, and that child is not Jack's. Not genetically, anyway. And no, I was never asked for a DNA test. Not a cheek swab. Not a whisper. Looking back, I have to wonder if that was the plan all along---just slide me out of frame before the credits rolled. Let Jack play daddy while I got written out of the script.

Maybe people think I'm an asshole. Fine. But I'll say this---I make damn good-looking, highly intelligent kids. And I wish to God someone would've had the balls to let me in on the secret. Instead, it was another one of those life-altering decisions made about me, not with me. Middle of the blast radius, no say in the detonation.

Breaking up a family---especially one that's trying like hell to believe in itself---isn't my style. I've made my share of bad choices, no doubt, but ripping apart people clinging to some version of "happy" isn't on my list. And with nothing but whispers and sideways glances to go on, I didn't have a leg to stand on. No DNA test. No paperwork. No courtroom. Just a gut feeling and a name I wasn't allowed to say out loud

There was no fight to fight. No custody battle. No demand for answers. Just the quiet sting of being cut out like a bad scene from a movie---edited out without consent. A decision made for me, not with me.

As Maria promised, I never heard from her again. No calls. No texts. No apology. No trace. Her vanishing act was surgical---cleaner than most. No drama, no theatrics. Just silence. Just gone. And with her, any chance at closure evaporated. No proof. No trail. Just another unsolved chapter in a book full of what-ifs.

But maybe that's the risk built into all of this. Hope is not a plan. It's the gamble you take when you play games with no rules and pretend feelings don't accrue interest. When you fuck like it means nothing, and love like it means everything. When you write yourself into someone's life with a Sharpie---and they erase you with a whisper.

That's the cost. And sometimes, you don't even know you've paid it until you're broke.

All in all, it was one hell of a ride. An adventure, sure---but one stacked with warning signs, regret, and a few harsh truths wrapped in designer leather and bad decisions. The kind of story that leaves you with more questions than answers. Maybe a little shame. Maybe not enough.

Now, if you've made it this far, let me offer a disclaimer: don't try this shit at home. I'm a professional driver. It's just not a car I've been steering---it's my life. And I've crashed more than once.

The group? We shattered. Everyone peeled off in different directions. Divorces came in waves. Those who made it past a year didn't survive the next. Turns out, glitter fades fast in the daylight. The glue holding us together was never real. Just lust, shared secrets, and temporary highs.

So you decide---before you cannonball into this pool, ask yourself if it's worth it. That 8 to 11 seconds of euphoria we chase with such obsession---orgasm, climax, whatever you call it---it's the most powerful drug there is. But we rarely question the cost. We just chase it. Lie for it. Bleed for it. Lose for it.

As for me and Bridget? We unraveled like a bad stitch. You saw the fallout in Chapter One. No mystery there---just decay dressed up as denial.

And Jay? He latched onto my daughter. I wish I could tell you that it ended well. I wish I could say he became the man I once believed he could be. But reality doesn't care about hope. After giving us the most beautiful grandson---a kid with eyes like his mother and a crooked smile like mine---Jay overdosed. Just like that. Another needle. Another statistic. Another absence.

Now my daughter raises their son alone. My grandson. A little boy born from chaos, now being shaped by resilience. Not in a million years did I see that twist coming. But that's my life---plot twists stacked like wreckage. And even I don't always see the crash until I'm already pulling glass from my skin.

Chapter 13

Situational Awareness

I've Loved These Days
Performed and written by **Billy Joel**

The phrase "I loved those days" was never about me. That sentiment belonged to my customers---the ones who lined my pockets night after night, wide-eyed and half-drunk, chasing the fantasy I sold by the hour. They weren't in love with the girls, not really. They were in love with the lie. The promise. The illusion that for the right price, they could touch something sacred, something forbidden, something that made them feel like men again.

They came in aching for connection, pretending the winks were personal, the laughs were genuine, the moans were more than just part of the act. And every night, they left with nothing. No numbers. No names. Just an aching hard-on and a lighter wallet. Empty hands. Empty hearts. Some didn't even realize the damage until they were pulling crumpled singles out of their sock drawer the next morning, wondering how the hell they'd explain the overdraft to their wife.

That's what they meant by "loving those days." It wasn't love. It was addiction dressed up in dim lighting and overpriced cologne. And I was the dealer.

Why would anyone sell a thriving, cash-heavy business that practically ran itself? One that required minimal oversight, came stacked with wall-to-wall eye candy, poured top-shelf liquor like water, and gave you just enough local fame to make you feel untouchable---hell, even noble in certain circles. Why walk away from something most men would trade their souls for?

I didn't inherit it. I didn't franchise it. I bled for it. Built it with no business degree, no map---just a sick work ethic and a tolerance for chaos. I named it. I painted the walls. I paid the DJs, paid the girls in the beginning, and the guys who kept the peace when things got loud. I turned it into a machine---a well-oiled, neon-lit, cash-slinging monster. And then, one day, I walked.

So why did I leave?

Let me tell you exactly why.

"Five pounds from perfect. Five pounds from being single."

Yeah. I said that. Out loud. To the woman I loved. Dead sober. Eyes locked.

That was the line. The line. The one that cracked the glass beyond repair. Arrogant? No question. Cruel? Absolutely. Asshole? I won't even argue. That sentence cost me more than most people lose in a lifetime. And yet, in that moment, standing in the center of my kingdom, surrounded by smoke machines and silicone, it felt like truth. The kind of toxic truth that festers in places like Scarlett's Secrets.

Because when you live inside that world---when you own it---it doesn't just brush up against you. It gets inside your bloodstream. It rewires your compass. Every day, you're flanked by artificial beauty, airbrushed perfection, women engineered to trigger lust and surrender in every man that walks through the door. Over time, it doesn't just change what you want. It changes what you think you deserve.

Imagine this: you've got a garage full of pristine Ferraris. Fresh off the line. Polished. Growling. Built for speed, built to turn heads. And every night, you're told to walk past them---walk right by all that temptation---and go home to a Buick with rust on the doors and a missing hubcap. It's dependable. Safe. Familiar. But it's not the fantasy.

That's not a metaphor. That was my marriage.

The Ferraris worked the floor. The Buick waited at home with leftovers and bills. And eventually, the Buick didn't feel like a prize---it felt like a burden. You start wondering why you're settling. You start asking why your real life can't match the fantasy you built with your own two hands. It creeps in. It corrodes you. The entitlement. The hunger. The itch.

It's a brutal analogy. I know that now. It makes me sound like the kind of guy you warn your daughter about. But that's the nature of this business. It doesn't whisper. It shouts. It sells fantasy, but it doesn't come with a return policy. And if you're not careful, you start to believe the fantasy is the standard.

That's what owning a strip club does to a man. It warps the mirror. Distorts your reality. It doesn't just cost you money---it costs you your perspective, your empathy, your loyalty. Slowly, invisibly, it burns through everything solid in your life until you're left clutching a fistful of cash and wondering why your bed is cold.

And here's the part nobody wants to say out loud---the ugly truth buried under the neon.

You're not just selling sex. You're selling false hope. You're selling the illusion of connection to guys who haven't been touched in years---emotionally or otherwise. You're selling a brief, borrowed escape to men who are drowning in mortgages, divorces, dead-end jobs, and their own irrelevance. They don't just want to be turned on. They want to be seen. Heard. Respected. Worshipped, even if it's only for fifteen minutes and $400 in singles.

Some of them came in with wedding rings and left with nothing but guilt. Others pawned their guitars, emptied their bank accounts, borrowed money they had no intention of paying back---all for one more hit of the fantasy. You could see it in their eyes. The desperation. The grief. The addiction.

They'd sit front row like kings---backs straight, shoulders high, eyes locked on the stage like something holy was about to happen. For an hour or two, they lived in the glow of attention they didn't get anywhere else. They tipped heavy, laughed loud, barked out compliments like they mattered. And then they disappeared like they were never there. No swagger, no presence---just shadows dragging their shame out the front door, past the bouncers, back into the life they came to forget.

And the worst part? I knew it. I saw it every single night. Hell, I counted the cash that came from it. And still---I kept the lights on. Still spun the music, still got paid from the girls, still opened the doors at seven and closed them at three. I fed the machine. Smiled while it devoured people.

That's the business. That's the game. And yeah---I got tired of playing it. I got tired of being the guy who turned desperation into profit. Tired of watching people come in full of hope and walk out gutted. Some nights, I felt like a priest taking confession and a drug dealer handing out guilt all in the same breath.

Some of those customers? They weren't just spending disposable income. This wasn't extra cash from a good quarter or poker winnings from a lucky hand. These were men cashing in rent money, pawning wedding rings, pulling twenty-dollar bills from their sock like it was the last trick they had left. They were trading dignity for fifteen minutes of illusion. Begging to be seen, heard, wanted---even if it was fake.

You could see it in their eyes. It wasn't sex they were after. Not really. It was something harder to name. Validation. Power. Escape. Some were broken in ways they didn't have the words for. Some were trying to rewind the clock, claw back youth, manhood, relevance. Some just wanted a warm voice and a soft lie before they went home to silence.

And yeah, some were lonely enough to call it love. They'd come in wearing their pain like cologne---thick, heavy, impossible to ignore---and pretend the connection was real. A dancer would laugh, touch his shoulder, say his name just right, and that was all it took. He'd believe. Not just in her---but in himself. For a moment, he wasn't invisible anymore.

Most wouldn't admit that part. Not out loud. But I saw it. I watched the illusion swallow them whole. And I let it.

Because that's what we sold: the feeling of being wanted. Not touched. Wanted. There's a difference---and we made a killing off it. The illusion of being seen, admired, desired… like you mattered for more than your job title or the shit in your garage. For some guys, it was the only place they felt alive. And there's a price tag for that kind of hunger. Always.

They'd stumble out of the club broke, empty, humiliated---shirt wrinkled, credit cards maxed, dignity in tatters. Shame clinging to them like sweat. And then, like clockwork, they'd come back the next night. Like nothing happened. Sit at the same stage. Tip the same girl. Order the same watered-down whiskey. Smile through the same pain. Their destruction wasn't dramatic. It didn't explode. It dripped. Quiet, constant, like water carving a canyon. A slow erosion of self-worth and sense. A spiritual bleed-out in real time.

And I watched it. Night after night. Pretending I wasn't part of the machine, chewing them up and spitting them out. Pretending I wasn't fueling it. Paying girls to fake it, paying DJs to set the mood, comping drinks to keep the wallets loose. I built the trap, and I polished the bait.

That's the problem with selling fantasy---you start to believe it's real. You start thinking you're not just peddling dopamine and desperation, but something noble. You tell yourself you're giving people what they need. But it's a lie. And lies rot everything they touch. Including you.

I'd be remiss if I didn't speak plainly about the deaths---yes, the deaths---that hung around Scarlett's like smoke that wouldn't clear. This wasn't some rare, tragic exception. It was a dark rhythm, a side effect of the culture we built---or let rot---inside those walls.

The engine behind the money was never just the girls---it was booze. Always booze. Alcohol kept the cash flowing, the customers loose, and the tips fat. Company policy technically prohibited over-serving, and on paper, it looked solid. We had meetings. We had signs. We had rules. And I'll be honest---I did try to enforce it. With sincerity. I really did. I sat managers down. I warned bartenders. I cut off regulars when I could tell they were on that edge.

But like everything else in that world, the rules were mostly theater. People found ways around them. Management would say one thing to keep corporate or the county happy, then turn around and greenlight another round for the guy spending thousands. Bartenders looked the other way. Security didn't want the fight. And some of the dancers? They'd sneak drinks to their whales like it was part of the fantasy.

And so, people died.

Patrons would stumble out onto the highway, into traffic, into cars they had no business driving. Some of them didn't make it home. Some of them took innocent people with them. There were customers who left with dancers and died a few hours later---maybe from drugs, maybe heart attacks, maybe just bad luck. And the girls... the ones who gave everything on stage, then went home to silence and demons? Some of them never woke up. Pills, fentanyl, needles, desperation---take your pick.

At first, we lit candles. Made a flyer. Shed tears in the locker room. But eventually, we stopped. The grief hardened into routine. Another obituary, another shift. Call it coincidence. Call it collateral damage. But I call it culture. A culture of numbness, of shortcuts, of chasing the dollar harder than we chased decency. And I wish I could say I was above it, but I wasn't. I was in it, trying to do right in a place that rewarded wrong. And that's a weight I still carry.

So yeah, I walked away. Because if I didn't, I knew exactly how my story would end---just another burned-out casualty in designer shoes, convincing himself the money justified the damage. I would've become one of those men too---just in better clothes, with my name on the license and a front-row seat to my own moral collapse.

It was painful to watch. Because I knew what it was costing them. You'd hear things. You'd see the signs. Kids went to bed hungry. Power got cut off. Repo guys rolled in at 3 a.m. to drag off what little pride was left in the driveway. Maxed cards. Bank accounts overdrafted to death. And still---they came back. Hoping that one more lap dance, one more flirty conversation, one more wink from a girl who was paid to pretend might patch the hole burning in their gut. It never did. It only made it deeper.

But the worst moment---the one that stuck in my chest like a rusted nail I still can't pry loose---was the day one of them showed up outside the club in broad daylight. No music. No lights. Just raw reality. His wife was behind the wheel, her face red and hollowed out from crying for too long. The car was packed with everything they owned---blankets, trash bags, a broken lamp, and a microwave on the floorboard. Two stuffed animals. The back seat held their kids, maybe six and eight, wide-eyed and confused, staring through the window like they were watching the last scene of a movie they didn't understand.

He asked to speak to me. Not with anger---but with shame. Head low. Voice cracked. He couldn't even look me in the eye. Told me how the rent money vanished, how he was chasing a win that never came, how he sold off their last bit of savings, hoping that if he just came one more time, the dancer he obsessed over would give him something real. Just one more night. Just one more chance. One more lie he could afford to believe.

That moment didn't feel like business. It felt like judgment day. A gut punch from the universe. Because while we peddled glitter and fantasy inside those walls, I saw the brutal reality parked right outside---a family unraveling in real time, collateral damage from one man's desperation and my willingness to let it ride.

It wasn't just a strip club to him anymore. It was an addiction. A sanctuary. A slow-drip poison in a champagne bottle. A place that promised escape, and instead dragged him deeper into the wreckage of his life. And no matter how well I ran Scarlett's Secrets---how tight the books were, how smooth the operation---moments like that reminded me of the truth: behind every bill stuffed in a garter, there was a story unraveling. A lie being fed. A life being mortgaged for a taste of something that was never real to begin with.

And I built that house of mirrors.

What this looked like for me---in terms of everyone else's fallout---was a $6.5 million payday in today's dollars, courtesy of what the locals once mockingly called the "rainbow express." Call it what you want, but it cashed like any other deposit. Not bad for a kid in his twenties with no business degree, no investors, and not a clue what the hell he was doing when he stumbled into the game. I paid just under $400,000 for that building---roughly $1.16 million by today's standards---and flipped it into a monster. One of those mythical, podcast-worthy turnarounds people drool over in hustle culture circles. The kind they dress up in TED Talks and self-help books.

On paper, I won. In the headlines, I was a success story. A renegade entrepreneur who saw potential where others saw problems. A guy who bet on chaos and walked away with a check.

But what they don't print is the cost. Not the financial kind---the soul kind. The sleepless nights, the betrayals, the moral gray zones you convince yourself are just "part of the hustle." What you don't see in the spreadsheets is the weight of watching good people burn while you rise. The ethical gymnastics. The isolation. The sacrifices that don't make it to closing tables or bank statements.

That's why I walked. Not because the money dried up. Not because the deal went south. But because somewhere along the line, I did. And no payday, no matter how fat, can make you feel whole when you've hollowed yourself out to earn it.

So let me help you understand the decision. Try stepping into my shoes for a second.

Imagine being a local celebrity. Not the kind that signs autographs, but the kind people whisper about in bars. You've got the swagger, the car, the plane. A Ferrari in the driveway, your own jet in the hangar. You can afford to disappear for a weekend without checking your bank account. You live like a rockstar before your frontal lobe's even finished developing. And everybody wants your life---or so they think.

Now drop that into the context of a relationship. Maybe you're in one. Maybe you've built trust, love, and some kind of routine. Now ask yourself---how the hell does that relationship survive when you walk through the door at 3:00 a.m. reeking of stale perfume, cigarette smoke, and liquor? Or worse, when you show up emotionally fried after hours of being immersed in flesh, flirtation, and fantasy?

How does your partner react when they know damn well you've been offered threesomes by drunk bachelorettes or whispered propositions from waitresses in the back lot? You didn't ask for it, but you didn't exactly run from it either. What does that do to someone who's waiting at home, holding on to the idea that you're still hers?

Even with a supportive partner, cracks form. Trust starts to erode. The late nights pile up. So do the questions. For me, there wasn't even a strong foundation to begin with. I walked into this business already dragging vulnerabilities behind me---and in a place like Scarlett's, weakness doesn't get healed. It gets fed. Exposed. Exploited. That kind of environment doesn't just test a relationship---it disassembles it.

Now let's take it a step further. Extend the fantasy.

Say you dabble in drugs---pick your poison. Coke, pills, molly, blow by blow, night after night. In my world, access wasn't a problem. It was practically room service. If that was your thing, you could get high before your car even cooled down in the parking lot. Girls would offer it. Customers would bring it. The bathroom stalls weren't just for makeup.

I never touched the stuff. Not once. I treated it like a loaded weapon. I knew the second I took that first hit, that first line, that first pill---I might never get off that train. It wasn't willpower. It was fear. Self-preservation. I had too many demons already---I didn't need to hand them a switchblade.

But make no mistake---just because I didn't use didn't mean I wasn't surrounded by it. Gentlemen's clubs are breeding grounds for substance abuse. It's part of the rhythm. Dancers, bartenders, even some of the bouncers---they all needed something to get through the night. Booze, benzos, blow, doesn't matter. For many of them, walking half-naked into a crowd of hungry strangers with rent due in two days required more than confidence---it required chemical help. And once you go numb, it gets easier to fake the moans, the laughs, the touch.

It wasn't just their problem. It was the culture. And it was mine to manage. I had to run the club like a business while babysitting a bomb. I was the guy who had to smile at customers, balance payroll, handle cops, spot cokeheads, break up fights, and talk a crying girl down from a bad trip---all in the same Friggin night. And somehow, I had to keep myself from falling into the same hole.

So yeah, I made money. I made more than most people do in a decade. But I also watched people unravel right in front of me. And if you think that doesn't leave a mark, you've never owned a place like Scarlett's.

Then there's the ever-present threat of law enforcement. You want pressure? Picture being handcuffed in front of your family during dinner---fork halfway to your mouth, your kid watching with wide, confused eyes---because someone in your club, someone you barely knew or maybe trusted too much, broke the law. Could be a dancer running a side hustle. A manager laundering cash through his girlfriend's salon. A customer caught selling pills in the VIP lounge. Doesn't matter. Once it touches your club, it touches you.

There were always whispers. Always someone watching. Undercover agents posing as high-rollers, as casual regulars, even as staff. Confidential informants who acted like friends, partied like family, and then wrote your name down on a report the next morning. Smiles across the bar, microphones under their shirts. You never knew who was who. Everyone was a suspect. Every hug could be a setup.

With a Ferrari in the driveway and a private plane sitting pretty in a hangar, I was low-hanging fruit for prosecutors, cops, and media vultures. Easy to paint as a villain. A rich young club owner? They eat that shit up. I wasn't just a businessman to them---I was a story. A trophy. A headline that could make someone's career.

I lived in constant fear of losing everything. Not because I was reckless, but because someone else was. I ran my business clean---tight books, legit licenses, fire-code compliant. But I couldn't control every dancer's choices, every bouncer's behavior, every backroom deal that might happen when I wasn't looking. And in the eyes of the law, the owner is the one who pays. Period. Doesn't matter if you were ten miles away. If it happened under your roof, you're the one in the courtroom.

But the legal risks were just one flavor of hell. The daily grind came with its own demons.

Running the club meant managing chaos---because people are messy, emotional, impulsive creatures. And when you throw in ego, alcohol, and fast cash, it turns into a goddamn circus. I was juggling egos bigger than mine---dancers with cult followings, DJs with coke habits, bartenders who couldn't keep their hands out of the till. And the managers? The ones who were supposed to have my back were usually too busy lining their own pockets. That little betrayal? It wasn't a one-off. It became a pattern. An epidemic. One I'd keep fighting in the years to come.

Theft was nonstop. A slow bleed I could never fully stop. Cover charges skimmed at the door. Locker rental fees rerouted into someone's purse. Drinks rung up wrong---"accidentally," of course. Some nights, I'd spot thousands missing from the count, and no one would admit a thing. It was like trying to plug a leaking dam with bubblegum.

No matter how much cash flowed in---and there was a lot---someone was always trying to carve out a slice that didn't belong to them. It was survival of the greediest. And the worst part? If I cracked down too hard, they'd leave. They'd run to a rival club and take customers, dancers, and drama with them. So I walked a razor's edge between being respected and being feared---never fully landing on either side.

There's no playbook for that kind of leadership. No handbook for managing a group of emotionally raw, half-drunk, hyper-sexualized employees in a setting where every dollar is a temptation and every compliment is transactional. You either learn fast or you drown.

And most nights, I felt like I was gulping water just to stay above the surface.

And while the money was incredible---the kind of stacks that make your accountant call twice---it came at a cost. A big one. The smoke-filled rooms weren't just a mood; they were a daily, slow-death sentence. Every night, I inhaled a toxic cocktail of cigarette smoke, body spray, and whatever was burning in the back alley. It clung to my clothes, my skin, my lungs. There was no escaping it. It got into everything.

I'd lie in bed some nights and feel it in my chest---a weight, a tightness. My breathing was off. My nerves on edge. Lung cancer didn't feel like a risk anymore; it felt like a countdown. I started picturing my kids visiting me in some hospital, lungs full of tar and regrets, all because I stayed too long in a place that reeked of fantasy and decay.

And that was just one piece of it.

Add in the constant anxiety of managing theft, dodging law enforcement, and trying to keep a morally gray business from tipping full black... and I had to ask myself the question no one at the top ever wants to face: Was it worth it?

And then there's the inevitable IRS. At any time, they can come swinging, trying to reclassify dancers as "employees" instead of contractors. They've been chasing that fight for years. What used to be called the 20-factor test has now been boiled down into three buckets—behavioral control, financial control, and the nature of the relationship. Push those hard enough—like setting schedules, taking house cuts, or making the dancers part of the club's core business—and it's not hard for the IRS to argue they're employees. And once they do, the owners can get hammered with back wages, unpaid taxes, benefits, and penalties. We're talking millions. They ran that play more than once at Scarlett's Secrets. A big concern.

Sure, I did well. Very well. But let's set the record straight. I never got close to owning a jet---not even sniffed that level of wealth. Just to give you some perspective, that's a whole different league. Different sport, even. Most people have no clue what it really costs---not just to buy the damn thing, but to keep it flying.

You could easily drop $300,000 a year just to pay someone to fly it for you. That's before you even hear the engines spool up. Before the first wheel leaves the runway.

Flying it? That's a money pit in the sky. Try $300 an hour per engine---and that's the base rate. You want to know what model jet? What engine series? What maintenance program you're under? Buckle up. Every variation is more expensive than the last. Every hour flown comes with a ticking invoice behind it.

Then come the mandatory inspections---non-negotiable, federally regulated, and always expensive. God help you if something breaks, because it's not if, it's when. Turbines don't care how full your wallet is. They fail on their own schedule. And when they do, the repair bills hit like a steel-toed boot to the ribs. A cracked fuel cell? That's your kid's college fund. An avionics issue? There goes the lake house.

People say boats are money pits---Break Out Another Thousand. Cute. With jets, it's Break Out Another Hundred Thousand. Every time something fails, it feels like your wallet just took a crowbar to the knees.

And let's talk fuel. Don't even get me started on fuel. Take the thirstiest, most gas-guzzling muscle car you've ever driven, multiply that by ten, and maybe---maybe---you're in the ballpark. I've seen jet fuel spike to $14 a gallon. You think filling up your SUV hurts? Try filling twin tanks on a Citation and then flying it across the country.

And when you land? That's when the nickel-and-dime game really kicks in.

Landing fees. Ramp fees. Overnight parking fees. Hangar space. Crew accommodations. Catering. Charts. Insurance. Everything's charged in units of hundreds or thousands. You get nickeled and dimed with hundred-dollar bills until you feel like you're bleeding green.

So yeah, when you see someone with their own jet---not fractional ownership, not a timeshare, but a full-blown personal aircraft---don't let their laid-back, cool-guy act fool you. That's one-percenter territory. Rich-rich. The kind of rich that doesn't flinch when they drop a million on maintenance or fuel in a year. That's the realm of hedge fund CEOs, oil heirs, and the kind of money that remembers Prohibition. They're not lucky. They're not just successful. They're swimming in it.

And I wasn't. I was doing well for a guy with no college degree, a knack for reading people, and an appetite for risk. But private jet rich? That was a galaxy away. I had the taste, but not the means to feast forever.

That's the truth behind the curtain. Not every baller you see is flying high. Some of us are just leasing the dream---trying to keep the wings on long enough to land without crashing.

But that? That was never me. My planes, the smoke, the cash, the chaos---it all looked impressive from the outside. It sparkled. It roared. But I knew the truth: the shine was only skin-deep. Underneath it all was corrosion. And no matter how much polish I applied, the rust kept creeping in.

Selling Scarlett's Secrets wasn't just a smart decision---it was a life-saving one. Hands down, the best move I ever made. That wire transfer didn't just buy me freedom---it bought me peace. It bought me oxygen. It brought me back.

The financial independence gave me the rarest luxury of all: clarity. I finally had the space to look around and realize how toxic the whole damn ecosystem had become. I walked out of that smoke-stained warzone with my mind intact, my body clean, and my future wide open.

My wife at the time, Bridget? She didn't see it that way. She fed off the chaos. She loved the power, the infamy, the attention. The backstage passes to the underworld, the clout that came from being married to the king of the club scene. For her, the party was the purpose. So when I pulled the plug, she saw it as betrayal. Her exit was quick, cold, and expected.

And honestly? Good.

Because her leaving made space for something real. For someone real.

Kate came back into my life like a breath of clean air after years of choking on poison. There were no threesomes, no backstage politics, no fake laughs or transactional love. Just truth. Real connection. The kind of love that doesn't need to be shouted across a crowded VIP section to be felt. She grounded me. Reminded me of who I used to be before the spotlight, the fast money, and the fake friends.

After the sale, my stress levels didn't just drop---they evaporated. For the first time in years, I slept through the night. No more lying awake wondering if the feds were about to knock on the door. No more checking my phone for police reports or staff overdoses. I could breathe again.

And I didn't coast---I pivoted. I took everything I'd learned from that firestorm---the instincts, the hustle, the management, the sharp radar for bullshit---and I built something new. Legal. Clean. Scalable. Profitable. No stage lights. No G-strings. No cops. Just progress. Just peace.

Do I miss the easy money? Sometimes. Sure. That kind of fast cash is like heroin---you never forget the high. And yeah, I miss the notoriety now and then. Being the guy everyone wanted to know, the one they couldn't quite figure out. But you know what I don't miss?

I don't miss the paranoia.

I don't miss the theft.

I don't miss wondering which one of my employees was going to set the place on fire---figuratively or literally.

I don't miss the smell of sweat, desperation, and lies.

I don't miss managing addicts, or coaching girls through breakdowns, or cutting off a drunk regular who thought he owned the place because he dropped $500 on bottle service.

Scarlett's Secrets was a fantasy---but it came with a real cost. It was a dark, smoky pressure cooker where truth suffocated, and deception paid the rent. Every night, I ran a circus of fire-breathers and escape artists. And it nearly burned me to ash.

Looking back, yeah, I'm proud of what I built. I turned nothing into something. I created a brand out of thin air and sweat. But I'm even prouder that I had the balls to walk away. I didn't cling to the empire. I didn't ride it until it imploded. I sold high, stepped off the ride, and walked straight into reinvention.

I didn't lose the game. I flipped the board and started a new one.

I reinvented myself. Re-challenged myself. Built a life rooted in truth, health, and peace---real peace, not the kind you rent by the hour.

Do I miss the job? The chaos? The risk?

Hell no.

Not for one second.

Breaking News (10 Years Ago)

The headline bled across every TV screen in Galaxy, Georgia, and across the nation:

"Two gunmen stormed Scarlett's Secrets, a gentlemen's club on Highway 17, in Galaxy, GA, Seven killed. Thirteen wounded. Identities withheld. Suspects still at large."

Scarlett's Secrets had been mine. My idea, my sweat, my gamble. I built it brick by brick, neon by neon, only to watch it turn into a slaughterhouse in a single night. Two of the partners I'd brought in never walked out.

The place never reopened. Couldn't. It sits there still—dark, boarded up, candles long burned out at the door, only a tale of what was. Folks drive by and whisper, like the walls themselves carry the screams.

The shooters? Caught. Convicted. Waiting to die by needle and steel. Justice on paper, maybe. But justice never scrubbed the blood from those floors, and it warped every good memory. Scarlett's Secrets was meant to be a monument to escape — not a memorial to the dead.

Chapter 14

To Be as a Has Been you Must have been a Once Was

Photograph
Performed by **Nickelback**
Written by: **Chad Kroeger**

At the end of all the reflecting, it really comes down to the memories we manage to hold onto as we age---the ones that don't rot or fade with time. Everything else gets shaky. Names, timelines, places---they blur like fog on a windshield. But the real ones? They stay. Burned in. Branded.

Maybe it's an old photo, edges curled, color bled out like it's been through a war---but the moment? Still razor-sharp in your mind. You remember the smell. The sound. The way someone laughed before they disappeared from your life. Or maybe it's a thumb drive crammed with digital snapshots, frozen flashes of who you used to be. Little fragments of your chaos, your wins, your screw-ups, all locked away in a piece of plastic smaller than your thumb.

Either way, that's the inventory of a life. That's the proof we were here. That we mattered. That we lived. Even if the rest of it starts slipping away, those moments fight to stay---scars and all.

Why This Title: Let Me Get My Underwear on First?

I told Kate---if I ever drop dead on top of her, coming out of the shower, or God forbid, while taking a dump---please, for the love of whatever dignity I've got left, get my underwear on first.

The last thing I want is for my final legacy to be how they found me: naked, face-down, saggy balls tangled in a bath mat, looking like a deflated corpse balloon with an inverted chode. That's not the closing scene I want people remembering. No dramatic fade-out. No peaceful final breath. Just full frontal failure and a pair of lifeless eyes staring up from the tile.

Worse yet, imagine the poor bastard first responder who has to walk in on that crime scene of a body. That image would burn into his skull for life. Or even worse, what if some Gen Z EMT gets trigger-happy with their phone and I end up as a viral TikTok---#FlatlinedNakedDude trending while the comments roast me from here to eternity. That'd be the final insult. All that I've built, undone by one last humiliating headline.

So yeah, that title? It's more than a punchline. It's a damn plea for dignity.

The sale of Scarlett's Secrets and the other clubs marked the end of an era. Stepping away from the gentlemen's club world was liberating---but don't let that word fool you. It wasn't some movie ending where I walked off into the sunset with stacks of cash and peace of mind. It was a fire escape. One I barely got down without choking on the smoke.

My marriage to Bridget was already a cracked foundation, and the 2008 financial crash turned it into rubble. You couldn't run from it. You couldn't hustle around it. It swallowed everything---equity, safety, trust. The world was imploding, and I was trying to steer a nightclub empire through a Category 5 shitstorm. I sold just in time. She left not long after. For her, the party was over. For me, the reckoning had begun.

If I had a do-over card, I'd play it on my dad's business. That was my fork in the road. I'd have come in sharper, more calculated. Would've made his partner my best friend, learned everything I could, and then branched off and built my own damn empire of car dealerships. Played the long game instead of chasing fast highs. That was the smart play. But I missed it. Immaturity and ego blinded me.

Most of the guys I know with jets? Car dealers. Not crypto bros or influencers---real operators who figured out how to scale. Inventory, systems, brand loyalty. That could've been me. Should've been me. But instead, I was playing blackjack with my future while they were stacking passive income in climate-controlled garages.

When the crash hit, I scrambled to pivot. I scraped together just enough to land a franchise deal with a national rental car company. They supplied the fleet, I ran the counter. Simple in theory, brutal in execution. I earned overrides on revenue, clawed my way back into the transportation industry. It wasn't retail car sales, but it scratched the itch.

For a while, it worked. I expanded to three locations across Georgia and Florida. Added airport shuttles and limos to the mix. That part wasn't new---back in the Scarlett's days, I already had a foot in that world. It was just smart business to bring it with me. I even had my own Cessna 206--- a single-engine workhorse---so I could stay airborne, stay sharp, and write off the fuel while I was at it.

The idea was simple: grow it, polish it, sell it. Build something I could hand off or cash out. Something clean. Something with staying power. But then COVID came in like a drunk bouncer with a God complex and shut the whole thing down in one violent shove.

Travel froze. Inventory vanished. Customers disappeared. No one was renting cars or booking rides---they were hiding in basements, spraying bleach on Amazon boxes. One boardroom decision in a corporate tower wiped it all away. A piece of paper signed by someone I'd never met torched years of work.

Just like that, it was gone.

I don't even want to tally up how much equity vanished in that wave. It still makes my teeth grind. So I did what I've always done when life throws a Molotov cocktail through my window---I downshifted. Third time now. Reinvent. Rebuild. Again.

That's when jets came back into the picture---not just admiring them, managing them. Getting behind the yoke myself. Eventually, becoming a professional jet pilot. That wasn't the plan. That was survival. A chance to take control again, to get above the bullshit---literally.

And like most relationships, even when you know it's time to move on, that familiar weight pulls you back. Nostalgia is a liar. It shows up smelling like perfume and regret, whispering old songs in your ear. That last 1% of hesitation? It was fueled by memories, bad timing, and my old buddy Jose Cuervo---who's never shown up with good advice.

I was 99% out the door. But that 1%? That's the part that can wreck you if you let it.

Not this time.

Redemption in Reverse

One fateful night, under the dual influence of tequila and catastrophic judgment, I did something unwise even by my own standards. Somewhere between shot number six and a full-blown emotional tailspin, I convinced myself I was on the cusp of creative brilliance. A drunken visionary. A tortured artist with a cracked iPhone and something to say.

I decided---God help me---that I'd make a home movie. Not just any movie, though. No, this would be my magnum opus: an X-rated, deeply personal, dimly lit, emotionally chaotic to my soon-to-be ex-wife. Shot handheld, narrated with slurred poetry, and starring me in all my regretful glory. This was going to be art, dammit.

In my Cuervo-drenched brain, it didn't feel pathetic---it felt poetic. Tragic, sure. Messy, absolutely. But raw and real, the kind of vulnerable shit Instagram therapists swear women eat up. I convinced myself it was a grand, cinematic gesture---heart-on-sleeve, bottle-in-hand, a man finally laying it all bare. Maybe she'd laugh. Maybe she'd cry. Maybe she'd remember the good times, get swept up in nostalgia, and come sprinting back---mascara streaking, voice shaking, whispering that she still loved me. But if I'm being honest? I just wanted her jealous. I wanted her to see me with Kate and feel that twist in her gut. I didn't want her back---I wanted her haunted.

What I should've done was go to bed.

Instead, I filmed it. I directed it. I starred in it. I even gave it a working title in my head---Redemption in Reverse. I poured my twisted little heart into it. I moaned. I monologued. I whispered sweet, bitter nothings to the camera. And then, in the most symbolic finale of all time---I finished. Brilliantly. All over my chest. Another Friggin mess in my life to clean up. A metaphor so obvious even a hungover version of me could understand it.

Then, with the unwarranted confidence of a man who had no business operating a smartphone in his condition, I hit send. In my haze, I thought I was sending it straight to her inbox. A private showing. A midnight miracle.

Then came sunrise. Like a slap from God. The light sliced through the blinds. My mouth tasted like drywall. My stomach did barrel rolls. And my phone buzzed like it owed the IRS.

First call of the day: unknown number. I answered, still groggy and assuming it was some robot trying to sell me roof panels. Instead, I was greeted by a man's voice---loud, angry, and disturbingly familiar. A guy I vaguely recognized from my kid's T Ball league. And he was livid.

He was yelling about some "filthy, inappropriate video" I sent his wife.

I blinked. My brain was still rebooting. No clue what he was talking about. I told him he had the wrong guy.

Thirty minutes later, another call. New number. This time, a mom from the same league. Her voice was equal parts moral outrage and straight-up revulsion. She mentioned children. Community standards. Biblical judgment. And then---like a film critic from hell---she ended her rant by absolutely eviscerating my "performance." Apparently, I lacked conviction. Believability. Passion. In her words, "If you're gonna ruin lives, at least commit to the role."

That's when the fear kicked in. Not hangover fear. Existential, stomach-in-a-vise, "your life is now permanently altered" fear. I sat there, sweating tequila, wondering how this woman even knew what I looked like naked.

Then came the call that made it all make sense.

It was my wife.

"WHAT. THE FUCK. ARE YOU DOING?!"

Those six words hit harder than any tequila shot I'd ever taken. My soul briefly left my body and hovered above the wreckage I had caused. And then it hit me. Like a slow-motion car crash, I couldn't stop.

I hadn't sent the video to her.

I had replied to the entire T-Ball team group text.

The one they'd just used to send out the game schedule.

So instead of confirming that little Timmy had a 10 a.m. game at Field 3, half the community got front-row seats to my tequila-fueled meltdown. In full HD. With commentary. No plot, no pants, no friggin dignity---just a sad, drunken one-man show where I mistook heartbreak for performance art. What was supposed to be a group text turned into a personal highlight reel of "What Bridget's Missing," shot like a low-budget home porno. No soundtrack. Just shame.

To say I wasn't invited to the end-of-season potluck would be an understatement.

And just to complete the humiliation trifecta? That very afternoon was my turn to drive the kids to practice. Nothing says "walk of shame" like pulling up to the ballfield surrounded by minivans full of horrified, barely-contained snickering parents---each one now an unwilling subscriber to Walker After Dark.

I sat there, engine running, sunglasses on, praying for spontaneous combustion. The looks I got ranged from pity to perversion to pure schadenfreude. No one said a word. They didn't have to. Their faces screamed it loud enough.

There are moments in life when you just have to sit in your own filth and nod. Own the disaster. Accept that you are the main character in a story you'll never live down. This was one of those moments.

In case you're wondering---no, she wasn't moved. No tears, no soft music swelling in the background. No sentimental regret, and sure as hell no hint of a comeback---not that either of us wanted one. There was no redemptive arc, no warm reunion years later, no clinking glasses over wine while laughing about "that one time." Just silence. A blank space where I used to be. A memory she probably filed somewhere between *What the fuck* and *Never again*.

I didn't just burn the bridge---I strapped C-4 to it, hit record, and made sure the whole neighborhood got the director's cut.

Redemption in Reverse indeed.

The Rearview Mirror

At Scarlett's Secrets, I was the man---at least in the circles that mattered back then. The guy who held court at the bar like a king without a crown, made it look effortless. I didn't walk through that club, I glided. The bassline bowed to my tempo, and women noticed. So did men. Power like that hums in your blood. It makes the lights brighter, the nights longer, and the consequences… invisible.

But that was then. And time doesn't just pass---it grinds. Perspective isn't something you're born with. It shows up years later, dragging a suitcase full of regret and a mirror you can't look away from. The things I once thought made me invincible? They were just red flags waving in my blind spot. Funny how life plays you. First, it hands you power---before you've earned it---then strips it away right when you start to figure out what the hell you were doing. You get the appetite before you get the bill.

Truth is, life's a rigged game---especially when it comes to how youth sees age.

The younger crowd looks at older men like we're rusting antiques. Obsolete. In the way. No longer dangerous, just domesticated. Once you hit a certain age, society treats you like sour milk with a charming smile. You could walk into a room dressed like royalty and still get reduced to "sir." The unspoken label is always there: Expired. Do Not Open.

I've lived it. Hell, I've been the contradiction that pisses everyone off. A Ferrari idling outside a five-star restaurant, out steps a man who's clearly not in his twenties---tailored, sharp, carrying the gravity of earned confidence---and on his arm, a woman half his age, radiant, untouched by cynicism. And you can feel the sidewalk sneer. You hear the whispers without hearing a word: What a waste of a Ferrari.

What they don't get is---I used to be that guy inside the Ferrari, too. The driver, the shot-caller, the man who made you question your own life choices. The car, the clothes, the girl who made heads swivel, and other men's dates shift uncomfortably in their seats. I didn't just rent the image---I was the image. But here's the part they never saw: those women? They weren't rented. They weren't arm candy or Instagram fodder. They were with me because they wanted to be. And I was proud as hell to be chosen by them. I never once had to beg to be seen. I was the scene.

People used to toss out jabs like, What are you, driving Daddy's car?---but that was never about me. That was a projection. Pure, uncut insecurity dressed up as sarcasm. I see it now. I see how hot the truth burned in their throats, so instead they spat sideways and tried to laugh me off. It's easier to mock a man than admit you're afraid to be him.

I tasted success at full throttle---when I had the body to throw at the night, the stamina to chase every thrill, and the reckless confidence to bet everything on one more high. Ferraris. Planes. Limousines. Whatever the world told me meant I'd made it, I owned it, drove it, flew it. But time? Time doesn't care. Time peels the paint, dulls the chrome. The engine might still roar, but the applause fades, and eventually, you're just another man behind the wheel, wondering why nobody's looking anymore.

Still, my name hasn't disappeared. Even now, people remember me as the guy who ran Scarlett's Secrets. That place still echoes. The walls knew me. The staff adored me or feared me---sometimes both. The city remembers. It's funny, the way people still ask about it. Still want the juice. The stories. The chaos. That curiosity? It's its own kind of currency. Proof that relevance isn't measured by youth---it's measured by impact. I carved my name into that place. Into people. Into legend. That shit doesn't wash off.

There's my saying: "To be a has been, you must be a once was." That one lands different the older you get. Just because a man's gone gray doesn't mean the fire's out. There's still heat in the coals. Still a flicker of that young bastard who thought he could bend the night to his will. I've slowed---not because I wanted to, but because the body started filing complaints the brain couldn't argue with. I tap the brakes more these days, but time? It doesn't. It's flooring it. And I'm chasing something I know I'll never catch again.

The days blur now. The months disappear like smoke. The years hit harder and faster, like waves that don't care how well you used to swim. I find myself looking in the mirror, not to fix my hair, but to recognize the man staring back. He's got scars. Stories. And a stare that says he's still dangerous---just a little quieter about it now.

That's the part no one prepares you for: not the fading fame, not the aching joints---but the silence that follows when the crowd moves on and the night stops calling your name. And yet, somehow, I'm still here. Still standing. Still driving my own damn car.

Because underneath it all, I was never just the man who ran Scarlett's Secrets.

I am Scarlett's Secret.

Today, Scarlett's Secrets tells a different, sadder tale. Once it pulsed with neon and sweat, a place where the lonely and the reckless came to lose themselves for a night. Now it stands hollow, a boarded-up tomb on the edge of town. The laughter is gone, the music long stopped—only the ghosts remain. Every brick whispers the names of the dead, and every passing glance reminds me that what I built with fire and ambition ended in gun smoke and silence. Back in the prologue, I told you about smoke in the cockpit. What I didn't tell you was how calm it all felt---right up until the moment it didn't.

Back in the prologue, I told you about smoke in the cockpit. What I didn't tell you was how calm it all felt---right up until the moment it didn't.

We nailed the landing. Textbook-perfect. Greased it in so smooth it could've made a training video. Everything felt controlled. Safe. Then came the betrayal. A mechanical failure no one saw coming. The gear folded like wet cardboard, the nose dropped, and the fuselage slammed into the pavement with the kind of violence that makes you believe in second lives. The wings tore away. We went from gliding like gods to skidding across the runway in a screaming mess of sparks, shredded rubber, and adrenaline.

My copilot that day? My grandson. Fresh off his instructor certificate, buzzing with that electric confidence that only comes with new wings. His fiancée joined us too---wide-eyed, excited, ready to make memories. It was supposed to be a day of firsts.

It ended with emergency crews cutting us out of a crumpled airframe.

Instead, it became a brutal lesson in aviation's darker truths: machines fail---even when you do everything right. Perfect checklist? Doesn't matter. Textbook approach? Doesn't guarantee shit. You can play the game by the book and still get blindsided.

But here's the part that matters---we walked away. All three of us. Not a scratch. The plane was totaled, but our will to fly? Untouched. That wreck didn't define us---it confirmed us. Resilience isn't some bumper sticker pilots slap on their flight bags. It's coded into the bloodstream. It's what keeps your hand steady when the engine coughs and the ground's rushing up faster than you can think.

Next up---the badge from Chapter 1. Yeah, that one. It showed up the same day I got slapped with foreclosure papers. Three days---three damn days---before the short sale on my house was supposed to close. Most people would've folded right there, started packing boxes, and whispering prayers. But not me. I dug in. Went full trench warfare. For the next eleven years, I went to war with the bank.

It all started in the bloodbath of 2008. The market collapsed. Panic set in. Insurance premiums shot up, property taxes doubled, and two mortgages crushed any hope of breathing room. The wolves came sniffing, jaws open, fangs out. Everyone around me bailed---sold at a loss, walked away, gave up. I didn't. I stayed. Never made another payment. Eleven years. Roughly $750,000 saved. No shame in that. Just strategy.

Am I proud of it? Not exactly. But ashamed? Not a damn bit. The banks weren't victims. They were predators, betting on fear, counting on people to flinch first. I didn't flinch. I had just enough legal instinct to be dangerous, and just enough rage to weaponize it. Lucky for me, I had an attorney with more skeletons than a cemetery---he bought me time. Then he passed the baton to a no-bullshit, steel-spined lawyer who played chess while the rest of the world played checkers. I still call him a friend. I still owe him a drink. Call it hustle. Call it karma. Call it survival. Doesn't matter what you call it. The bottom line? I'm still standing. And the house? Still mine.

The Boogeyman

Most people never meet the Boogeyman. They just let their imagination gnaw at the edges of their sanity---those late-night whispers that maybe, just maybe, something's watching. A shadow behind the curtain. A car parked too long across the street. Static on the line that wasn't there before. The brain starts to itch. The gut tightens. But they shrug it off, pour another drink, scroll past the feeling, and tell themselves it's nothing.

I didn't get that luxury.

I met him. Shook his hand. Sat across from him while my stomach did cartwheels and my mouth went dry. I lived with that crawl under my skin for months---months of looking over my shoulder, second-guessing every text, every phone call, every unfamiliar frown in a crowd. I became fluent in gut warnings and silence that felt loaded. It wasn't paranoia. It was real. There was an investigation. My name, printed cold and clinical on a file that lived in some sterile office. A badge in a drawer. A few green lights blinking somewhere in a government basement, giving strangers permission to dissect my entire life like a frog in high school biology. They went deep---bank statements, phone records, surveillance. Not because they had proof, but because they had questions. And I'd made the mistake of living loud in a world that doesn't like its secrets exposed.

Then came the football game. Packed bleachers. The crowd roaring in unison. That tribal, chest-rattling energy that only small-town Friday nights can conjure. Parents buzzing with pride. Kids amped on Gatorade and hormones. Adrenaline in the air like static, snapping off the concrete. It was the kind of night where memories get made---and for me, a memory I'll never forget was standing on that sideline, thinking I was finally clear of it all. That's when Keith walked over. One of my closest friends. My business partner. A guy who'd been in the trenches with me when shit got loud. He was also the Boogeyman's former partner in law enforcement---something he rarely talked about but never denied. He leaned in, calm as ever, and said, "There's someone you need to meet."

No heads-up. No context. Just dropped the hammer. And then I was face-to-face with him. Ken. The guy whose face I'd never seen but whose name had haunted me for months. The one who'd been combing through my life like a bloodhound trained in humiliation. A man whose job was to break people apart with surgical precision---and whose instincts had led him straight to me. The fear that stalked my dreams just got personal, and it wasn't angry. It was worse. Calm. Stone-carved. A stare built for interrogation rooms and last chances.

No handshake. No small talk. Just four words, dropped like a grenade: "How does my dick taste?" That line didn't just cut the tension---it executed it. Shot it in the face, dragged it behind the bleachers, and buried it beneath the end zone. I stood there, completely leveled. Fear crumbled. Pride took a knee. And all I could do was stare back as the wall between us buckled like soaked drywall in a hurricane. There was no escape hatch. No clever comeback. Just the raw, exposed reality that I'd been living inside this man's crosshairs---and now, here he was, real, breathing, and not nearly as mythical as the paranoia had painted him.

And the twist? We're tight now. Yeah---Ken and I shoot the shit. We text. We grab lunch. We've double-dated with our wives and laughed over drinks like we weren't ever mortal enemies. Life's funny like that. It finds the most twisted ways to bend the plot. Ken still has that badge energy tucked under his skin like a concealed weapon. Every now and then, he'll flash it in his voice just to remind me who he used to be. He's told me, without blinking, "If we'd found anything real, you'd be doing time." That part still haunts me. Cold food. Concrete mattress. Bologna sandwiches stamped with expiration dates nobody wants to read. Steel doors that don't open when you scream. That was the reality I brushed up against.

But they didn't find anything. Because I wasn't a criminal. I was just a complicated, fascinating son of a bitch who refused to go down. And that? That made me dangerous in a whole different way.

Bridget's Mansion

Bridget left.

She married Oscar---a plumber, of all things. But not just any plumber. This guy owns a fleet. Sixty trucks, a hundred employees, and a payroll that probably rivals mid-sized corporations. He doesn't crawl under sinks anymore; he's the guy writing checks to people who do. The only thing that comes out of his butt crack is money. Oscar farts hundred-dollar bills and lives like his life was storyboarded by the Hallmark Channel and financed by Goldman Sachs.

He showed up after her predictable, pathetic rekindling with Ira. That rerun went exactly how it went the first time: Ira still married, Bridget still the side piece, and me---stuck somewhere between victim and volunteer. And yeah, I'll own my part. I deserved it. I was the idiot who believed a history of chaos could somehow rewrite itself as a future of stability. Spoiler alert: it can't.

So she chose Oscar. Stability in a Rolex. Clean cut, well-off, and deeply Southern in that "bless your heart" kind of way that makes you want to throw a chair through a window. Together, they bought a beachfront palace in Georgia---think sand-colored stucco, wraparound porches, custom wood shutters, and gas lanterns glowing just enough to make it look like money whispers instead of screams. It's your classic "southern charm meets obscene wealth" setup. The kind of place where the air smells like magnolias and money. Where you can almost hear the real estate agent saying words like timeless elegance while handing over the keys to your new fantasy life.

It's also the kind of place self-proclaimed princesses dream about while sipping overpriced rosé on Pinterest boards. A life curated in sepia tones, complete with monogrammed towels, a labradoodle named Tucker, and a perfectly filtered existence designed to tell the world: I made it. And maybe she did. I'm man enough to admit that. I'm also man enough to admit that, yeah, there's still some bitterness when I think about it. But there's also honesty. I am happy for her. I really am. And I know---deep in my bones---that she's damn happy for herself. And in her world, that's the only happiness that really matters, right?

Now Oscar? Here's the kicker---he's actually a great guy. So great, in fact, that if the circumstances had been different, I probably would've ended up calling him a friend. We share a love for aviation, a head for business, and just enough alpha to get away with saying the kind of things most men keep buried behind polite nods. In another version of life, one where things weren't so tangled and poisoned with history, I could've seen us grabbing beers after a flight, shooting the breeze about engine temps and fuel flow, maybe even flying together---him in the left seat, me in the right, swapping stories at 10,000 feet.

First, let me rewind and tell you about our first encounter with Oscar and Bridget, which was... interesting, to say the least. This was our big attempt to break the ice and ease into a new reality---one where "divorced" applied to Bridget and me, but not to the children who still counted on us to be something resembling stable. So, we made a plan. One of those well-meaning, high-risk, paper-sound plans that look okay in a group text but feel like walking into a fire wearing a gasoline suit.

The idea? Meet halfway in Atlanta. Grab dinner at some velvet-draped, overpriced restaurant where the waiters wear vests and the wine list is longer than the Constitution. Then, for good measure, stay the night---together---in a suite at the Grand Hyatt. Because parenting doesn't stop at divorce, and if there's a manual for co-parenting with your ex and her new man, I sure as hell haven't read it. But I'm pretty sure the chapter titled "Share a Hotel Room" wouldn't come highly recommended.

Oscar---her new guy---was a couple of years older than me. Same height. Genetically blessed in that casual, effortless way that makes you hate yourself for noticing. Built like a guy who lifts not for vanity but for sanity. His arms were inked in a way that said: I had free time and disposable income. The vibe? Calm, grounded, never in a rush, never insecure. Like he'd never once asked himself if he was enough---because he already knew. Spoiler: he was.

Bridget, who had known Kate and me since before the emotional wreckage and court filings, slid into her hostess role with ease. She handled the dinner like she was managing a high-profile merger---decisive, composed, tactical. The drinks came quick, the small talk quicker. And beneath it all, just barely audible beneath the wine glasses and polite nods, was the tension. Quiet. Loaded. Waiting.

Oscar broke it first.

With a story---of course. A charming, not-so-innocent anecdote about the time he brought his pet boa constrictor to high school gym class. He told it like theater---his snake slithered out in the locker room, made a surprise appearance in the showers, and sent a fellow student screaming. Principal's office. Suspension. You know the drill. Everyone at the table chuckled. Oscar smiled.

But make no mistake---that story wasn't about a reptile. It was about his snake. The whole thing was one long, perfectly timed dick joke delivered like a TED Talk. He wasn't trying to be subtle. He wanted me to know. He was the python in the room. And me? I couldn't compete with my 2-inch punisher in shrink wrap. Ok, maybe that's a little understated.

And look, I caught it. I got the message. Loud and clear. If I didn't already have my own insecurities trying to crawl out of my fly and fight for its life, I might've unzipped and laid it next to the breadsticks in protest to show I had no fear. But I didn't. I let him have his moment. He strutted like a golden retriever who just brought back a goose. And honestly? I didn't hate him for it. I respected the delivery.

Then Bridget upped the ante---because if there's one thing Bridget has always done with surgical precision, it's stir the pot.

The waitress arrived, notepad in hand, smile nailed into place. Bridget looked up like she was presenting nominees at an awards show. With a calm, measured voice, she gestured around the table. "This is my husband," she said, pointing to me. "This is his girlfriend, Kate." Then, like she was introducing a co-worker at a networking lunch, she added, "And this is my boyfriend, Oscar."

The waitress blinked, mid-sentence, eyes darting like she'd been dropped into a scene from a show she never auditioned for. Her pen floated above the page like it wasn't sure whether to write or run. I swear even the air paused. You could almost hear her thoughts: *Is this a prank? A cult? A reality show I missed the pilot for?*

I just took a long sip of my drink and let it all wash over me. Because, in that moment, it really did feel like Bridget had hit play on the strangest reality show ever aired---and somehow, I had a starring role. No script. No cue cards. Just raw, exposed life at its weirdest and most brutally honest.

And as I watched her lean into Oscar, laughing in that natural, effortless way I hadn't seen in years, I got it. I saw it. It wasn't about money or a beach house or monogrammed bath towels. It was deeper. Primal. He had that unshakable, quiet confidence. The size, the charm, the don't-give-a-damn edge that comes from knowing exactly who you are and never apologizing for it.

And me? I wasn't jealous. I wasn't bitter. I wasn't angry. I was... free. For the first time, I wasn't clinging to the scraps of a love story that ended years ago. She had moved on---completely. Physically, emotionally, sexually. And I wasn't standing in the wreckage anymore. I was watching the rebuild. And oddly, it felt okay.

Then came the top of the wedding cake---the awkward, poetic finale to our twisted little reunion. We returned to the hotel. The same Grand Hyatt where, once upon a time, Bridget and I had whispered promises and cried goodbyes. The same place we'd once said everything. Old love. Dead love. Now, something else entirely.

The night back at the suite was full of exchanges. Some light. Some loaded. But all of it civil. Measured. Almost… mature. No one stormed off. No one cried. No one bled. And when it comes to modern family dynamics, that's a win. We were all doing our part. Progress.

Then came the encore performance---Bridget's version of a Broadway show.

It was late. The mirrors were fogged from hot showers, the monogrammed robes stripped from their decorative placements. Everyone had retreated to their respective corners of the suite. Then came the noise.

Enter stage left: the moans.

Not squeaky-bed moans. Not vague thumps and rustling. These were intentional. Projected. Theatrical. The kind of sounds that could drift off a fifth-story balcony and land somewhere near Times Square. Oscar and Bridget were putting on a show. A one-act play in lust and volume---just loud enough to make sure at least one audience member couldn't miss the performance. I laid there, eyes open, ceiling staring back, listening to the final confirmation that she was his now. Fully. Viscerally. Without hesitation or apology. And weirdly… I didn't flinch.

I didn't feel gutted. Didn't want to punch the wall or shoot off some sad, late-night text to a number that stopped meaning anything. I just felt still. Not numb---just finished. Finished chasing smoke. Finished playing chess with snakes. She'd found her guy---the one who made her laugh across the table and moan through the drywall. And me? I found something too. Not peace. Not closure. Just the edge I'd lost somewhere back there.. Maybe not closure. But peace. The kind that doesn't shout. The kind that settles. Because sometimes letting go doesn't come with a bang or a bottle or a breakdown. Sometimes, it comes with a smirk across a dinner table, a sip of bourbon, and the slow, steady realization that the war's been over for years---you just forgot to leave the battlefield.

But life's got a twisted sense of humor. It gives you a taste of what could've been just long enough to remind you what won't ever be. Instead of that friendship, I get the front-row seat to the highlight reel of their perfect life: vacation selfies, sunset porch swings, Fourth of July barbecues with kids in matching polos and red Solo cups full of sweet tea and smug contentment. She got the life she always chased, the one I never could give her---probably because I never wanted it in the first place.

So yeah, Bridget lives in a mansion now. She got her castle. Oscar got the girl. And me? I got the moral of the story. But don't confuse that with a sad ending---because it's not. Sometimes, walking away empty-handed is the only way to keep your soul intact. No prize. No parade. Just peace. And peace is worth more than any fairytale ending that wasn't built to last.

The truth? Bridget and I are friends now---genuinely. And we're a hell of a lot better at that than we ever were at being obligated to each other. Getting there wasn't easy. It was uphill, sideways, backwards. But we made it. And that friendship? It's something I protect like a scar I earned.

So if Bridget ever does read this---this paragraph's for her: I hope you see the value in what we finally figured out. That connection doesn't always have to come wrapped in romance or wreckage. Sometimes, it's stronger when it's stripped of all the things that once made it heavy. We're not who we were. And maybe that's the point. Here's to keeping what matters, without burning it down first.

Piper.

She's been my rock---then, now, always. An extraordinary woman who somehow managed to finish law school (because of course she did), raise three beautiful kids, and still have enough presence left in the tank to remain a steady force in my chaotic life. We still stay in touch regularly. And when I say "we," I mean Kate and I.. Yeah---that Kate. Life's wild, isn't it?

The three of us have ridden some serious waves together. Highs, lows, shipwrecks, full-blown storms---and yet somehow, we're all still afloat. She's still one of the most influential people in my life. Our lives. Time never really wore that down. If anything, it polished the truth into something shinier, more valuable.

And listen---I'm not saying I'm holding out hope, but if I dust off a few of my old antics, crack a few nostalgic jokes, maybe---just maybe---I can talk them into a little *ménage-a-tious*. Hey, stranger things have happened. We've already rewritten the rules once. Who says we're done bending them?

Mom and Dad

While I was navigating the wreckage---strip clubs, rental car franchises in chaos, and a trail of broken relationships I couldn't outrun---my father was fighting his own, quieter war. A losing one. His opponent? The American Dream. The one that promises if you work hard enough, stay loyal, and grind through the decades, you'll come out the other side with something to show for it.

But that dream turned into a nightmare dressed in business casual.

Between the so-called "economic meltdown" and GM's ruthless franchise realignment, he got gutted. Left with nothing but memories and a stack of letters that sounded polite but carried the weight of a guillotine. One day, he was managing a dealership with a full lot and decades of goodwill. The next, he was a name on a spreadsheet someone at corporate deleted before lunch. The new car inventory disappeared. The used lot sat empty like a graveyard. And then came the final blow---a carefully worded letter thanking him for his service, telling him he was no longer part of the plan.

This, after GM had already killed off half its legacy---Pontiac, Hummer, Saturn, Oldsmobile---like a corporate firing squad executing its own children. And guys like my dad? They were the fallout. The casualties. Men who'd built empires from dirt and chrome, suddenly told they were irrelevant. It didn't matter how many late nights he'd worked or how many families he'd helped into their first car. He was just another bootprint in the mud.

In his later years, all he had left was a hollowed-out version of what used to be. A couple of service bays still running. A few used cars on consignment. But the soul of the place---the energy, the spark, the pride---it was gone. You could see it in his eyes. That look he used to get when a deal came together, when he'd toss someone the keys and clap them on the back with a grin? Gone. Burned out. He eventually sold what was left---pennies on the dollar. A lifetime of sweat and sacrifice cashed out like some Saturday yard sale. A closing shift with no one left to turn the lights off.

And just when you think life might show him a little mercy, it tightened the screws. He sold everything just in time to ride the front edge of the 2008 financial collapse. His pennies still amounted to a decent pile of money, by perspective, of course. He did everything right---played it safe, invested smart. Lost half of it overnight. Gone, like it was never real. He retired, technically. But not the way a man like him should've. No retirement parties. No golden parachute. Just a smaller house than the one he raised us in, a rusted lawn chair, and a chipped mug of coffee. I've watched him sit on that porch and stare at nothing like he was waiting for an apology that would never come.

Then there was my mother.

Sharp as a scalpel. Driven like she had something to prove---and maybe she did. She didn't come from privilege. No leg up. No family name to coast on. Everything she had, she earned. Scraped her way through med school, beat back doubt at every turn, and wore her white coat like armor. She was built for greatness. Five years into her practice, she was just starting to see the payoff. A full roster of patients. Respect. A future. Then her body betrayed her.

Multiple sclerosis.

Just like that, it was over. The hands that once held lives steady began to shake. The legs that had carried her through a thousand call nights started giving out. One week, she was performing procedures. The next, she was a passenger in her own life. The framed degrees on the wall meant nothing when her fingers couldn't hold a pen or her balance turned on her. Everything she'd fought for, planned for, and earned, evaporated. Not from failure. Not from lack of will. Just fate. Cruel, blind fate. She had the brain to change the world, and instead, she had to sit back and watch it spin without her. That's the kind of shit life throws at you when you think you've finally figured it out. When you think the worst is behind you, it shows up with a new mask and says, Not yet.

So while the rest of the world was out chasing hashtags, filtered joy, and fairy-tale endings, my family was busy writing our story in broken contracts, medical charts, pink slips, and foreclosure notices. There were no slow-motion airport reunions. No tearful Hallmark-style breakthroughs. No life lessons wrapped in soft lighting and warm music. Just grit. Just grief. Just enough fuel to keep the damn engine from stalling out completely.

We didn't get the dream---we got the wake-up call. And somehow, against the odds, we kept going. Kept moving. Kept holding it together with tape and willpower, until the chapter finally closed.

At 90 years old, both of my parents passed away---just two months apart. Mom went first. Dad followed, like clockwork. I'm convinced it was a broken heart. They spent more than 70 years side by side. Whatever kept them alive that long, it wasn't medicine. It was each other.

Kate

But here's the kicker---I got the girl.

Kate. My dream girl. The one who slipped through my fingers the first time around because I was too blind, too reckless, too wrapped up in the noise to recognize what I had. I lost years with her. Years I'll never get back. But somehow, through the wreckage and reinvention, the stars realigned. Releasing Scarlett's Secrets made space in my life---and in my head---for something real. For someone real. Timing's a cruel bastard, but sometimes it throws you a bone.

When things with Bridget fell apart---slowly, then all at once---Kate was also at the tail end of her own long relationship. We came back into each other's lives like two puzzle pieces that had spent years getting sanded down by life. She wasn't just a second chance. She was the missing chapter. She encouraged me to finish my degree, pushed me to earn my ATP---the highest certificate in aviation, a badge of honor I used to only dream about while bartending in the shadows of the clubs I owned. Kate believed in the version of me I hadn't even met yet. She saw the pilot long before the plane took off.

This book started as therapy. A way to bleed the poison out---rage, heartbreak, regret. But it became something more. It became proof that survival isn't just about staying alive---it's about becoming.

Less than two years after I walked away from the strip club world, I jumped headfirst into a new business venture. One that chewed me up, spit me out, and damn near drained me dry---mentally, physically, financially. At the same time, Bridget and I were unraveling. I thought leaving that wild chapter behind would somehow save our marriage. I thought choosing normalcy would bring us closer. Instead, it magnified the distance. I believe it was clear, Bridget was searching for her own identity, her own voice, and I couldn't be what she needed. The truth is, we were never building the same life---we were just renting space in each other's story.

Life has a way of torching your plans and handing you something better in the ashes. In the middle of all the collapse---business losses, emotional landmines, financial hell---Kate was there. A steady hand when everything else felt like freefall. She became a lighthouse in a storm that never seemed to let up.

When the mortgage crisis hit, I found myself trapped---owing more than the house was worth, swimming in uncertainty, trying to keep a roof over our heads while the rest of the country was losing theirs. I made impossible choices. I leveraged everything. And somehow---maybe by stubbornness, maybe by grace---I held onto that home without a single payment. It wasn't just survival. It was a defiant middle finger to the system. It was a chance to rebuild, brick by brick.

Leaving the gentlemen's club industry didn't just open doors---it blew the whole wall down. I stepped into new arenas: finance, aviation, leadership. Places where people shook your hand without looking for a tip. Flying jets, something that once felt like a fantasy scribbled in a notebook, became my daily reality. I earned respect in circles that had nothing to do with nightlife and everything to do with discipline and grit. Along the way, I built real connections. Some came from unlikely places.

Like Ken the Boogeymanwho once investigated me, the guy who tore my life apart with a badge and a mandate. We're friends. I trust him more than I trust most people who claimed they had my back when shit hit the fan. Go figure.

Even Ira Rosen---Bridget's partner after we split---ended up in my corner. Our history was complicated, sure, but we both took heavy hits during the financial crisis. We both lost. We both rebuilt. And in that shared suffering, there was understanding. Eventually, we put down the weapons. He became a friend. A confidant. When he passed suddenly, it hit harder than I expected. Not because he was perfect---he wasn't. But because there was something real between us. A strange kind of brotherhood forged in the fire most people couldn't comprehend.

And with, Kate.

We blended our families. We built something that feels real in a way nothing else ever had. Not the kind of real people post about on social media, but the kind forged in the fire---day by day, choice by choice. There were no secrets. No scorekeeping. Just mutual respect, shared decisions, and the kind of unwavering support that doesn't flinch when things get messy. She's not a trophy on my arm---she's the Friggin foundation. My anchor. My mirror. My equal. The kind of woman who doesn't just stand beside you when the cameras are rolling---she rolls up her sleeves and builds with you when the lights are off and the bills are due.

We've seen storms. Real ones. The kind that break people. Financial stress. Family drama. Grief. Doubt. Pressure that makes most couples crack or cave or quietly drift apart. But we didn't. We dug in. Every fight, every low moment---it didn't pull us apart. It made us harder, stronger, sharper. We didn't aim for perfect. We aimed for honest. And every morning, I wake up next to her and think, damn---so this is what peace feels like. Not silence. Not stillness. But peace. Earned, not given. Shared, not assumed.

And yeah---I did get everything I wanted. Because people underestimate just how crucial the right relationship is. It's not some subplot or side quest. It's the blueprint. It's the bedrock. It's what holds everything else up when the weight of the world starts pressing down. Without that solid ground beneath your feet, the rest of your life starts to crack. But with it? You've got something that can stand through anything. A storm. A drought. Even time. Something that not only holds up---but builds you up. The kind of love that doesn't just keep you afloat; it teaches you how to fly.

In the end, I didn't just survive the chaos. I came out on the other side with everything that actually matters. I didn't just limp away with a story---I walked away with a life. I won.

But here's where it gets real---because there's a part of winning that comes with a twist. Let's talk about the age gap between Kate and me. Yeah, we've got off-the-charts chemistry. We click in all the ways that count. But the truth is, I'm creeping into my seventies, and she's still riding her early fifties with grace and power. And while I'm still more than capable---five, six times a week without reaching for a bottle of anything but water---there's this ticking clock I feel in the back of my mind. The kind of internal pressure you don't talk about at dinner parties.

It messes with your head. You start doing mental math in the middle of the night. Start imagining a future where you're not there---where your wife, your partner, your everything, keeps living after you're gone. That's when the sharp part of love cuts through. Because as much as I want her happy, the idea of her building a new life with someone else? It burns like hellfire. If I drop dead tomorrow and she ends up in heaven telling me about a twenty-year love story she had after me? That'd slice through my chest like a blade.

And I think that's normal. I think that's human.

I love my wife from the deepest place I've got---but I'm still a man. Still wired to protect, to provide, to matter. Do I want her broken forever, paralyzed by grief, unable to move on? Of course not. But am I cool with the idea of her finding comfort in someone else's arms? Hell no. That image alone can wreck a good night's sleep. And anyone who says they wouldn't care is either lying to themselves or they've never really been in love. Be honest---what man, in a strong, ride-or-die partnership, fantasizes about the woman he gave his life to waking up next to someone else?

That fear, that sting---it's real. And it doesn't vanish just because you wear a wedding ring or hit a milestone anniversary. It only gets louder when the age gap widens. When your wife's closer in age to your kids than to you, it becomes impossible not to think about the what-ifs. Even if you're the same age---mid-forties, happy, healthy---all it takes is a twist of fate. Cancer. A drunk driver. A random moment that pulls the rug out from under you. And suddenly, you're not in the story anymore. Someone else is.

It's a brutal truth. One thing most people don't talk about. But if you've ever loved someone so much it rewired your DNA, you get it. That ache, that primal fear of being replaced---it's not about jealousy. It's about value. It's about being that guy. Her guy. Forever.

Even if you don't get to be there to see it.

Yeah... that reality doesn't go down easy. But it's real. And it's always there---lingering in the shadows, showing up uninvited in quiet moments or restless nights. We don't talk about it every day, but we feel it. That ticking clock. That quiet truth that no matter how strong our love is, time is undefeated. Mortality doesn't ask for permission---it just shows up.

But here's the thing: our relationship isn't beautiful because it's perfect. It's beautiful because we're both all in. Every damn day. No halfway. No one-foot-out-the-door bullshit. We show up. We compromise---not out of obligation, but out of desire. We put in the work, and in the middle of putting each other first, we still manage to protect pieces of ourselves. It's a balance we earned the hard way, through pain, through failure, through moments when it would've been easier to walk away than to stay and grow.

Respect? That's not just something we throw around in conversations. We live it. I had to earn that word. I learned the hard way---through years of wreckage and mistakes---that love without respect is just possession in disguise. I've called women I once claimed to love, things that still make my stomach turn. The C-word. Slick little jabs dressed up as humor. Rage camouflaged as wit. I talked down, talked over, or worse---just stopped talking altogether. Silence as punishment. Sarcasm as a blade.

And what did any of that ever get me? Nothing but scorched earth and echoes of regret. There's no glory in being a clever asshole. There's no prize at the end of the road for emotional cowardice. I wish I could go back and rewrite some of those moments, take back the damage I caused---but I can't. That version of me had to die so this one could be born.

Kate doesn't get the broken man. She gets the man who finally learned to love himself first---not the ego-stuffed version, but the kind that owns his shit and knows his worth. Because that's the only way I could love her the way she deserves. She gets the version of me that doesn't weaponize affection or treat vulnerability like a weakness. The man who doesn't see emotional honesty as a threat to his masculinity---but as the backbone of it.

What we've built? It's solid. We don't go to bed angry---ever. We don't let the sun rise on unresolved tension. We hug. We say I love you. Not out of habit, but because it's armor. It's the thread that holds everything else together when life tries to pull it apart. And no, it's not Hallmark crap---it's real. It's necessary.

We're honest. Brutally honest. We stripped jealousy from our lives by dragging the past into the light and staring it down. We didn't deny where we came from. We didn't Photoshop our journey. We acknowledged the chaos, the bad choices, the wild years---and we chose to build anyway. Not on top of lies, but with the truth as foundation.

And yeah---let's talk about unconventional. How many people can say, with a straight face, that their current wife and ex-wife once made a sexual sandwich out of them? I'm guessing not many. Probably for good reason. Some would call it twisted. Others would call it the stuff of late-night fantasies. But for me? It was just a symptom of a sick era in my life. A time when I led with lust, blurred boundaries, and pulled people into my orbit without understanding the collateral damage I was causing. I called it freedom. I called it charisma. I called it power.

But let's be honest---it was pig leadership. And I was the mascot in the mud, snorting lines of ego and calling it strategy.

That was then. This is now.

Now, I don't need chaos to feel alive. I don't need a crowd to validate my worth. I need this---a woman who walks beside me, not behind. A partner. Not a prop. Someone who challenges me, calls me out, lifts me up, and never lets me shrink into the smaller version of myself just to make her feel big.

What Kate and I have is rare. Not because it looks good in a photo or plays well in polite conversation---but because it was forged in fire. Not that Instagram-filtered love people pretend to have, but the kind that's clawed its way through hell. We didn't come together clean. We came together raw. Dragging our pasts. Dragging our pain. And then we stood face-to-face, dropped the bags, and said, Let's try this anyway.

It's not perfect. It's not always pretty. It's made of real fights, real silence, and real forgiveness. It's the kind of love built on decisions, not feelings---because feelings fade and change and come back again. But decisions? That's where the staying power lives. We chose each other. We keep choosing each other. Through the mess. Through the memories. Through the doubts and the days that test us.

What we have is built on truth. And truth doesn't break. It bends. It bleeds. But it doesn't break. This isn't a fairytale. It's real. It's gritty. It's full of sharp edges and soft landings, of hard truths and beautiful moments that hit harder because they're fleeting. And most importantly---it's ours. Built from scars, honesty, and the kind of love that doesn't flinch when it hears a ticking clock.

That's why the age difference between us isn't just a casual detail or a quirky little footnote---it's a flashing signpost we both see coming a mile away. We don't pretend we've got endless time. Because we don't. Time, in our story, isn't some gentle companion growing old with us. It's a loud, relentless metronome in the background---reminding us with every passing second that nothing lasts forever.

I'm not in my thirties anymore. Hell, not even in my forties. I'm deep into the back half of the game. Closer to the finish line than the starting blocks. Kate's still vibrant, still got decades ahead with the kind of fire most people spend their whole lives chasing and never find. We've got this rhythm, this incredible sync between us, but under all that harmony lives a silent truth: I won't be there for the whole ride. Maybe not even half of what's ahead for her. And that thought? It cuts.

We've never bullshitted each other about it. We don't romanticize the inevitable or put rose-colored filters over the facts. We feel it. That weight is always there---an invisible gravity that tugs at the edges of our joy. But in a strange, beautiful way, it's what makes our love sharper. More deliberate. We don't waste the days. We don't gloss over the little stuff. Every hug, every fight we resolve before bed, every shared meal, every stupid laugh over nothing---it all matters more. There's urgency woven into the everyday.

Time isn't our friend. It's our challenger. Our shadow. And---fucked-up as it sounds---it's also our gift. Because we know what we have. And we hold onto it with both hands. Fiercely. Desperately. Gratefully.

We're told to plan responsibly. Wills, trusts, insurance policies, burial instructions---whatever makes the numbers line up and the lawyers happy. We prepare for death like it's a checklist. But no one prepares you for what comes next for the one you leave behind. No one teaches you how to make peace with being the chapter that ends before the book is finished. That's the part they don't write songs about. That's the part that keeps you up at night, staring at the ceiling, hoping the love you leave behind will be strong enough to outlive you.

This chapter of my life---this unexpected, late-in-the-game miracle---has taught me that life's curveballs can turn into home runs when you stop trying to hit perfect pitches and just swing hard. Letting go of the past, facing the mirror, cutting the dead weight, owning your failures, embracing the discomfort of change---that's the real work. That's where the good stuff is.

I stopped chasing illusions and started holding on to what's real. I stopped needing the world to clap for me and started clapping for myself. And in doing that, I found something I never thought I'd have: a life that feels full. Whole. Grounded. Not despite the chaos---but because of it.

That whole past life---my so-called interlude---is now reduced to a head full of noise and a hard drive full of pictures. Lots of pictures. Smiles frozen in time, moments that look warmer than they ever really were. Proof it all happened, even if it feels like someone else lived it.

Today, I didn't just build a new chapter. I built a new damn book.

Happiness these days boils down to Kate still hanging on, my kids and grandkids calling me back, and being able to take a leak without praying to God or cursing the urologist.

And for the first time, I'm not afraid of the ending.

I'm proud of the story.

1951-2025

Dear Reader,

My name is C.J. Striker III, and I'm writing to you on behalf of my father.

C.J. Striker Jr. passed away peacefully in his sleep before he could finish this book. What happens to Kate and Cole in the end? We may never know---not exactly how he would've told it. Or maybe we will, in our own way. The story, raw and beautiful as it is, was nearly complete when my brother and I found it tucked away---unfinished but still burning with his voice.

My father was, first and foremost, a pilot. Flying wasn't just his job---it was his lifeblood. His escape, his discipline, his church in the sky. The rest of what you've just read? The strip clubs, the betrayals, the longing, the sideways redemption? Let's just say that my mother---God bless her---would rather walk barefoot across hot coals than be caught dead in a swinger circle or a ménage à trois. Those are most definitely not my parents. Where he got the inspiration, the detail, the emotional messiness? That's part of the mystery that died with him. And maybe that's exactly how he wanted it.

As his son---also a Corporate Aviator, and a literature major, with just enough ego and heartache to try---I took on the task of editing and preparing this final manuscript for publication. It wasn't easy. Some passages made me laugh out loud. Some made me flinch. Some made me set the pages down and stare out the window for hours, just missing the man behind them. But more than anything, they made me proud. Proud of his guts. Proud of the raw, unapologetic way he chose to tell the story.

My father was never one to shy away from the hard truths, and his voice didn't care whether it made people uncomfortable. He believed in telling it like it was---even if it was messy.

We've found additional manuscripts. Fragments. Chapters. Scribbled outlines on cocktail napkins. Letters he never sent. Whether they're truth, fiction, or something swirling in between, they deserve to be read. They deserve daylight. And I may just be the curator crazy enough to bring them to life. I've taken it upon myself to carry the torch, to keep his voice alive, and to continue the legacy he left smoldering in these pages.

On behalf of our family, thank you. Thank you for reading. For your time, your curiosity, and your willingness to sit in the fire with him. That's the greatest compliment he could've ever hoped for.

This was his final story.

And it's the beginning of mine.

Sincerely,

C.J. Striker III